CROSSINGS 18

Tosca
The Cat Lady

Tosca
The Cat Lady

a novel

Gina Lagorio

translated by
Martha King

BORDIGHERA PRESS

Library of Congress Cataloguing-in-Publication Data 2009920223

All the characters and events portrayed in this story, although based on a faithful chronicle are entirely fictitious. Any resemblance to real persons, living or dead, is coincidental and not intended by the author.

Printed in the United States.

Published by
BORDIGHERA PRESS
John D. Calandra Italian American Institute
25 West 43rd Street, 17th Floor
New York, NY 10036

CROSSINGS 18
ISBN 978-1-59954-002-3

TABLE OF CONTENTS

Part One

1

"I'm here waiting. You remember the father, don't you? No one in the village had more spunk. What an awful death! I can't bear to think about it. And before he died he brought his woman into the house. I couldn't send her away afterwards, could I? He had made her his very own, got her pregnant. I didn't have that much courage, and so now I'm here waiting. But this time it's taking too long, she's already overdue and so big. Let's just hope it won't be a difficult delivery."

The woman lit a cigarette. Her hair, tied in a ponytail to give her some relief from the midday heat, bobbed and swayed as she continued her monologue in the lobby of the small condominium. Her listener had stopped on the first flight of stairs, forcing his face to remain impassive, but with surprise written in his eyes. The person Tosca had detained as he came from the beach was a calm man from Piedmont, who had become completely tranquilized in his retirement. He had never been much at ease with women and animals, but he was well mannered, and as he had passed the woman leaning against the door with her eyes fixed on the little garden below, he had spoken to her politely, as he had been brought up to speak to his neighbors. She had responded eagerly, immediately inquiring if the water was clear and if he had had a good swim. Signor Audiberti realized that she was feeling talkative at that blinding, sweltering time of day, and after rapidly reviewing the situation at home — a cold lunch on the kitchen table to be eaten whenever anyone was hungry, wife and children still at the beach — he courteously acquiesced. After going up the first few steps, glancing at her and saying the few necessary words, he had stopped, put his things down and leaned against the stair railing. To please her, he started the conversation by asking a question. "Why in the world are you here at this time of the day? You're not going to the beach?"

With a wide, grateful smile, in a deep, hoarse voice, she had given him the first chilling bit of information, "I can't. . . my emphysema, you know. . ." And as though anticipating his logical observation, "I smoke a light cigarette. I used to smoke Nazionali, but I can't any longer, and I just can't quit smoking entirely."

She brought the cigarette to her mouth with a wink of wicked complicity, and began her monologue: "I'm here waiting."

When he had heard the word "delivery," Signor Audiberti felt he had done his good deed for the day and it was more than sufficient, considering the fact that the thermometer registered eighty-six in the shade. He bent down to pick up his things and went on up the stairs while murmuring vague good wishes in the woman's direction.

Why would anyone stand in the doorway waiting for someone to deliver? Maybe an ambulance was coming. He didn't feel like giving a hand. He was tired. He had already stayed at the beach longer than he should. He mustn't overdo it. The doctor had given strict orders. Short swims, not too much sun, light food, and not too much exertion.

She should ask his wife. Women know everything about having babies. Maria! Thirty-two years of marriage had been quite enough on that subject. Maria's pregnancies had been a nightmare. Now there was their first daughter to provide nourishment for his wife's libidinal narratives. A nice woman, after all, and almost always kind, but given to inexhaustible, sadistic descriptions if the subject was a pregnant woman's suffering.

Tosca was alone again. When the door closed on the third floor and she was sure there were no judgmental ears to overhear, she let go. Her pretty face, white and shining with perspiration, crinkled up in angry protest: "When are you going to make up your mind, you slut? I'm sick and tired of waiting for you, do you understand? You could have stayed in the house! But no, the lady wants the fresh garden air, she wants it under the trees! With me standing guard. . ." She interrupted herself with a short fit of dry coughing. Crushing the cigarette under her clog, she bent over to pick up the butt and went to the back of the lobby where two small steps led to the outside. Three noisy children erupted through the back gate. Apprehensive, Tosca immediately stepped out to warn them. "Watch out! Don't go near the oleander bush!"

Busy arguing over a little plastic boat, the children dashed in without a pause in their yelling and shoving, while Tosca explained to the mother coming along behind them that they shouldn't frighten "the poor little thing."

The mother was young, burdened with three children after seven years of marriage; she was hot and nervous, laden with beach bags. She gave Tosca a pitying look and made no comment. In a flash she reached the smallest of the three who had separated from the other two already on the stairs, giving him a quick slap. His shrill protest alarmed his two sisters who clattered up the stairs in their wooden clogs as fast as they could go. Holding the little one firmly by the hand, the infuriated mother followed close behind the girls. Tosca watched until they disappeared into the darkness of the stairwell, the young woman's strident voice still within earshot. A door slammed violently, then silence.

"Tell me, Poppa, if having children is worth the trouble when you treat them like that. How unjust! Too many children for some and none at all for others. Those who would love them can't have them, and those who have them don't have as much patience as animals. . ."

She bent over to caress, with a white, puffy hand, something gray lying on the ground. Giulia, the girl at the beauty shop, had been watching it from the shop's balcony, where she had come to hang wet towels.

A slender young girl with blue eyes, straight hair like a shining helmet. The pink apron hugging her waist revealed, in the slight swelling of her bosom, that she was barely more than a girl.

Giulia was hungry, thirsty, and sleepy. Her friends were at the beach now. After getting up late and eating a hearty breakfast they had taken off for the seaside. Until a month ago that had been her routine, too. But then her mother found this job for her. She wasn't sorry, but it was hard getting up in the morning when sleep had tied every muscle and nerve in a knot. Each morning she felt like lead, like a rigid statue wrapped in the viscous tangle of sleep, and her mother almost had to pull her out of bed. In the bathroom, if no one called her, she would go back to sleep sitting on the toilet. Every morning it was the same. Drowsiness kept her from eating and later, when the beauty shop owner offered her a sandwich she could eat a dozen. The shop was cool in the morning, but as the hours went by the coolness vanished with the hot waves from hair dryers and the heavy, penetrating air from Via Aurelia, the road where your heels sank into the heat-saturated asphalt.

Now the shop was empty. The owner had gone for his customary snack at the bar, and her mother had not yet brought hers. Her mother worked in a restaurant and came after she finished serving the regular customers. Giulia wished she could go down to the garden. She called out, "Signora!"

Tosca turned and smiled at her. "Ciao, how are you?"

She sighed. "Oh, all right, I guess. . ."

"You'd like to be at the beach, wouldn't you? But just think how much nicer it'll be this evening. The water's warmer and the sea's calmer in the evening."

Giulia sighed again, but was already feeling better. "Nothing's happened yet?" she asked, but didn't wait for an answer because she heard a voice behind her and announced with a joyful, "It's my mother. Hurrah. Now I can eat!"

Tosca went back to stand in the condo doorway. It was easier to watch from there in the shade. "If she makes me wait much longer I'll go get a stool to sit on," she thought, as the roar of a car motor rose from below. A moment later the journalist raced up the stairs two steps at a time. He had a briefcase and a roll of newspapers under his arm. Tosca hadn't seen him for a year and felt an instinctive shyness. She bent over, pretending to pick up something she had dropped and replied to his greeting with a demure, "Good morning." When she straightened up the man was already on the stairs. "Oh, yes, he's in a hurry, lucky man; she'll be waiting for him!" Suddenly her long surveillance in that deserted doorway between the garden and Via Aurelia, both in blinding sunlight, seemed senseless. She hesitated, uncertain what to do. With a sigh she went down the few steps that led to the source of her concern.

2

That long, almost nightlong race in the car, alone, really was insane. But once the recordings at the radio station were finished, and he had taken care of the few routine things, Rome seemed more distasteful than ever. An atrocious heat from the famous west wind, scrawny cats rummaging through garbage bags left on the doorsteps of "historical" palaces, the general disorder, no friends. Everyone on vacation, everyone gone. And so Gigi had filled up his Alfetta and taken off for the seaside and Toni. He had stopped for a quick snack and soon a nagging thirst (the consequence of a ham sandwich as salty as herring) was added to the annoyance of headlights in his eyes. "I'm getting old, driving isn't fun anymore."

By this time he had reached Liguria and decided to get off the highway. He was bone tired, and thought perhaps it would be better to spend the night at Genoa. When he reached Caricamento he got out in search of some place that might be open late at night and, following the sound of muffled music, arrived at a door defended by a man in short-sleeves, with only a military cap to indicate his responsible position. The man roused himself just enough to hand him a ticket for ten thousand lire, and barely gestured with his chin in the direction of some red-lighted stairs. "Laconic Sicilian," thought Gigi, who collected the language of gestures since the sclerotic words currently in fashion no longer interested him.

He needed a bottle of mineral water badly, and dug into his billfold once again. The barman was a young Genovese who, in order to minimize the obvious difference of Gigi's drink from the other customers', served him his water in a whisky glass garnished with a slice of lemon and a mint leaf. With the smile of an accomplice he handed it to Gigi. Obviously he was a student who needed the money and in this job it was better not to notice things. Even something as insignificant as drinking water instead of alcohol. With the cold glass in his hands, Gigi paused to looked at the couples gyrating on a small circular dance platform.

Only two were entwined without any regard for the musical tempo. The others moved as they saw fit, in imaginary harmony with the person facing them; but for the observer it was difficult to determine who was with whom. The single common element was the ugliness of the bodies and the awkward movements that made the group a representation of sexual preliminaries.

"I'm really getting old. Even this doesn't interest me any more." And since it was the second time in a few hours that he had thought about age, he felt a sharp desire to be in his own home. But he didn't want to wake Toni in the middle of the night. Sleep was always a problem for her; he would rest a while in their house in Genoa and then make the last leg of the trip in the morning.

He turned to get his glass refilled and it was then he saw her going up to the dance platform, the only person there who seemed young in the ghostly light of those ridiculously sulfurous reflections. She was small and thin, even her arms, which unlike the other women, she covered with a lightweight shirt. She was blond and only her cheeks seemed made up, or perhaps it was merely the red reflection. The sailor who held her hand let it go and they began to dance facing each other. They moved well, with lightness and grace, but Gigi was especially drawn to the girl who was dancing without looking at anyone, not even boy. In the strong rhythmic dance her small breasts undulated under the fabric of her shirt, but there was nothing licentious in her movements and even her hips moved sweetly, like a ritual the girl was performing for herself alone. She lay her head on the

7

sailor's chest, her long blond hair covering her face when, with a final loud chord, the record stopped. Raising her head and brushing her hair from her face, her large, vacant eyes—they seemed greenish to him, the color of water—met his for an instant without seeing him. Gigi felt his heart skip from that stolen, entirely accidental glance. Those eyes were lakes of nothing, empty wells without depth, eyes that did not look and had not seen him. The girl disappeared as she had arrived, and the sailor was gone, too. Gigi asked the barman if he knew her. No, he had never seen her before, but the women who came here were all of the same profession.

Gigi threw some money on the counter and hurriedly left, followed by the boy's happy voice shouting thanks after him. He hoped to see her on the beach. But aside from the sleepy and disheveled doorman on his stool propped against the wall, without his cap this time, hoping to catch a cool breeze from the hot night wind, he saw no one.

Immediately beyond the nightclub a dark alley wound between the houses. Useless, perhaps dangerous, to go there. He returned to his car. There was no traffic, and by going along the coast road he was soon at Boccadasse.

Six hours later he continued his journey, surprising himself by the turn his thoughts had taken. He had slept more than he expected, but that apparition, without warning or logical sequence, continued to occupy his thoughts, heavy with a meaning that escaped him. A life had touched him that would never touch him again. How many others, even more familiar, had crossed his path, had shouted for help perhaps or merited attention or pity, and he had not stopped? Those eyes were innocent, and if what the boy said was true, they were innocent in spite of a sordid existence. Or perhaps she had simply erased it, like guilt or disgust. She lived it out of necessity, and that was that. And when she danced, she emptied herself of everything, of daily events (but every event is sordid in different ways), and she had recovered the feeling of pure naturalness, of movement that became rhythmic, of blood that ran freely, of the parenthesis that forgets what precedes it and what will follow. That was what had bothered him: his own charge of awareness while watching the girl dance, and the absolute vacuity that met his eyes. Writing was a similar process. When he wrote about others and not about himself, that same skip of his heart always accompanied the first sentence tapped out on the keys. Outside was the innocence and naturalness of life itself; inside was his presumptuous weaving of plots, of transforming free and autonomous beings into puppets dancing a story.

That's how it was. You just had to accept it and try not to find a way out that wasn't there. Didn't that German writer say that perhaps of all writing, that which camouflages the "I" is still the best? There is only one reality, but it changes by the way one looks at it. A half glass is a half glass, but his mother said it was half full and his father said that it was half empty. His mother smiled easily, his father almost never. It's all in one's point of view.

When he reached the village the sea was bright under the high sun. In the emporium they were busy sacking fresh fruit and vegetables, a few cyclists rode calmly down Via Aurelia. The great crowded, noisy day by the seaside was observing a moment of quiet in the streets and houses.

He left his car in the garage and sprinted up the few steps leading to the condo door. He thought the woman who spoke to him looked familiar. But by now Gigi had Toni on his mind and he ran up the stairs. As his door keys were in his bag, he rang the bell. He heard the cat mewing and then, immediately after that, Toni's morning voice in an astonished interrogative that Gigi smothered in his arms.

3

Tosca peered into the oleander bush. She was approaching fifty, still youthful-looking, but pudgy and shapeless. Her fine complexion contrasted oddly with her swollen body. In the light-weight dress her bosom and stomach, shoulders and arms revealed the puffiness and weakness of ill health, childlike dimples in aging muscles. A large child marked by the years, a woman not totally without youthful grace.

Signor Pino Audiberti had understood this unconsciously when he had accepted her invitation to exchange a few words with her; Giulia's boss, the white haired hairdresser (who in his youth had been the tender friend of many idle women) knew it with a tiny pinch of annoying desire and shame every time he thought about her. When she ran into him Tosca always rearranged the funny, elastic-bound ponytail on her neck. "One of these days I'm coming to have my hair done." She was naively flirtatious, and the man reacted proudly with a never-failing compliment: "You don't need me, Tosca, you know you're beautiful just as you are." The woman would laugh and the conversation would proceed with her frivolously innocent seduction and the echo of his past gallantries. If his wife should appear in the doorway at the back of the shop, Tosca would immediately dart away and he would return to the shop without another word. But a day or a week later when they met the scene would be replayed—in the warm months, because the shop closed in September when the owner went back to his home in Loano. Only Giulia remained behind in the village.

Emphysema played a part in Tosca's private little theater in the Ligurian village where it had brought her from her beloved Lombardy—beloved but foggy and cold. She had learned it was emphysema only a short while ago, after another very trying series of tests to determine the cause of her allergies. In Milan springtime had made her eyes swell and filled her lungs with irritating pollens. Sometimes at night she had been afraid she wouldn't survive the constriction that closed her throat and made everything go dark around her. "Asthma" had been the doctors' first diagnosis. This was followed by rare visits to the sea—the only remedy that could make her happy when she woke up in the morning. After that it was the solitude following her husband's death that had persuaded her to leave her home, too melancholy a place to wait for the attacks all alone. And so she had decided, thanks to the law that gave five years to women, to take her pension early.

The choice of where to live had fallen almost naturally on the seaside village where her husband had taken her as a bride to meet his sister, his last remaining relative in the world. It was really her sister-in-law who suggested the move when she had come to Milan that first Christmas to visit Tosca, alone and confined to her home by a cough. Afterwards it was she who had written that an apartment had become available in a little condominium almost on the beach. A retired woman had spent her last years there as the building custodian.

A little nervous because she was superstitious ("she was retired, I'm retired, she was a widow, I'm a widow; it's true that she was old and I'm not yet fifty, but then I'm not well. . .") Tosca agreed to take the woman's place. There weren't many stairs to wash and only a few apartments, divided by two stairways rising from the little lobby with a large fig tree growing in an old oil jar. Watering that tree was one of her jobs. Anyhow, the steps stayed cleaner longer after the beach closed for the winter, and the paddle boats were put in dry dock, the doors of the concrete cabanas nailed shut, and the wooden ones dismantled. Then voices in the building gradually grew silent, and wooden clogs on the gritty stairs grew less frequent until finally she was left all alone after the son of her apartment owner left—a fanatic for underwater fishing whom she had once bumped into at night, black as a hotel mouse, gun and flippers in hand. She had screamed in fright.

The first winter had been difficult. The empty, deserted stairway was frightening. She kept thinking that if someone with bad intentions wanted to hide while she was away he could wait there undisturbed for her return. But to do what? There was nothing precious in her house—she hadn't wanted to get rid of everything in Milan and had left some things with a friend's daughter who had come to work for the phone company. Besides, she knew she was no longer desirable, wasted as she was by continual poor health. Nevertheless, that vague, indistinct darkness in the stairwell always made her heart freeze and the blood pulse furiously in her throat. That was when she decided never to turn off the light in the two stairwells during the three darkest months. She asked permission from the condominium's administrator to do it as a matter of personal safety. That was when she got to know her neighbors better, during the meeting held in August in the portico among the flowering oleanders and bougainvillea. The administrator, who had authorized it immediately, presented her request along with the regular administrative business pertaining to the apartments. The three women whom she saw less often because their apartments were on the other stairway, Signora Audiberti, the cardiologist's wife, and the journalist's friend had no objection. In fact, they asked if she was fairly compensated. The woman who asked about the cost of the "innovation" (as she called it) and requested a review of the electric bill, was the owner of Tosca's apartment, the engineer's wife. Tosca then understood why her husband came to the seaside so rarely, and almost always when his wife and son weren't there.

Tosca had never had a proper conversation with him. He greeted her, went away hurriedly, his hands behind his back, a blue linen cap on his bald head, a newspaper in the pocket of the linen jacket he never removed, even on the hottest days. When he was there she never heard a sound in the house. He was considerate of her, unlike his wife and son, and made them wear rubber sandals instead of clogs. Their apartment was over hers; they owned the largest apartment in the building, occupying the entire top floor, with an inside stairway leading to an apartment on the terrace where their son lived. She always knew immediately which one of them had arrived, because the son dragged his feet in orthopedic clogs bought at the pharmacy, and his mother had the stride of a gendarme. She wore high heels inside the house and out, sophisticated sandals and clogs that she must have bought in expensive boutiques, a pair for every dress. But all her shoes, whether blue, white, red, or yellow, made the same implacable hammering over her head. The son didn't have the imagination or sufficient concern to think he was bothering her either, but Tosca forgave him. Men, as everyone knows, don't come to this nicety naturally. It takes a woman to suggest it, and his mother certainly wouldn't think of it.

Tosca had never liked her, even though she admired well-groomed, nice looking people, and Signora Bergamoni was that. Maybe too much so. Something about her slender body (that must have been statuary in youth), high breasts, soft hips, trim waist, alarmed her whenever Tosca happened meet her face to face. Perhaps it was her slanted, greenish eyes like a snake's. Or maybe it was her perfect set of teeth behind lips pursed as from repressed rage or continual suffering. One day on Via Aurelia Tosca had walked behind her for a while and noticed that she stamped her feet on the pavement or the asphalt as she walked. Therefore it wasn't a question of the surfaces echoing according to their particular composition, but a matter of the balance and majestic gravity of her elegant body, supporting her unusually (for a woman) broad, straight shoulders. The shoulders of an athlete, perhaps of a lance or disk thrower. Every time Tosca saw her from a distance she fled. Those shoulders and that unmistakable step mortified her own fragility, making her feel more sick and alone than ever. She knew now that her intuition had been right, because at the August meeting the woman had also wanted to check the bill from the preceding year to see the difference, as if she alone were paying it. The administrator explained that there had been a rate increase, and so the true difference for the nightly use was actually very little for each apartment. The woman justified herself by saying that, as the owner of Tosca's apartment, she had to protect her own interests. "After all, I'm the one who has to pay." The other women had greeted that statement with smirks, because she raised some time-wasting question at every meeting, and they just wanted to finish in a hurry and get on with their day.

Tosca heard all about it from beauty shop owner's wife, who always found out everything without prying, because her customers wiled away the time with gossip. "Watch out, she's a stingy, sly old fox." But Tosca wasn't worried. She paid her rent, cleaned the stairs, and watered the plants. Since she had come the garden was nicer than it had ever been. She had had the walls of her three rooms painted at her own expense. She had never complained about anything. So she had nothing to watch out for.

Anyway, Signora Pierina may have exaggerated everything she heard. Lorenzo's wife was caustic by nature and because of resentments accumulated over the years of married life. She was faithful to a butterfly, according to her view of the situation. She was a heavy burden to a sensitive man, according to the customers who over so many seasons of sunshine and freedom had appreciated Lorenzo's expert hands on their temples and necks, his discretion in their confidences, his affectionate complicity in their brief but burning summer peccadilloes. Sometimes he was their consolation and, as is natural, sometimes also the protagonist, remembered forever after, and returned to over the years as a trusted friend in whose tender and slightly skeptical eyes it was a pleasure to read the memory of younger and happier summers.

Tosca had imagined this more than she had heard it from others. She was new to the place, as noisy and varied in the summer as it was closed and indifferent in the winter. In the winter she was and always would be an outsider, "a furiner," as they said. The few local inhabitants—fishermen, some shop keepers, young men working in neighboring villages from which they returned in the evening—shut themselves up in the houses that they took back again at the end of September with a possessiveness equal to the detached manner they left them in the summer for personal profit. Each one worked out a system to make money on his house as a temporary rental. Some lived in boat houses, others in cabanas. But when the summer vacationers left, the community returned to what it was, a world closed to anyone not known for at least a generation.

4

Tosca sighed, pushed the oleander branches aside, and crouched down beside the cat. Her swollen body was soft and distorted, as though squashed shapeless like a discarded rag or a worn out pillow. Clearly exhausted, the animal didn't even lift her head off her paws.

"It's cool here. Poor little thing, are you feeling better?" She seemed to find comfort in Tosca's voice and the gentle stroking of her fur — made thin and scraggly from the strain of carrying the extra weight.

"How many of them are you making for me this time? Hurry up, Poppa, or you know what might happen! Do I have to call the vet again? I'll call him if you want, but you're so wild! If I tell him it's for you, he won't want to come. Don't give me any trouble! You know I'm alone and don't want any trouble. I can't have it. The people here are so bad about animals!"

Poppa showed her approval of the discourse with a faint movement of her long tail, wrapped around her shapeless body like a protective ring.

Tosca stood up. Hesitant to leave, she was afraid someone or some thing might bother the cat. After her beloved Miciamore died this cat had been the object of her care and the main concern of her days. A few feet away she saw the nice woman who lived on the second floor of the other stairway, the journalist's wife. The villagers said they weren't married, affirmed most recently at the baker's by a woman from Genoa who was their neighbor at Boccadasse. But Tosca didn't care. They were always calm and smiling, constantly chattering away, even in the stairway. Married or not, it was obvious they weren't bored with each other's company. The woman jumped back with a little cry.

"I didn't see you!" And then, "What's wrong with the poor little thing?"

Tosca smiled at her, immediately grateful. "She's about to have kittens, but I don't understand why she hasn't had them yet. She's ten days overdue."

"Excuse me for asking, but why are you always standing at the door?" She was curious. Like everyone else she had asked herself why in the world the custodian was always in the lobby, often talking to herself. That made Tosca realize that she had been an object of interest once again, and she immediately smoothed her hair and started to talk, even to defend herself; in any case, it's better to be a protagonist than a mere onlooker. What a long time she had waited! June was half gone, the apartments were all occupied and no one had yet asked her what happened to Miciamore. No one paid much attention to her. Only the children were interested in the cat here under the oleander bush, because it was ugly to look at, so large and threatening. If anyone came near she would hiss, fur standing straight up on her back — a back she couldn't arch because of her heavy stomach. But last summer, the journalist's friend, Toni — that's what he called her, but letters came addressed to Antonia Dasta — had found a kitten a few days old, with one little eye closed, and Tosca had helped her take care of it. After that they had talked many times. One day, when the kitten had recovered the use of its eye and had become sure footed after all the care and milk suckled from the baby bottle Tosca had provided, they invited her to have a glass of white wine with them.

The journalist had been very kind. He wanted her to tell him about herself, and when she left he gave her a bottle of rosé in an unusual shape, like a canteen, with a foreign name that told her it was a good brand. When she tried to object, he had smiled and said, "Don't worry, I get so many! With the job I have, the problem is how to drink it all."

That was how she learned that he wrote about food for a magazine with colored photographs and shiny paper, because he gave her a copy along with the bottle. Toni wrote too, but Tosca didn't know what about. In their apartment—one large room where the dividing walls had been torn down—there was a desk with a typewriter at each end. It had been a memorable day for Tosca who had never seen a house like that, in disarray but very comfortable, open and easy, full of pictures and cushions, with large baskets full of magazines and one with bottles and glasses. A house of adults still children, where music filled the space with a light, continual wave of sound, and where it seemed impossible to hate or raise angry voices. Tosca went away happy. They hadn't laughed when she said that Miciamore was her only companion, that he kept her from feeling lonely.

Now Toni held out her packet of Muratti, lit both their cigarettes with a smooth enamel and gold lighter, and then said to her, her face attentive, like someone really ready to talk and who isn't just faking interest. "I'm sorry. I wanted to let you know that I was here, but we just arrived a few days ago. Gigi had to attend a wine conference and I went too. I won't tell you what it was like to take Paletta on a trip like that! And in fact, I refused to go on to Rome with him and that cat."

Paletta was the rescued cat. She had been named by the little girl belonging to the woman Tosca didn't like because she was constantly harried and unhappy with her three children. When Toni had brought into the garden the trembling kitten, with its tearing eye and its little body so thin you were afraid to hold it, the little girl —who knows why—had called it "Paletta." That summer she was two years old and just beginning to discover the world. She took possession of the beach and the happiness that came from it with words. She always wanted stay at the seaside, and could repeat everything: beach, swim, boat, bucket, shovel [paletta]. And so Toni had accepted the name casually, just as her adoption of the kitten had been casual, and so Paletta had remained Paletta. The name proved apt with time because she turned out to be female and Paletta sounded similar to Anna or Emma or Edda. Toni told Tosca she had bought a wicker basket for their travels, but they were continually on the go, and sometimes had to change their plans because of the cat that didn't like to travel and got carsick.

"And it's a disaster on the plane because some airlines make you keep animals in the baggage area, and if she isn't with us she cries the whole time."

"She was lucky to meet you," Tosca observed. "Just think, I've never been on a plane!"

Toni laughed. "Lucky, yes, but it's obvious I can't teach anyone how to behave. Do you remember last summer when she was so famished she would eat paper or grass? You should see her now! If she even stoops to eating a piece of ham, she takes the fat off first, wants her fish cooked, and leaves the heads on her plate."

Now Tosca was truly happy, so happy that she lit one of her own cigarettes off the Muratti. Finally someone who thought as she did, someone she could talk to freely and openly.

"And what do you think about Poppa?" – she returned the ball quickly. "Now that she's in this condition she needs to eat but isn't hungry in this heat. I buy her the whiting she likes and boil it and bone it for her. But even before, when she was always on the prowl, going around like a gypsy, if she came home and didn't find what she wanted to eat, she'd go away without touching her plate. She knows how bad I feel if she doesn't eat and that's how she punishes me. She can't do it now, but you'll see. As soon as she's free we'll start all over again. I'll fix her something to eat, look for her, call her, and if she bothers to come, it's her way or not at all. Either I give her what she wants or she goes back to her prowling!"

Toni had settled on the portico steps. " Sit down, aren't you tired? I can't sleep with this heat, and by this time of the day I'm as limp as a rag."

Tosca smiled at her. "No one would know it. You're as fresh as a rose. I think you look wonderful."

She accepted the compliment, but a slight ripple of her mouth signaled the repression of a retort, and Tosca noticed she didn't have the same familiar open look. A shadow of tiredness was cast over her face, lightly emphasized by her eye makeup.

It finally came. The question she had been waiting for since the beginning of summer.

"Where's Miciamore?"

Tosca waited a moment, and then, "He's dead."

"Dead?"

"Poisoned."

Tosca waited for the exclamations of dismay and indignation to end. She had the audience worthy of the great drama, so many times rehearsed alone, and which she was now ready to perform. Tosca sat down next to her, at the right distance for watching her expressions. Leaning against a column of the portico, a little apart from Toni who leaned back against another, Tosca clasped her hands around her knees and launched into her monologue.

"They poisoned him this winter, in January. They poisoned all the cats in this neighborhood. Only those in the old part of village were spared. Why? Because they own the town. Everyone else is a no-good outsider, a "furiner." Oh, you don't know how mean they can be. I admit that the vacationers can be a nuisance. It's not nice the way some people abandon their animals from one summer to the next, leaving them to forage by themselves for ten months. The animals always return the next summer, and not just because they're hungry. No, it's because they want a home, too, a haven, a quiet place, even if it's only for the summer. Why else would they come back? I'll give you an example. As soon as the Alciones open their house—I water their garden and know their schedule—it's not an hour before Rossetto appears, and how he purrs, how he rubs against the legs of that poor woman who would take him to Turin if only her husband would let her! You know, animals are nicer than people. I'm sure Rossetto understands that poor woman better than the man she's lived with for twenty years.

"But Miciamore didn't bother anyone, not Miciamore. He didn't go mewing around the villagers' houses. He had his own home and ate like a king. They all knew that very well. I went to the butcher's and fishmonger's more for him than for myself, and never tried to hide that from anyone. Why should I be ashamed? I'm alone and Miciamore made my life more interesting, because—you remember how tough and fearless he was, free as the air. How many nights he made me spend out on the street calling him! I was afraid if he didn't come home, and I couldn't leave the door open after the thieves broke in. You didn't know? Not in my house. They tried to break into the jeweler's shop by making a hole underneath the floor, from right here, from the cardiologist's garage. I heard them, and just to do something (I was frozen with fear), I went to the door and called Miciamore. He was actually right next to me, and you should have seen the look he gave me. Like he was flabbergasted. I think he thought I'd lost my mind. But then he seemed to get it and ran in circles around me. I telephoned the police who came quickly in a squad car but didn't find anyone, only the tools. They even had an electric drill.

"What was I saying? Oh, yes, I was thinking about Miciamore, and if they wanted to laugh behind my back because I called him "Amore," they could go right ahead and do it. I didn't need them. With Miciamore I didn't feel useless and I wasn't alone. But one evening I called him for a long time and he didn't come.

"I hoped he was in love again, with some cat from the old part of the village. When he was in love he would go to little hiding places above San Lorenzo with his ladylove. If I climbed up that far and called him, he would come out for a moment to reassure me and then return to his lover. After a day or two, he'd come home and stuff himself! He would gobble up everything I gave him—love wears you out—but the nights! The nights were his again. He would look at me before going out, as if to explain that he couldn't help himself. He'd rub once against my legs and then out he'd go! You know? Other female cats from the old village would come here, the hussies, but he wouldn't even look at them. After he had made his choice, he wouldn't think twice about another one for a while, and I wouldn't see him again. It happened twice. On the other hand, if he wasn't really madly in love, he would just have casual affairs. He'd disappear for a few hours and then come back when he heard me call. And he slept with me. In the morning I'd find him in bed, next to my head. Sometimes if he was hungry he would gently pull my hair. He'd tickle me with his tiny teeth and I'd wake up and go fix his milk. He drank it warm, with cookies, while I drank my coffee. I'd talk to him, and together we'd decide what I'd buy for lunch. If I turned on the radio and there was some bad news and I said something he'd get up, arch his back and stiffen his tail. Believe me, he was more intelligent than those announcers on the radio. Oh, I know I'm exaggerating, but that's the way it seemed to me, like he understood and took part in what I was doing or saying."

Tosca's eyes were lost in the distance, not watching Toni anymore, not caring if she believed her or not. In her mind she was seeing Belmondo, Jean Gabin. Miciamore's amorous nights were home movies lighting up her eyes and Toni thought that her too-white skin was still youthful and perhaps desirous of love.

"That night he didn't come back. Early in the morning, before anyone was up and around, I went as far as San Lorenzo and called and called, but he didn't come. I found him three days later, here, behind the door to the garden, stone-cold dead. He had dragged himself this far, to die at home, my poor Miciamore. . ."

Toni didn't know what to say. That sorrow and pain embarrassed her because it was as real as any sorrow she had had to face, and she knew it was no different in intensity. All tears are salty, and no different if shed over a cat. But Toni felt she had gone too far into some unknown territory, and it disturbed her. She felt uncomfortable and wanted to run to Gigi's arms. When she left the house she had told herself it was to let him get some rest after his trip, but that was just a pretext: it was to avoid the sour mood he was always in when awakened brusquely from a deep sleep. She stood up.

"Come see Paletta whenever you want. I keep her in the house because I'm afraid she'll get pregnant, and she's acting so strange these days she may be going into heat. As soon as we go back to Genoa I'll have her spayed."

Tosca's outcry astonished her. "No! Don't do it! Not before she has become a woman!" She stopped, momentarily embarrassed. "Because I live with cats I know I must say things that sound weird to others. I meant that if she doesn't have a male, and doesn't have a litter, she'll never be a healthy, normal animal. Even animals become neurotic, don't you think? But if you let her have some kittens, and have her sterilized before she goes into heat again, she'll be all right, she'll be a gentle cat. Because she'll know what she should know, and will have had what's hers by right."

5

For several mornings Tosca had awakened with a vague uneasiness that was not exactly illness, but a kind of intimation of it. A tremor in her bones, a nervous agitation spreading over her whole body, perhaps in her blood, that she explained to herself with a name she couldn't remember where she had heard it. Tachycardia. "Here it is again," she said to herself, "I'm shaking all over, and yet I'm sleeping no worse than usual. Poppa doesn't even complain about the heat any more, poor thing. The air is fresher after the sprinkle last night, and maybe I'll skip the inhaler this morning. Too much cortisone's not good for you. Well, what else can I do? Nothing, but I'm shaking all over. If I had a tail like yours, Poppa, it would be like a straw in the wind."

Tosca stood up and the cat followed her with her eyes without moving her head, dejected like the rest of her—ears, body, paws, tail. Tosca caressed her, then slowly moved closer to her the bowl of milk that the animal had not touched during the night. Poppa breathed faster, and Tosca understood. "You don't even have the strength to hiss at me, but I get the message. You don't want it."

Then she went into the bathroom. Tosca had always taken good care of her appearance, even though she commented ironically to herself, "No one wants you any more, but you keep at it," and then, "So what? I have to please myself."

Once she would have added, "and Miciamore." Now she sighed and stopped herself in time. She had Poppa to look after, but she wanted to do it with loving care, not in the careless, hasty way one cares for mothers-in-law, or daughters-in-law, or neighbors.

Love inspires love. Hers for Miciamore had been returned—lazily, with intervals of absence, with egotistical stubbornness, with caprice and changes of mood, like the most beloved, tender, cruel lovers, able to dominate because never completely dominated.

Tosca returned to the kitchen. As she was pouring a cup of coffee, the sound of the doorbell made her jump and she scalded her hand.

It was the gasman coming to read the meter. Poppa's first litter, three small tabby cats shot in behind him. Tosca exclaimed, suddenly cheerful, "Here are the three musketeers! Poppa, look, you have visitors. Aren't you happy?"

The three young cats surrounded their large pregnant mother, each head trying to reach the milk source, mewing, anxiously trying to communicate to her. Poppa stirred; her long tail whipped the air. The three leaped back, stiff with fright. Tails and ears straight, they watched her with glassy eyes.

The gasman got off his knees after reading the meter under the sink and wrote the numbers in his book. "You don't lack for company," he observed, and after a pause, "but they smell bad."

Tosca exploded. "It's the heat. Not the cats. Instead of raising the rates you should check the pipes. Can't you see there's more rust than solid metal? And there's no water pressure."

The man answered placidly, "That's not up to us. Tell your apartment owner. They've used cheap material to cut costs. It takes special pipes for salty water."

He headed for the door, but Tosca stopped him with a touch on his arm. "I'm sorry. I know you can't do anything about it, but it makes me mad when someone blames the poor animals, who couldn't be cleaner! And as far as the owner of this apartment is concerned, it's better to let sleeping dogs lie. I'll keep these pipes as long as I can. This year I painted the walls, and the year before I re-did the bathroom." A pause and then, "Do you want some coffee? I just made it."

The man refused with a smile, and Tosca was left alone again with the four cats. In a flash the three small ones surrounded her, rubbing against her bare legs. Laughing and shying away from their tickling that brought the inner tremor to the surface, Tosca filled three bowls with food from the refrigerator.

Tosca always had some extra food on hand for their occasional visits. She had wanted to keep Miciamore's first offspring and had raised them herself because Poppa wasn't a good mother. She went back to her nighttime prowling too soon and sometimes stayed out all night. Tosca had fed them with a baby bottle.

When the landlady came from Turin in May with her maid for the big yearly cleaning, there had been some difficult skirmishes. Every day a complaint, every day an insult. The deodorants Tosca sprinkled around didn't help, and neither did the daily disinfecting with alcohol, rubbing each step by hand. If Tosca crossed paths with the landlady and her maid, an elderly woman who spoke only Sicilian dialect, they unfailingly pretended disgust, holding their noses or covering them with a handkerchief. When Poppa got pregnant again, and the other three were weaned and healthy, Tosca gave up and sent them out into the world.

The three hadn't made a fuss. If they saw her in the street they ran up to her. Sometimes they mewed in the garden if they hadn't found anything to satisfy their hunger, or because some other cat had finished the food Tosca hid under the bougainvillea. At times they begged to come in. And they always sought out the maternal breast. Now that they had cleaned up the bowls, Tosca opened the door. Slowly, one by one, they went out and down the stairs.

Their mother hadn't moved. A thin thread of saliva bathed her face, a violent contraction passed like a wave over her belly. A sound torn from her viscera forced Tosca to face the obvious. She dialed the veterinarian's number she knew by heart and got his promise to come at once.

Squatting down beside the animal, she slowly massaged her as she had been taught, but she couldn't keep at it. Tosca's tremors had become quick jolts, her breathing labored, "I'll be right back, don't be afraid!" she called. The inhaler gave her temporary relief, while Poppa's voice rose in tone, lacerating and yet low, the modulation continuous and varied with constant pain. The veterinarian arrived in time to give assistance to the woman who slumped to the floor after opening the door--her last lucid moment before falling unconscious.

6

Three days later Tosca told Toni about "the happy event." She was in the garden again because of another problem. Poppa refused to stay in the house and care for her newborn, a little male with closed eyes, who was now lying on a pillow under the oleander. Giulia, from the beauty shop, had seen Poppa roll him down the stairs and put him in the shade under a car parked in a no parking zone. After that Tosca improvised a bed for him under the bush. The mother cat came around every once in awhile, but all attempts to bring her back into the house failed before her stubbornness, first cold and then furious.

"She had seven," Tosca said to the kind woman bent over the still shapeless, ugly little creature. "The veterinarian helped me get rid of them. I was trouble for him. Just think, I fainted from one of my asthma attacks the moment he came in. He put the kittens in a box and covered them with cotton soaked in ether. They didn't suffer that way."

And answering Toni's tacit question, "I kept this one because she chose it. Believe me, they understand everything. She knew she would lose them, so she hid this one inside the cupboard. I didn't see her do it, but she must have taken advantage of the open cupboard when I offered the doctor a beer. When I found him I didn't have the courage to kill him by myself. And so now I've started all over again."

Toni observed, "I think he has blue eyes, from what I can see."

"Wonderful! Oh, she made a good choice, poor thing! She saved him, but won't feed him. And look at those other three." She ran to the cats that had appeared out of nowhere and were already lying beside the mother to suckle the fresh milk.

"He's your brother, you beggars! Leave some for him. He's still little. Go away!"

Hissing, their claws visible, the three relinquished their position. Poppa seemed indifferent as Tosca talked to her. "You hid him in the house for me to take care of, eh? Oh, no, slut that you are. You take care of him, and send these ugly spoiled cats away who just want your love."

Toni took advantage of Tosca's concentrated indignation to slip silently away through the little door leading to the alley, where palm trees stood against a background of blue sea.

That morning, after Giulia noticed the little kitten, Toni had seen it under the car, when a friend who had spent the weekend with her and Gigi had heard the mewing and had just missed backing over it. Toni informed Tosca, who hadn't been aware of anything. She had left her apartment door open in order to hear the telephone while she cleaned the stairs, leaving the two, mother and son, asleep and satisfied. However, Poppa's craving for freedom had been too strong. Tosca scolded her again, "You're a gypsy. You didn't deserve Miciamore. Your children are even better than you. They want to nurse because you're a worthless mother and didn't feed them when they were little. But do you see them now? They clean their little brother, not you."

Just then a ray of sunshine suddenly broke through the branches. Quickly, agilely Poppa took the kitten in her teeth and moved her to the shade. Tosca felt encouraged. Maybe that cat had more sense than she thought. Tosca called the other three away so there would be some milk left for the little one. In the kitchen she watched them eat. Later she would think what to fix for herself; it wasn't worth going to much trouble when you're alone, when you aren't waiting for someone to come home!

Her house was more a refuge for the cats than for her. Love is nourishment and rest, something cats know and remember. But what did she have to think about? The newborn. That was all. After it gained enough weight she would give it to Giulia, because she couldn't aggravate the landlady with another animal on the stairs. For some time the woman had barely spoken when they met, and Tosca felt so tired. . . She lit another cigarette. The three were now huddled together, their bellies full, their faces happy, their eyes shut in the innocence of sleep.

With her free hand she put on one of her two favorite cassettes. Songs from the days she lived with other thoughts. Popular singers Mina, Ornella, Paoli, salty tastes, sky-filled rooms, sweet sleep with someone breathing next to you! She hadn't had a friendly body to depend on for such a long time. Embraces, the stolen hour, is a gift, but there is nothing like the peace that comes from the warmth lying next to you that you recognize in your sleep. The cassette ended and she put in her other favorite, "Verranno a te sull'aure," "Un bel dì vedremo," "Una voce poco fa," "Tutte le feste al tempo," "Amammi Alfredo." She turned down the volume. A subdued wave of sound was enough for those songs that had accompanied her daily life in the Milan apartment where she had gone as Mario's bride. How tender and far away were those songs in their absolute freedom from any real misery! Listening to them always made her uneasy, made her feel sharply nostalgic for something she couldn't define, but something that had touched her and then vanished. An angel's wing that would never touch her again. She stood up and went to the window. Even the sea was off limits for her. She could smell it, but no swimming. Sun and beach were bad for her. Once, at night, she had violated the order, but she hadn't been alone — otherwise she would have been too afraid to go. The harpy must have seen her from her upstairs window, because Tosca heard about it from some gossip that reached her ears. She smoothed her hair. She didn't want to think about that. The blue out there and the singer's caressing voice were too perfect! She longed to embrace the sun-warmed palm trees, embrace the sea, drink the sky. A light tremor shook her. The familiar tachycardia. She laughed and spoke out loud, as she did more often now. "But this time it's not my illness! It's my sensitivity. Mario told me I'm sensitive, and Bruno did, too. . ."

The cassette ended. And melancholy weighed on her chest like a hostile, suffocating hand.

She opened the refrigerator and took out a bottle, a tomato, and a ball of mozzarella. On the windowsill a pot of basil offered comfort to her suddenly hot face, while her body was covered in cold sweat. She pinched off two basil leaves to flavor the mozzarella and tomato, poured a glass of wine, and drank. "Here's to menopause, to bad moods, to cats, to the damn awful things that get me down!" At the first mouthful she placed the fork on the plate and lowered her head onto the crook of her arm. She was crying, but she wanted to wail as women in the south are said to do.

It was the quiet time of day, the hottest and most sultry time. No voices or human sounds came through the open window, only the occasional drone of a car on Via Aurelia.

The cats looked like sculptures, their bodies abandoned in the absolutely immobile sleep of adolescents. When Miciamore or Poppa slept they never lost awareness of their surroundings. A creak, a whisper, a blade of light were enough to set off alarms in their nervous systems. Not these. They were sated, young, inexperienced, or only experienced enough to know they slept under watchful maternal eyes. Hers. Mother of cats. "Oh, Mario, Mario, if you could see me now you would know. . ." She got up to look for a handkerchief. Tears bathed her face. She had lost any desire to eat and blew her nose loudly to check the sensitivity of her three musketeers. Only one lifted an ear; the other two gave no sign of life. She smiled and poured another glass of wine, sipping it slowly. The cool liquid brought a kind of physical comfort; she felt better. Incredible how a drop of wine can change your mood. She filled her glass again, and this time drained it in a single long voluptuous gulp that filled her throat with intense pleasure.

Quickly she tossed the oily mozzarella and tomato slices into the garbage pail. She hadn't eaten anything but a bite of badly cooked bread — tasteless, thready, like rope. Ah, Lombard bread was for her — fragrant and well cooked like French bread! It wasn't possible to find decent bread on the Riviera. The kitchen was tidy again, not a crumb on the floor. With a damp cloth she wiped away a stain the bottle left on the plastic tabletop. There was still a bit of wine left in the bottle. No use cluttering the frig with such a small amount; she poured it into her glass and drank it down.

Tosca felt almost good and was growing sleepy. In the bedroom the shadow on the wall made by the lowered blind gave the illusion of a fresco. Lying down she began her preparatory ritual for sleep, not allowing her head or heart to churn with harmful, angry thoughts. She went over Mario's life — not the part he spent with her in their married life, but the part he had walked alone before, when she knew nothing about the man she would meet, tender and full of imagination, so much richer in experience and culture than she. Even if he only had the fifth grade written on his workman's papers, while she lacked only two years training to be an accountant. When she told her mother of their plans to marry she had had to overcome her mother's resistance to the idea, just because of his work and lack of education and money. He was a shoemaker, but didn't own the little shop he opened in the old quarter of Corso Garibaldi when he came back from the war. He paid a modest rent and worked with the same precision and grace he put into everything. They had a comfortable life without money worries, and a richly enjoyable life because Mario knew everything and read everything. She learned much more from him than she ever learned in school. He acted with an amateur group and in this way, little by little, Tosca became exposed to things other than figures and current accounts. Those things belonged to her not particularly difficult office life. The rest was the fantasy, the witty patter that Mario acted out for her on winter evenings. Then, with happy heart palpitations, she remembered opening nights, books, music, and get-togethers with friends, suppers at one of the many neighborhood restaurants or along the canals, Sundays on the banks of the Ticino or at the stadium.

Mario didn't come from Milan as she did. He had grown up in the country between Cremona and Crema, where he learned his craft, and where he worked the land in his free time. Then he went to war and was gone a long time. Nine and a half years. He came back a sergeant major with a bronze medal and decided that working the land wasn't for him any more. He became a craftsman; they met, and were married for sixteen happy years.

Tosca sighed. If he were still alive he would be seventy-seven years old, almost seventy-eight. She quickly calculated how many months it was before his birthday. Mario was born in 1914, belonging to the generation Mussolini hurt the most. Perhaps, she thought (ashamed of herself), I wouldn't be so happy anymore. She moved around in search of a cool spot in the bed. Fifty-three years is a lot, but too few to give it all up. . . If her thoughts took that track she wouldn't be able to stop them before she hit bottom, but she managed to pull herself up before it was too late. Cigarettes and matches were on the dresser. She lit one and tried to detour her imagination by thinking only about Mario.

So many times she had thought about his ability for improvising, with a gentleness that was strange and unexpected in someone born in the country. The skill in his hands! In the early days of marriage Tosca would sometimes break a plate, a cup, a knickknack, always nervous about the housework, because the office took up most of her time. The first time it happened she felt desperate. Then she stopped worrying and even enjoyed herself, because there was nothing Mario didn't know how to fix and make work smoothly again. If an appliance burned out or a sink leaked, he soothed her complaints, and calmly, precisely, got out the tools he kept neatly in two different colored boxes, and in no time at all things began to work, the radio to play, water to run, lamps to shine, objects to reappear in tip-top condition.

"The war forced me to make-do the best I could," he told her, and the war became a familiar event by listening to him talk about his unit, companions, marches, friends, Africa, Russia, the many Italian cities he had seen before leaving for foreign fronts. She would think "the war" and immediately one of her privately created and perhaps absurd little films would appear in her imagination. A Russian hut, a wasteland of snow or sand, a choir of soldiers in the courtyard of an old barracks, a mess hall full of ravioli prepared with a local cheese and nettles gathered by the whole unit, and always him, Mario, with his accordion that kept a thread of memory or an illusion of happiness alive. He played so well, so sadly, also so strangely—he called those his "variations." But somehow the music became different when Mario played. More difficult, but it touched your heart when he played slowly, or made you forget everything when the notes flew by.

Tosca thought once again how friendly Mario had been. His companions must have liked him when he was an enlisted man like them, and his soldiers after he was promoted. Even the prisoners at Loano liked him.

In August, when she had her vacation, Mario would close his shop and give himself three weeks by the sea with his sister. Tosca helped him cook for an elderly couple from Turin who rented the living room with the convertible divan. She and Mario fixed up the storeroom where his sister's husband kept his peach crop in the winter, and Mario, free and happy, managed to make himself useful as always. Even his last summer, she remembered, he tired himself out with the many things he did for different people in the village, and he worked on the annual Feast of the Assumption performance at Loano prison, giving up many hours of sleep.

He brought the scripts from Milan himself, with the parts for each of the principal actors. The prison director was a friend. The time of atrocious prisons and prison guards was still to come, and the prisoners were calmer—more unfortunate than delinquent. A few thieves, some swindlers, a murderer who had served so much time that no one could remember (or pretended not to remember) the reason why a man from the south had ended up in that Ligurian village, in the ancient monastery where the iron bars had changed the monks' voluntary isolation to enforced segregation. Tosca also helped with these performances, along with the wives of the director and the three guards. The first time with dreadful shyness, then more at ease, feeling herself among friends, just as at the little theater on Corso Garibaldi.

Many times Mario had asked her to take a part in the plays, but she always refused. Her timidity kept her from saying out loud the lines she had learned by heart with a voracious appetite, and which she would sometimes recite for him, mischievous and triumphant, like a secret adventure she finally got enough courage to confess. These were their most indescribable hours of love, impossible to recount to her sister-in-law, or a friend. How explain the plot of seduction that thickened around the two of them, making them forget everything outside themselves that was there before and would be there after them, a need that flowed from her amorous body and made Mario touch her with his delicate and knowing hands—hands that must have made sparks on her skin like male caresses on Poppa's back. And there were those absolute moments, a losing of themselves in the other that she couldn't remember because nothing of those words, those gestures, were fixed in her memory. Only a hazy but strong feeling, like some strange music, like a melodic wave, came back to her with the same intensity every time the memory of that love ran through her.

The cigarette was finished. She lay down and tried to recover the drowsiness that had brought her to bed. Suddenly she remembered a detail of that time she hadn't thought of since. Once when Tosca, with a last good night kiss, had expressed her lover's gratitude to him as a blessing from fate, Mario had replied, "You should give your thanks to God, if you believe in Him. Not to me. I'll tell you something about fate." And he told her about an episode that for some reason he had never told her, but she understood it was shame that had kept him silent for such a long time.

It was at El Alamein, at the height of the war, in a little outpost where English fire rained down day and night, with ten men stuck behind the lines, abandoned and lost in the desert after a grenade cut off the last contact with the others. Mario, a corporal, had been sent on a mission with three soldiers to connect the telephone lines a few yards away. But that unknown tract of sand they had to cross frightened them. They left the trench they had dug deep enough to feel protected, and with one jump had reached a natural ditch formed by the wind. They must have been seen because the shelling immediately sounded different and more intense. They had to hurry because the horizon was growing lighter.

"The three soldiers next to me were shaking so hard they couldn't speak. I was as scared as they were, or maybe even more so. I couldn't stand another minute in that no man's land between us and the others, so I gestured for them to get down as low as they could, and I dashed out. It took a few minutes or maybe an hour, I'll never know. I connected the wires and crawled back during a lull in the explosions. All three were dead, lying in the same position, big boots touching, arms at their sides, wide-open eyes, at an equal distance from each other like three points of a monstrous three-leaf clover. A grenade had hit them head-on and they had fallen like that, a triangle of senseless death I've never been able to understand. Why them and not me?" Mario had held her close again, and she understood that he had let her into one of the most secret corners of his mind. After a little, with his voice already lost in sleep, he had said, "And that's how I earned the rank of sergeant and the bronze medal."

Mario was right to speak of fate, and not to understand why. What sense did his death have, so many years later, from an accident on Via Aurelia?

A little boy had been crossing the road. The driver saw the boy suddenly appear in front of him and managed to miss him, but the car skidded and hit Mario, who was returning home with the shopping bag hanging from his bicycle handlebars. They took him to the hospital at once, but he was dead on arrival. Desperate to understand, Tosca looked at him lying there without any apparent sign of injury. They explained that his brain had been fatally injured in the fall on the pavement. The bandages framing his ashen face made him look younger and more pure, a surprised angel, with the shadow of a smile on his lips. They had to carry her away, and perhaps her illness had begun then. During the first days of mourning she couldn't breathe because of the agonies wracking her breast. When her normal breathing rhythm didn't resume, the doctors talked about allergies. "Allergic to accidents, to being alone, allergic to desperation. What do the doctors know about it? The poor things talk about what they've studied, but no one really understands anything, the real reasons, the why and the how of things . . ."

A noise woke her up. The cigarette pack had fallen off the nightstand. One of the three cats was watching her from the dresser. She exchanged glances, not fully awake. He stretched out a paw toward her and moved it in the air like a greeting. She spoke to him soothingly, and with a leap he was next to her, acquiescing to her caresses a moment before jumping down. Now all three cats were together, rested and satisfied, wanting to play. By the door, tails high, they were waiting. She laughed. "Look at the hypocrite. I thought he was happy to see me, but he just came to get me to open the door."

They filed out slowly, with dignity, and the last of the three, in gratitude for what she had done, rubbed against her legs before following the other two.

"A true gentleman," Tosca said, and she felt hungry. Humming, she picked up her billfold and went out. She would give herself a present of a nice cheese sandwich cooked to a T.

7

On the way to the coffee bar—her only social outing in the summer, which had to end when the bar closed at the season's end and the tourists left—Tosca was thinking about the homage just received from the male of the trio. Puss resembled Miciamore, even in character, she thought, though he was still so much smaller. "He's just a young fellow, like these boys here," and she tried to maneuver past the group of mainly bare-chested boys blocking the entrance to the bar. They stood in the space enclosed by a low red brick wall, furnished with tables where customers could sit. The boys considered the wall their private property, something everyone accepted, even the owners, even the policeman who came twice a day to put tickets, accompanied by yells of protest, on the windshields of illegally parked cars. But the boys had gotten a bit out of hand this summer. The bar's owner, standing between two tables overturned in a pile of broken glass, was yelling at them. She grabbed one of the boys by the arm and he, a stocky fellow with a curved snout, turned on her, letting loose a flurry of swear words.

Tosca stopped to give him an indignant tongue-lashing. In the meantime the other boys made a circle around the snarling fellow who they carried off almost bodily. One of them, whose hairline was already receding, asked the owner how much they owed her for the broken glasses and cups.

When the owner came back into the bar, Tosca was waiting for her, and smoking a cigarette. "Every year it gets worse. I don't know where it'll end or how much of it we can stand."

The other woman, still red faced, made no reply. Nervously her hands moved in a succession of careful, practiced motions: the broom, the dustpan, a damp rag for the floor, a sponge for the tables, new ashtrays to replace the broken ones. Finally, she asked Tosca what she would like. Gradually her natural color and normal tone of voice returned. The woman, coming from Germany, had lived in the village for ten years, and though the villagers thought well of her, they still called her "La Tedesca." She was very clean: her glasses always gleamed like crystal. And although she didn't forget even the most insignificant debt that the boys tended to forget, in compensation the entire population of summer visitors would swear to her honesty. The mothers of the youngest boys entrusted their sons' finances to her, and paid the bill as soon as they received it.

Grete was corpulent, with her great bust held high by a rigid, armor-like corset that gave the impression it might suffocate her when, as now, the blood flowed to her face. She was often disturbed by indignation, which she almost always kept in check or gave vent to in her native language through clenched teeth.

Sitting down next to Tosca, she also lit a cigarette and sighed. Now she was pale, and Tosca noticed the violet circles around her eyes, poorly concealed under makeup. Almost to herself, the woman said, "I won't be back next year."

Tosca was alarmed. Grete was one of the few people she could talk to; she he knew everything about her and her cats and never made fun of her. And Grete had confided things about herself that she never told anyone in the village: her Jewish origin and her plan to earn enough to go to Israel and start over. Sometimes, during the slack hours, when the sun was hottest, Tosca would go with her to the pier where, screened by the rocks, Grete would sun herself and immerse her stiff whale's body into the sea with surprising ease. She swam well, with a grace that fascinated Tosca. Grete always managed to amaze her, and Tosca had learned to accept without question the sharp contrast between her large body and everything about her that wasn't physical—feelings, thoughts, behavior. Even now Grete postponed her moment of relaxation because of Tosca's forlorn expression and asked how she was feeling and how Poppa was getting along.

Tosca answered her questions and timidly concluded, "But don't be angry, and please don't think about going away forever!"

Grete smiled, took a bottle from the refrigerator under the counter, and offered Tosca a drink on the house.

At that moment her husband arrived. If he was annoyed, he didn't let on. A small, sturdy man, he was always impeccable even during the sultry hours of the day. Everything about him was smaller than normal size: height, hands, eyes, but in harmonious proportions; a gnome, with a clean apron always wrapped around his perfectly creased trousers and fresh linen shirt; a ferret-look in his black, shining eyes, two basalt blueberries, rarely a smile on his well-shaped little mouth under a small mustache, trimmed twice daily.

As she looked at him Tosca thought she had never seen him with a hair out of place and, as always, she felt uneasy in his presence. She could never talk to him without embarrassment. She hadn't yet figured out which of the two ruled the roost. Grete looked at him without animosity, but also without love it seemed to her. He affected a tone of authority when there were witnesses to his exchange of opinions with his wife, and Tosca had wondered more than once if the brain in that little head was equal to Grete's.

Now Pasqualino's hand brushed his wife's back, and Tosca lowered her eyes, scolding herself for such wicked thoughts. Who could say what kept a couple together, what the alchemy was between two people, which no outsider could ever completely understand? She rose, said good-bye, and only when she was back on the street did she realize she had forgotten to eat.

Tosca didn't want to turn back or go to the nearby dairy store where the villagers congregated. She felt too many cold eyes on her when she went there to buy milk for her cats.

Suddenly Tosca felt deprived, not only of a sufficient reason for living (that's how she put it, surprised at how little pain it caused), but also deprived of the freedom to choose whether to eat or not. In addition to that, she had no desire either to open her mouth and face the people or to fix the food. The hunger had passed. She would buy a big bottle of white wine, and even before cooling it would get the only kind of lift possible for her now.

Oh, please don't let her run into him! And to avoid having to come back soon, she decided to buy two liters. Every time she set off toward that stretch of Via Aurelia she felt her heart pound harder in the fear of running into his wife or one of his children. She had reduced her errands to the bare minimum in that part of village for this very reason. Every once in awhile she preferred to take the bus to shop in the nearby city and do the few bureaucratic chores that required going to a public office. They knew her at the village post office and she knew that the young woman, very nice on the surface, but with hostile eyes (she wasn't wrong, the cats had taught her to understand the flash of an eye, the subtlety of a glance, the barely contained threat of movement) was his wife's friend, perhaps because she also had a sickly air, and Tosca understood the basis of that friendship too well. There is almost a clique among the unwell, with a common language, an understanding that goes beyond personality or environment. They belong to the tribe of the unhealthy in the deaf and indifferent world of the physically sound.

She, too, was now part of that tribe, but an outsider, and had become even more of an outsider just when she thought she had broken the barrier of mistrust and difference that she had brought with her. In this town everyone knew everyone else, and they helped each other even when they didn't like each other, sticking together especially in their hate of outsiders. The more they disliked them the more they flattered and fawned over the non-natives in order to squeeze money from them. She had never understood the locals, and Mario certainly would have chided her for it. He was tolerant, ready to understand. But she wasn't. She had never been able to tolerate the nasty remarks that came out in the winter about the people she had seen them cow-tow to and make over like pimps in the summer.

When the *thing* had happened. (She called it that out of shame, unable to say *love* anymore; she didn't even know what it was: drunkenness, illusion, need for warmth with one of villagers.) She had tried to understand the others through him, and had hoped to become friends with them. After a time she realized it had been her greatest mistake; but she also knew that when Bruno went through incredible detours on his way to her, sometimes even being delayed for as long as an hour by stopping to drink or play a game of cards with whomever he might meet, he was demonstrating his loving regard for her. She didn't want their secret to be discovered, because she was afraid of everyone, of the village, of its condemnation, of the blackmail potential. She wasn't kidding herself. Someone in those six years (they seemed so many, to think of it now, that for almost three years had been only a tormenting memory) must have seen him go in or out of the little back alley gate that was closed in the winter, and it hadn't helped that he always came to see her with his waterproof jacket and fishing gear. Perhaps one of the card players at the dairy had become suspicious, or some woman, pausing by chance at her banging shutter, had noticed someone in the deserted alley. And so they put him under surveillance and discovered that Bruno had a lover while his wife was in the mental institution.

Bruno's marriage had been a Calvary from the beginning. After their first child his wife began to show signs of emotional instability. They treated her by filling her with pills that after a time made her calm and sleepy. But one day (no one knew why) the madness woke from its lethargy and made her do something that had everyone talking, and he took her back to the city for another interval of exile from the living. She had never been violent, and was mild in her ravings, but no one would have left her in charge of a child. Yet she had three children and took good care of them when feeling herself. When the malignant winds began to blow inside her that gradually filled her mind with melancholy, she started looking at her children like a caged animal. She didn't recognize them, and if they cried or asked her for help, she would hold her hands over her ears and shut herself up in the farthest room. Then she would begin her game, different every time, that made no sense to anyone. She would pile everything in the middle of a room, working hard to move the heaviest items. She would slice up mattresses, letting the wool fly around the house like snow. The last time she had cut up all the sheets in small strips and wound them around herself like bandages, and then folded them up neatly in the wardrobe she had emptied of clothes. Bruno later found the clothes in the dumpster, and when he scolded her she ran off crying. Everyone in the village felt sorry for him and helped with the children when he was alone. One would take the smallest child to nursery school; another would shop so he could cook supper when he returned from his repair shop. Tosca had heard he was very good at repairing televisions, even those as old as hers, and that is how she met him. He had come to her house, more tired from adversity than from work. The rest was the natural result of their being alone. But that long parenthesis had been beautiful, with excitement, waiting, carefully prepared meals, tender and sometimes fierce embraces, such as those after the holidays when he had spent all the time with his children, because watchful eyes on those special days were harder to avoid. Tosca had hoped the villagers would accept her also because Bruno had recovered his good humor, was in better health, and she had allowed herself to think: "Perhaps no one will mind if I help him, mend his children's socks, and knit them nice sweaters."

How many times she had thought, "If only his wife wouldn't come back!" And she felt ashamed, even though there was nothing bad in just thinking it. If his wife was doomed to a madness that meant exile and oblivion, Tosca could have raised the children and made Bruno's life less difficult. She didn't think she was bad, or that she was doing anything bad, but if Bruno guessed her thoughts from something she said, he would grow glum and withdraw into stubborn silence. She had never dared talk openly to him, never had a plan other than their eating supper together, and always in her house. She had suffered when he withdrew, as she suffered now from his unremitting hardheartedness. When his wife came back the last time, dismissed as "cured," he had never again come through the alley gate, nor had he phoned, after that single awful communication made in a breathless voice. He was leaving, he had to go get her, they were sending her home, there was a law he had to obey, she should never expect to see him again.

Tosca went into the shop on Via Aurelia where boxes and dollies filled with liquors and wine were stacked outside; the owner greeted her kindly. "The men are always nicer than the women in this village," she thought while waiting to be served, reflecting that it was still a few hours before sunset. God, how awful the summer was for someone who had nothing to look forward to! When it grew dark the traffic would slow down for a while and the place would be left in silence for a short time. In homes and boardinghouses they were eating supper and making plans made for the evening. Most of the adults settled on a walk

as far as the dock or under the palm trees. The young people gathered by the wall and then took their motorbikes and cars to
discos or to towns offering more diversion. Their village was
lazy and reserved; and just because it was like an oyster stuck to
a rock, it allowed them greater freedom at all hours and for
every age than the more elegant vacation spots.

How many of the vacationers she had seen come as small
children, then turn into adolescents from one summer to the
next, involved with their first love. Later, some of them, their
youthful beauty too soon lost, with thinning hair and encroach-
ing flabbiness, would pass her pushing baby buggies. Evenings
for Tosca were always the same after her affair with Bruno. Even
when it was hot in her apartment she didn't have the courage to
go out alone to enjoy the cool air on the dock. That would mean
crossing the village at the time when everyone stood chatting in
the doorways. The street resembled one enormous corridor
where news went from door to door, mouth to mouth, and there
was no goodwill in the eyes that glanced at her if she ever impulsively decided to go out.

"It's not like I have the plague; I don't owe anyone anything," and she would reach the benches at the dock as exhausted as if she had climbed a mountain. That wasn't living. She took
the big bottle, rested its coolness on her belly that was always
swollen these days, and set out for home. A motorbike passed a
few inches from the sidewalk and slowed down. She felt weak; it
was Bruno. Not a greeting, not a gesture. The look they exchanged would be enough to fill her time as she waited for
night.

8

Tosca had just about finished washing the lobby, rinsing the detergent for the third time, because the landlady — the Nazi was what she called her when she talked to her cats — had accused her of leaving the stairs sticky, "a real danger to everyone." That accusation was making her perspire more than the effort, when she found herself face to face with the journalist, in a linen suit, holding a briefcase and overnight bag, his diet-thin face looking younger with a suntan. They exchanged smiles and greeted each other in low voices because the horizon was barely pink, and a nighttime coolness was still in the air.

He was leaving for Rome, a hurried trip to the airport by car, a quick job and, "Tonight I hope to be back in time for the concert. By the way, will you come with us? I have an extra ticket. Tell Toni about it. The two of you can go, and if I'm late, I'll go straight to Finale to join you."

Tosca blushed with pleasure and gratitude and stammered her thanks. What a nice man! Surely he remembered how they had chatted together the previous summer when she had visited them. They had talked about the amateur theatrical troupe in Milan, her lifelong passion for the theater and music, and how much she missed Corso Garibaldi and the Navigli canal.

Tosca put the broom and rags away and looked over the garden. The plants were smiling in the early morning sun. After giving them a good soaking, Tosca was sure they were smiling. Poppa raised her head to look at her and meowed. Thank goodness the little one was nursing.

"I understand now. For the time being I'm to bring him to you. Well, I'm glad you're finally beginning to be a little bit responsible."

That early morning encounter was pleasant and she climbed the stairs without gasping for breath. Puss and Bisi, Poppa's two adolescent males, were waiting for her at the door. They came back home more often now. The female, Fifi, was more self-sufficient and independent and could stay away for days.

"You didn't think there would be any milk for you here, did you?" Tosca smiled when she saw them, but suddenly became concerned. A red line parted the fur on Puss's head, and he was licking the blood coming from a deep wound on his forepaw.

Tosca picked him up and went into the apartment followed by Bisi who sidled along, his slightly rough fur in constant contact with her legs. From that bristly, barely felt contact, Tosca could tell the cat was tense: what had those two been up to? If Puss had been in a bloody fight and his brother was sticking to him like that, no doubt they had been in a tight fix together, and Bisi was informing her of it in his own way, asking for attention for himself, too. If he had run away leaving his brother alone they wouldn't have come back together. Tosca knew that. She spoke to him fondly and gave them both the food she had ready. While they ate she took care of the injured one.

It could have been that bully Mustafà who had dared to challenge Miciamore in the past. Now that the whole village, cats included, had united to get rid of the only one who could stand up to him, Mustafà was boss again. Perhaps he wanted to take revenge on the children for the humiliations suffered from their father. Tosca had seen him roaming the alley sometimes, but hadn't paid any attention. Now she realized the hollow, throaty sound she had heard over and over at night was Mustafà's call. He was inviting them out, the bastard, challenging them to fight. Puss, who was the livelier of the two and braver as well—she knew it now—must have taken up the challenge. "Poppa could handle him!" she said aloud, but no animal dared come near Poppa. She was already quite big, so heavy with her swollen teats, but as soon as a presumed or possible enemy came close, she doubled in size. Lightning seemed ready to strike from every hair, her whiskers stood out on her face, her upper lip rose over bared teeth, claws unsheathed. Only after the enemy's smell faded would Poppa retract her claws and relax her whiskers and return to a tranquil state—not without vigilance, however.

Puss cried and complained when the alcohol got into the wounds, but he didn't run away and Tosca was proud of him. As a reward, she fixed him a pillow under the living room window near a big pot of verbena, his favorite spot. The pillow had been made soft and pliable to his body by his father's long use. His brother curled up close to him. Shortly afterwards Tosca noticed the two had struck a compromise. Both heads were lying on the pillow, with their bodies stretched out almost perfectly parallel on the floor.

For the thousandth time Tosca thought how much better it would be to teach children animal behavior from life instead of from obscure poetry, such as Pascoli's poem about the wolves and two children.

She really should get in touch with Toni, but she was embarrassed, afraid Toni might resent her husband's generosity. In any event, she would be ready. She would wash her hair and make herself presentable "to make a good impression," as Mario used to say when their work day was over and they went out to the theater or to visit friends.

She would wear a pretty, cool dress, one she had never worn. It was to have been a surprise for Bruno if he had ever once invited her out to dinner in some nice place, as she had hoped. Its soft colors were in a pattern of large spirals like clouds blowing across a blue sky. The V-shaped neckline showed the beginning of her full breasts. Tosca's legs were still shapely and slender, and the wide, straight folds of her dress hid her ample curves. With some makeup, a black lace shawl on her arm and patent leather sandals, Toni wouldn't be ashamed of her.

Toni wasn't at all surprised and was extremely nice when Tosca, after much hesitation, chose to communicate with her by telephone.

When it was time to leave, Tosca had been ready for some time. Toni rang the doorbell for her to come down; Gigi hadn't arrived yet. The two of them would go on without him.

Tosca hadn't felt like this for ages, like a little girl on a holiday. She asked herself why, as she got into Toni's small car, and the constant beating of her heart paused for an instant. The surprise of that thought had made it stop, and immediately afterwards it started up in its usual wild gallop.

She laid a hand on her chest in a gesture that had become habitual, but she wasn't worried. The doctor had told her palpitations were to be expected in someone as sensitive as she was. She was happy because she finally felt free. Whenever Bruno had come to see her she had already been waiting so long, peeping through the shutters, listening for the slightest noise on the stairs, that as happy as she was to see him, her happiness was always the exhausted epilogue of a thousand worries, anxiety, guilt feelings, vague (and therefore even more distressing) fears. Now let anyone see her. She had nothing to fear. Nothing to answer for. She relaxed against the back of her seat while Toni drove fast and confidently on the road not quite yet enveloped in darkness. A slight pink glow still colored the coastline, but out at sea the fishing boat lights were already shining. She thanked Toni for the unexpected treat, but Toni dodged her thanks by shifting the conversation to the performance they were going to attend. If it was something worthwhile, as she hoped, she would review it for her paper.

Tosca asked about her work. She had never read anything Toni had written, or that Gigi had, either; her retirement check didn't allow for many unnecessary expenses. Once a year she would get some women's magazines after the summer season had ended when Giulia gave her those left in the beauty shop. But the weekly magazine that Toni wrote theater reviews for was not among them.

It was nice talking to Toni; she knew everyone—artists, singers, directors— and was friends with some of them. During the coming week a group of these people might stay with them on their way to tour France. This was exciting news to Tosca. She knew them from television shows and was curious, asking about different ones. By the time they were parked not far from the open-air theater on the outskirts of the small village, they had become better friends. With that thought melancholy gave Tosca's heart another quick bite. She had forgotten how she too could make a play on words, could ignite with a flash of imagination some spirited fireworks about a person or situation. More than once Toni had laughed at her way of singling out the style of an actor or singer; once she had been welcome at merry dinner parties in Milan. Even in her solitary house, Bruno had often laughed with her, and with her had become interested in things other than his tiresome daily problems.

An incredible number of people were packed into the field normally used for sports when school was in session. Even the windows and balconies of the houses that formed a quadrangle around the field were full of people.

It was growing dark and the lights of Finale seemed far away. The large blooming hedges bordering the platform added to the illusion of a magic space created for the music. A grand piano and baskets of flowers completed the illusion.

Expectations for the great tenor were running very high. He hadn't performed for years, but people still loved him. Tosca listened to those around her talking about him. This one remembered seeing him in an opera in Genoa or Turin, another one had his records, a group behind them (Tosca had noticed they looked smart in a different way, somewhat more sophisticated and elegant) called him a nickname that implied a long-time familiarity. She mentioned it to Toni who glanced back after a while and named a few of them in a low voice. Tosca had heard of them. Mario often mentioned them in awe. A great actress, a well-known scene painter, a soprano who had sung with Luchino and Callas.

At the tenor's appearance the theater boiled and foamed and rumbled until it thickened into powerful prolonged applause.

Tosca made herself comfortable in her chair, and pulling her shawl close because the air had become chilly, with a pleasant feeling pervading her whole body, she waited for the music to fill the space between the houses and the depths of their souls.

Torna caro ideal the tenor was singing. He had aged some, his jacket fit just a bit too tightly over his stout chest. Yet he was still vigorous and self-confident. He could control the audience and lead it wherever he pleased, singing as well as he could and enjoying the applause no less than when he had sung as he should.

After three songs something special grew between him and the crowd.

A few voices called out a specific request. The nickname the women had called him while clapping and shouting "You're still the best!" was used by others as well. The evening followed a definite "crescendo" movement. The music was an exciting family party for the one who dispensed it and for those who enjoyed it.

Tosca was relaxed and excited at the same time. A kind of joyful fever made every familiar note seem a message addressed only to her. Life was beautiful. It could be again even for her. Why not hope for it?

And she too shouted "Bravo!" when the passionate Neapolitan barcarole, which she remembered hearing her mother sing so many times, had ended.

Toni was smiling. Once in a while she turned around to see if Gigi had arrived. During the interval they found him at the refreshment bar.

"There's no one here under fifty," Gigi remarked after greeting them, and Tosca felt offended. The music had relaxed her and she wasn't afraid to say what she thought. Toni took her side and Gigi enjoyed teasing them, complaining about female irrationality.

"Without women romanticism wouldn't have existed," Toni blurted out, naming glorious poets and artists that Gigi jokingly disposed of as "feminine temperaments."

But after the concert began again, even Gigi agreed that Toni could make a colorful article, adding, "don't forget a touch of irony. Dress up your enthusiasm with a few sharp remarks or you'll alienate your readers under twenty."

"I don't agree," Toni retorted. "They are the ones who turn to love and romance, my dear. *Il caro ideal*, with different music if you like, is always the same."

It was a nice evening. Gigi took the two women to a small restaurant where they were treated like queens. Toni explained that restaurant ratings depended somewhat on him. Tosca enjoyed her food more than she had in months.

When they drank a toast at the dessert, and Gigi gently touched Toni's arm lying on the table, Tosca was as moved by that gesture of endearment as if it were meant for her. She quickly lit a cigarette; she wouldn't have let them misunderstand her feeling for anything in the world.

Of one thing, at least, she was sure. Her solitude had not corrupted her to the point of envying people more fortunate than she. Love, even if not hers, was a sweetness in life that she recognized as a blessing. Something to be thankful for whether it touched someone she loved or someone who was merely kind to her.

When she got home Puss and Bisi dashed like elves through the room dimly lit by the streetlights. They were chasing a rubber ball that Tosca had kept in the house from the days of Miciamore.

She petted them, gave them fresh milk to drink, and opened the door in case they wanted to stretch their legs on a nocturnal expedition like their father used to do. But those two must have decided they'd had enough of the universe and its risky charms for one day. For a moment they stood uncertainly by the door, their tails upright; then slowly, unhurriedly, they returned to the living room and resumed their play. "Next winter when that woman's no longer here to keep an eye on me, if I know anything about cats, they'll be here to keep me company," Tosca told herself while she put away her silk dress and headed for bed, quite determined to fall asleep without giving in to melancholy.

9

However, her night was a long nightmare. She must have been more agitated than usual, because when a prolonged mewing outside woke her—it was a famished Fifi waiting by the door—the other two jumped on the rumpled sheets like children wanting to play. She opened the door for Fifi and went back to bed. Then they didn't stop licking her arms and neck with their rough little tongues; they pulled her hair with their teeth; they shot from one side of the bed to the other, restless and wanting reassurance. She petted all three of them in turn, but Fifi gave her only a distracted instant before running to her empty bowl. "I know, I know. Just a minute. I'm going to the bathroom and then I'll take care of you."

The cool water felt good. Her nightgown stuck to her skin, her face was drawn, and there were shadows around her eyes.

While she fixed the cats' breakfast, she told them about the dream that had kept her tied to her bed like an instrument of torture. She spoke in broken phrases while moving around the kitchen, thinking over the horrible images she could still see, trying to explain the reason for them to herself and to them. That dream would not have returned to haunt her if she didn't have some remorse in her heart.

"So many years have gone by, and I'm still afraid of those days as though they were yesterday."

A year after they were married she had to have an operation, and complications followed what was otherwise a successful procedure. A bad case of pneumonia kept her in an old, crowded, prewar hospital for a long time. She was shunted from one ward to another and had to put up with the most unpleasant neighbors. The smell of those beds and medicines, of the food eaten by visitors in the narrow passageway between one sick bed and another, those packages opened with curiosity and consumed voraciously under the patient and happy gaze of old mothers. Or young wives with unkempt husbands who thoughtfully handed out oranges and inquired about their release with the expression of abandoned puppies. How many she had seen! And they always talked about their children. The words, smells, everything had taken root inside her strong enough to nauseate her even today by just thinking about them. It had been a difficult recovery, and when she returned home she was still weak, and often her stomach could not tolerate food. A little thing like a crack in a plate, a basin with the enamel corroded by rust, an odor of disinfectant coming through the window was enough to make Tosca grow pale. Mario had stayed tenderly close, even with these weaknesses of hers, and without a word spoken between them had understood her refusal to have children.

Mario had been careful in the early months of their marriage so that their life could be freer. But at about the same time Tosca had gone to the hospital they had decided to have a baby. They both thought it was the right thing to do. But when that long and dreary (more than painful) time was over, Tosca had built up an invincible repulsion for every kind of physical violence almost without realizing it. Those women talked about births and savage abortions with an ease that seemed insane to Tosca. Blood, urine, feces. They described everything and seemed to be liberated by talking about it with the other women who would add their testimony of suffering with the same ease and finality. Tosca would huddle under the sheets listening to them and hating them. She hadn't said a thing to Mario but, as always, he understood. He had been more attentive than before, and sweeter, as one must be with a frightened child. Perhaps he expected her to say she wanted a child after her health returned to make her pretty and secure. But Tosca never mentioned it again.

"That's what bothers me. I would have a child now, Mario. Mario, you should have said something. Yes, I was afraid, but I would have done it. Other women do it, why not me?"

Instead he had respected her wishes. His being older made him an attentive lover, but also a paternal husband. He asked nothing of her, and the years had flown by. Then it was too late; when she finally said something, he told her with a smile he didn't want to risk losing a nice real wife for a probable brat.

They had been so good together! Whenever she said that to herself she was reminded of the first evening she came home from the hospital. Mario had stretched out next to her and sighed, "Oh, my bed, how wonderful!" and that told her he hadn't slept there since she left the house. They had a divan with broken springs in the living room that was not at all comfortable to sleep on, and Tosca had been touched by the thought of her big husband punishing himself every night to keep her company in his own way, or as an exorcism. To hide her feelings she asked him smilingly if he had taken a vow, but Mario, who was not a believer and detested every form of bigotry, evaded the question and kissed her good night.

Every once in awhile after she lost him she had a dream like the one last night. She didn't recognize where she was, she only knew she couldn't escape, that there was a good reason for making her stay there. She was lying in such a way that she couldn't figure out what the noise was down where her feet were suspended in the void. Then little thudding noises began, a shuffling that ended as soon as it began. And she saw, by twisting her eyes because she couldn't move or raise her head, some little animals rolling around her. A marten, a squirrel, some newborn cats, all wet, with eyes closed; some mice, some hamsters, all without life or shape. In her dream she knew they were animals without bones. They were being born at that moment (from her? from her feet?), but they were born dead.

"My babies I couldn't make. The kittens I had to get rid of."

She tried to despise herself, but could feel only pity. Her mouth began to tremble, and tears streamed down her face. She decided to fix coffee. Who knows why that horrible dream returned last night when she had gone to sleep happier than she had been for a long time. Maybe she had eaten too much or had too much to drink, maybe (who knows) that music had awakened a desire for love, and the unborn baby had come to remind her she had never given him life. Or maybe it was Poppa's delivery that had brought her fears and those miserable days to the surface. . .

The telephone was ringing. It was Toni calling to ask how she was and if she had slept well. "Very well," she answered, and began to thank her, without, however, succeeding, because Toni immediately proposed another concert two days later."Just the two of us," because Gigi had to be at their house in Genoa to prepare a survey.

The sun was high. On the radio they were talking about the rate of inflation. She changed to a station playing some music she knew, a Verdi prelude Mario had also been able to play, and she sang along in a low voice. She could begin the day by erasing the dream with a different thought, something new, a suggestion of friendship, a little music. It wasn't much, but it was a lot in a life like hers. But one still vague thought mixed in with the others. Without really seeing them, she rested her eyes on Miciamore's three offspring who were sleeping with full stomachs. Yes. It was certainly so. They had poisoned Miciamore. Not those cats the vacationers left, but just him, on purpose. She had loved him too much. Like a child. And they killed him.

She realized she had always known it, but hadn't wanted to dwell on the details or look into the motives. Any cat could come upon poisoned food, not only hers. The vacationers' cats became the villagers' winter enemies, along with their owners. But no.

Now she felt sure about it. When Bruno had gone back to his wife and Tosca was alone once again (and naive!), she had talked about her pet as though he were a friend, and they saw her with him on the beach, and heard when she called him, and they must have seen her running as far as San Lorenzo when he was in love. Who knows what fun they had conjuring up a way to punish her. The plan must have been hatched in one of those houses on the beach as the men mended nets, the children did their homework, and the women sewed.

The outsider had to be taught respect for their customs. "It's not our way." It's not right to love animals that much. She saw their hard faces, the treachery that became malicious in words the men muttered through their teeth. She heard the fat, obscene laughter immediately afterward. Who knows who had brought the poisoned food. . . A boy. No one would notice a boy passing through the alley. But the bits he let fall from his hands would have been prepared by his mother. The saintly woman who must be respected because God, the parish priest, and his father say so; the woman who teaches her son that women can be divided into two kinds: his wife, mother, and sister on the one hand, and prostitutes on the other.

While anger reddened her cheeks and made her breathing labored, Tosca didn't even realize she was drinking. She finally looked with surprise at the nearly empty bottle, and sighed. Her mouth felt sticky. Knowing she wouldn't be going out, she headed to her room, to her stale bed with rumpled sheets, and without making the slightest effort to smooth them, she fell heavily across the bed. In a minute she was snoring.

Part Two

1

I ask myself if it is still legitimate to write a novel or if the presumption is no longer permissible. Basically, the question of first
or third person is only a euphemism. First person is humble,
they say, unassuming, doesn't think he is God almighty; third
person exhibits the arrogance of a profession. A whore who
holds court rather than someone who minds her own business. I,
Gigi Moncalleri, journalist and gastronome, may pass as a
shabby whore, but not as a whorish demiurge. No, that's not
acceptable.

When I began thinking about Tosca and her cats, about our
seaside retreat, Toni's and mine, and then of writing about it, I
did so only to feel more alive, or a little less dead, and the third
person (I don't know why) seemed professionally less compro-
mising, more serious. What do you do? I write novels. The *vexata
quaestio, le quérelles* and the diatribes don't interest anyone. If I
write novels I write them according to the rules because I want
to and — why not say it? — because I was born to, because I don't
understand computers and how I wish I did! Then Miciamore
would be smashing atoms in the Galaxies. So, if that's the way it
is, it's my duty to write novels. I don't see why, for some sur-
reptitious reason, it has to be my fault. Because you're an ass,
and no one gives a damn about your novel. That remains to be
seen.

Why should my thoughts about cats, and the human animals who believe themselves their masters, be less interesting
than a Dubliner's feelings about his kidneys, or melancholy
thoughts about drought and cold, or the soap bubbles written

about the greatest writers revisited, as they say. Thank you. I visit them in my own way; rather, I receive them in my living room, well furnished with things and memories. One is allowed a collection of bric-a-brac when on the threshold of fifty and with a just biography like mine. A little bit of Oedipus, an important, idealistic father intolerable to live with, a sweet mother too shriveled from the hot wind consuming her day after day to allow her to be what she should be, for me and for him, the giant of "magnificent destinies"—now no doubt grinding his teeth to digest the news of widespread political corruption. And then my studies afflicted by scoliosis, adolescent poetry, and even a pinch of ambiguity with a mad crush. Destiny revealed by names. I, too, an absurd infatuation, for my philosophy professor. They told me he was really that way, on the other sad shore of gays, but he never tried anything with me. I loved him with the absolute exclusivity of first loves and thrilling discoveries, *Enten Eller*, Husserl, Adorno and company. After that the newspapers, the film club, parties, waiting for the critic to get sick so I could sub for him, writing scripts. Then the wrong marriage, the need for money, America for the glory and the money that wasn't enough to save the endangered family ship, and finally, the wind falling that had filled the sails of the screen writer's American dream, the return. How about trying the wine business? Of course, a good sweet wine is well worth a politician like Forlani or a provincial Barthes. And here I am with play manuscripts in the drawer, and I keep on writing them, the more furiously the more others think me lazy and satisfied. With a beautiful woman beside me (and I'm lucky to have Toni, I know), with a job that pays well, the house full of bottles, frozen food, *panettoni*, food enough for any invasion or Martian siege.

I could do as Z. does, who talks about the novel he can't give up and writes correct banalities for establishment newspapers about terrorism seen at a safe distance. Or as N. does, who, on the other hand, believes the novel impossible and meditates laboriously over it with an intellect so subtle the pages can't sustain the temporal passage from the galley proofs to its appearance in the bookstores. One hundred thirty copies sold. Some he bought to give friends for Christmas, a thousand went to reviewers. Or I could be like A. who, with his neurotic dignity as is suitable for a great work-in-progress, pretends disinterest in the question of the unrealizable or impossible novel, and, whenever he feels like it, sends a story to the *Corriere* or to some magazine equally authoritative and is at peace. In the meanwhile time passes and maybe the right moment will arrive for the right novel.

And me? I'm ashamed of myself. I twist and turn, I do my best. I paid for the divorce with publicity about food. And now that I am so thoroughly prostituted, how can I come out in the open with a novel? The protagonist is not of great consequence, a lonely woman, more or less a contemporary, in a town anywhere, untouched, or nearly so, by political fulminations or ideological disasters. But this is where I'm kidding myself. Because this is precisely what makes me write. What I want to say is that intellectual or illiterate, lucky or unlucky, rich or poor, in the end it's always the same. No one is pure spirit or worth any special metaphysics. It's just life. And if I can say it in a way that others can empathize with as they read it, that's the only obligation that counts, the only aesthetic that is also ethical. What a relief! Finally I've said it, and in first person. I should add that the way of saying it is what counts, and if I had more courage I would use lofty words for this passing from existence to representation. But there is also a sense of modesty for matters of the mind as well as the flesh, so I'll stop here.

Now I'll go back to Genoa for appointments I don't have, and shut myself up in the house to write so Toni won't know. In the meantime my nets are filling with darting fish, because the two are becoming friends — maybe they already are — and I observe them up close and suck their life. Tosca's above all. Bizarre, tender, foolish, but most of all so incredibly alone and therefore so bare and absolute, the ideal measuring stick for a novel about living beings on this earth, at this moment, in this village.

But why write Tosca's story and not, for example, the story of those two who work together and type all day below our apartment at the sea? Because he fills his time by compiling statistics and she understands everything about anthropology, but doesn't even notice Tosca when they pass on the stairs. Books, political questions (possibly outside the regular parties) is more scientific, but no blood, no sweat. Everything for the people, but in the abstract. They see people only when they group at intersections. That these groups might be formed by individuals, each one different and suffering differently, does not enter in their postulants of equality and the democratic struggle.

And so I, yes I, must have the guts to admit it. I believe I am able to tell the life of Tosca or Toni or my own, because I have never believed deeply in anything I've been involved in — literary manifestoes or political programs, civil passions or career struggles.

For a long time now I've been feeling things as though it were not I myself who felt them, but two or three or many others. It's a superimposing of sensations, reflections, memories, moods that cannot be, cannot coexist in me alone as mine, at that moment or at that time of my life. I feel these things as my mother or my father might have felt them, when life ran quickly in their young veins or as it slowly deserted them in their dying hours. I feel like I imagine someone I loved might have felt when his life was filled with the time preceding and following it. It communicated its essence to me through a mysterious osmosis, or through what became a mirror in me, with the ability to reflect its life in me as it reflects my life in that of others. Moments of unrelieved turbulence and tension, due to the impossibility of expressing the undefined fullness of things only intuited in a flash, which now I would relish remaking as my own, grabbing them if my memory will give them back to me. I don't know if it's my age that gives me this emotional tension and the desire to communicate with whomever is near—attentive or distracted it doesn't matter, but alive, capable of understanding what is happening to me. That is what matters and needs saying. Not only what grips us at the moment and makes us different from each other, but what mysteriously unites us when "the thing" happens, when I feel how the dead and the living feel, and even those who cannot speak because less privileged or more unhappy.

I enjoy being by the sea. Perhaps because the waves express this sensation of intermittent and recurring continuity that overlaps and exalts, voice on voice, motion on motion, tenacious and constant as the flow of water or blood in the veins. The sea, a flat mirror of boring hours, the restless echo of painful ones. Everything—gestures, thoughts, everything, or almost everything—breaks over me like this, multiform and manifold, like the sea. Or like music.

Can I try to say it, to prove myself? Am I doing it to "make a novel," or simply to enjoy a craft I've learned, transferring the words that rise weightlessly from my soul onto the typewriter that scans my syllables just like time (ever more stingily) measures my remaining days? But is it a novel if others don't find the echo of their fragments in my fragments?

That is the reason I hide when I write Tosca's story, and also the reason why I put her at the center of my piece of the world, the part I know because I live in it, and therefore more legitimate, if the only legitimacy of the one recounting it is to have lived it. With the hope that someone might mysteriously (everything is mysterious, I believe) find himself in my story, or look there for a meaning all his own.

In third person, with a place and a time, and characters with their noses, eyes, shoes and houses, everything necessary to make it easier for me to decipher these companions of my existence, and I hope of others.

And now I'll turn off the gas, water, lights, close the door, and return to the little village, to Toni, my house cat, and Tosca.

Once in New York, during that other time of my life, in speaking to me about women, Saul Bellow used the expression "amorous community." It was affectionate, but also ironic. Women, he said, are "blackmailers who give their hearts away." He was smiling but only with his mouth. A wary prudence was in his eyes, a fear not completely masked by respect for that female solidarity that makes us feel excluded. He was asking me for agreement in male complicity, in that manner of judging them, and I gave it to him with an enthusiasm that amused him. At that time I was besieged by two women, defenseless as a sheared sheep that must withstand the good God's merciless wind. I had a deep desire for rest, for lowering my guard with men like myself, far from the sisterhood I thought cruel and unmerciful. And so I made the rounds of clubs and bars, joining with men who drank with my same determination.

It was an agreeable and hearty drinking that I wouldn't mind repeating as I prepare to intrude into the implicit but perceptible alliance formed by those two. I must collect the fragments of Tosca's story from Toni, and information about Miciamore and his cat progeny, innumerable in time. Or numerable only in that brief flash that is my time.

Do I write for the same reason they lick their whiskers after they've emptied their bowl? An observation that bothers me as it smacks of Marx; and what if it does? After all, Marx is often right.

2

"Is something wrong?"

Toni had looked at him by barely turning her head, but she hadn't seen him. Her eyes were on the uniform gray of the Parisian sky framed in the window. He could tell by the way her arms were wrapped around her body, by her crouched position on the kitchen stool, that she was aware of nothing else. Her gaze didn't take in roof tops or church steeples. Or perhaps Toni's visual tract was interrupted by the squat shape of the Pantheon covered by the murky gray cloak that lay over the city bathed daily in spring rains.

But she probably didn't even see that. While she had gone silently through the daily morning routine of tea, juice, cleaning the bathroom and kitchen of the attic apartment that a friend had lent Gigi for their visit to Paris, he realized that she was sliding into one of her troubled gyres whose duration was impossible to predict. He only knew it had begun. The spiral of silence, the drawn mouth, the wrinkled brow, the slumped back that transformed her suddenly into a woman weary of the years and the worries, and he asked himself why.

An ever-narrowing spiral descending into that mysterious darkness he could only occasionally illuminate in moments of love making, or sometimes a common project, discussing some plan, but never when he gave in to his irresistible need to tell her what he felt, understood, wanted, feared about living. At those times he would have loved to have a friend, wife, accomplice beside him. She was sweet, tender, docile, but without the key that might let him descend with her when the time came to face the darkness that everyone has behind or inside himself. Toni had been terrified by it for years before meeting him, and had loved him for his patience that had taught him to take her by the hand, meekly and discreetly.

But we are in Paris! Irritated, antagonistic, Gigi went over the signs of impending crisis. An imperious gesture, music at full volume from the record she put on the player as though snuffing out a fire, a blanket violently thrown back; a rapid stripping that left her naked in front of the wardrobe searching for something entirely different to put on: a fancy dress if she had tossed away a skirt and blouse, sweater and pants if she had been wearing an elegant dress; or a rapid hammering of heels on the floor, as though to get away from her thoughts. When the spiral drew her compulsively to the place she struggled against and became a vortex of unbearable violence, Toni would then begin to moan quietly like a sick cat, a sharp complaining whine gradually growing louder. Gigi would run to her, take her in his arms uttering the nonsense words one uses with an animal or a newborn baby. He would hold her tightly so she wouldn't howl or scream, or, as once happened, wouldn't throw herself against the wall in a self-destructive passion. Why in Paris? They had been there for four days, and it had been a happy vacation. He had called their musician friend Jean-Luc just back from his American adventure, no longer capsized and alone in the musical rivers of celluloid images, but performing with others, and Gigi had laughed and drunk with him and remembered the months of exaltation and hope. They had insulted and embraced one another, and Toni and the pale Alsatian who was Jean-Luc's new companion had appeared to be touched by their failed Fitzgerald and Gershwin.

The previous evening they had remained alone after their friends left for a round of concerts outside Paris. They had all eaten a light and tasty supper together in a small bistro on the Ile du Paris and shared a bottle of Sancerre that seemed perfumed by the lilies of the valley filling Paris that first day of May. Then at a theater they had enjoyed the malicious and slightly tawdry charm of Polanski, which Toni disliked, but Gigi found perfect when he imitated the infantile monstrosities of Mozart's genius compared to the wishful thinker Salieri. Later they made love while the rain coursed down their oblique mansard roof, and he had slept, feeling their closeness in his happy tiredness, in the unfamiliar heart of the foreign city. For her it was different. Perhaps insomnia had contorted the happy memory of the day, and she couldn't escape from the evil knots night had tied.

The memory of that May vacation had caught him by surprise as he entered their house by the sea. Toni had let herself be kissed, served him thoughtfully at the table, but something about her motor wasn't running right. That's the way he put it in jest, to give her the opportunity to get it off her chest. From past experience he was afraid of letting her silences lengthen. But Toni hadn't appreciated the joke and he had read his exclusion in her vacuous eyes.

That rainy morning in Paris had been terrible. When he tried to make her get up she had grown stiff, and when he kept insisting she had reacted fiercely and dashed off toward the living room. A low glass table was in front of the divan on the path to the kitchen and balcony. Running like a frightened animal, Toni hadn't seen it and with all the weight of her body projected forward in flight had hit the sharp corner. She hadn't cried out, but was white-faced as Gigi, who had followed her in terror, helped her lie down on the divan. The cut on her left leg was small but deep. He dressed it as well as he could with what he found in the medicine cabinet. But almost three months later the scar was still dark violet.

Toni let herself be put to bed without a word, quietly swallowing a sedative. Gigi stayed with her, reading without interest, feeling hostile in the foreign city for the four hours that Toni slept without moving, her face flattened against the pillow, her numb body taking up no more room than a child's.

On waking, she had wept in his arms and begged to go back to Italy immediately; he did as she wished because Paris wasn't a happy place for him anymore, either. They waited at the airport, on the waiting list, quietly passing the hours in the usual idle actions that at other times made them both impatient: coffee, duty free items, ugly ties and perfumes never used, superfluous lighters, stale candy, uninteresting magazines.

Life sweetly resumed its customary rhythm in Genoa, and Toni never mentioned the episode. Neither had Gigi broached the subject, even though he didn't know or think he would ever know what had set her off in Paris, taking her back through the years to the anxiety that had been her malignant and ever present companion for such a long time.

Supper was over. On the terrace the light had a rosy transparency; the last reflection of the sun, already disappeared behind the mountains bordering the sea, tinged the sky before growing dark. Chin in her hands, her elbows on the table, Toni's eyes looked as vacant as that morning in Paris. But he couldn't allow such a silence to continue. With a sigh he couldn't restrain, Gigi got up and began to clear the table. He was hoping her female proclivity for domestic chores would spark an automatic response in her. And so it did. Toni also got up, took the bottle from his hand and was about to carry it to the kitchen. Gigi quickly stopped her, taking her by the waist. Toni seemed to awaken from a dream. She looked at him for the first time since he had come into the house, really seeing him. Gigi, relaxed and relieved, quickly proposed a neutral subject for discussion. "Were you with our friend of cats while I was away?"

Toni seemed grateful for his not inquiring about her silence, and while quickly clearing the table, she began to talk. In this way Gigi learned that they had gone to another concert together and that Tosca had confided many things.

If Toni stayed well, as he hoped (he scolded himself for being so eternally anxious with her, with his children, with all those he loved) his game plan as secret novelist ought to work out fine.

After they cleared the table and cleaned up together (Gigi kept to his promise to collaborate), Toni said she felt tired and didn't want to take a walk. They stretched out on the canvas lounge chairs on the terrace and Toni began to tell him details about Tosca's life in Milan. Gigi listened, but something bothered him. Was the story that came illustrated with small details — dress colors, facial expressions, snatches of dialog — really Tosca's, or what Toni had invented as she listened to her friend?

And after Gigi himself reproduced it on the page, what would he have removed or added of his own to the order of events, or to the emotions and sentiments that followed or caused them?

He interrupted her. "Are you sure all this you're telling me is true?"

Toni looked at him, surprise in her eyes, resentment in her protesting voice.

"I didn't say that right. I know you don't mean to lie, I was only thinking that you have projected your personal film of Tosca's life in your imagination, where you are the director, and I'm wondering how true to life it is. For example, would Tosca recognize herself in the fogs of Milan in this story of yours *alla* Carné instead of those of *Quai des brumes*?"

Toni laughed. The cascade of her laughter was an enduring charm which time had not changed, a child's laugh, half mischievous and half playful. "And if I really did write the story of Tosca and Miciamore?"

Something in Gigi's face must have alarmed her, because she quickly added, "Don't worry, I won't write it, I won't write it. I'm only a journalist of things seen. I don't know how to invent anything, and my own psychological knots are quite enough for me." She slowly lowered her arms from around his neck and turned her face away from him.

"Tell me something. A proud old male like you wouldn't take advantage of us two poor women in order to write his novel?"

Gigi laughed, and while he defended himself, he was once again struck by Toni's ability to penetrate his deepest secrets. There was in her, in women (he corrected himself), a richer interior life, a lightning intuition capable of grasping the truth below the rational evidence of events. An emotional truth of feelings and imagination. This was her fascination that had first attracted and then ensnared him, after years of marriage to a woman incapable of ever going below the surface of others' reactions. If they clashed it was a dispute between Sophists and Byzantines. The hot, lazy, ambiguous, refutable truth of the senses didn't exist for her. If he pointed it out, she analyzed it, translated it into algebraic equations, made a hypothesis of it from which she deduced an obstinate and incontrovertible proof. In the end she remained triumphant with her personal geometry, and Gigi surrendered, each time more detached, with a painfully dry feeling in his guts and heart.

Toni had been the fountain one yearns for after a walk through the desert. And for her he had been someone who could keep her from falling into darkness, with the underpinnings of all the logic that his masculine nature found to shore up their common need for love.

This time, too, Toni intuited the truth. Her instinct suggested that in a certain way he was using her, and Gigi felt guilty, but didn't want to confess it. Not now at least, not right away.

In the early cool autumn evenings, with a fire burning in the little fireplace before the apartment heat was turned on, it would be nice to read Toni the fruit of the hours robbed from her in their house in Genoa—in that house facing the sea, where the wind made a ship of all Boccadasse, the houses creaking in their joints and framework like sails in a storm. He was sure she wouldn't be jealous. He imagined her next to him, curled up like one of Tosca's cats on one of the many cushions in the living room, her face clearly reflecting her feelings. There would be two readings: the book about Miciamore, and the transparent communication of her reactions, impatience, discomfort, happiness.

How genuine she was, and is even now, in her childish wish to understand and in her expert way of seducing him! How much a woman and how much a child! He silently drew her to him. Toni resisted only for a second, then she snuggled up next to him. She had the art of becoming tiny in her tenderness, and Gigi thought that without her he never would have imagined prying into the life of another woman to make her a character for a novel. Toni opened up a different way of looking at things and living with them. Every moment of their life together was genuine. He must remember that when overcome by impatience—or haste—because of the too many exhausting things work forced both of them to do. It wasn't always easy to make room for each other in the tangle of daily responsibilities. But Gigi realized, as he slowly stroked her silky, naturally wavy hair, that Toni also knew how to handle this. She refused any newspaper assignments, within reasonable limits, that would take her away from him, but her conscientious and careful work was always satisfactory. She wasn't a news reporter, but followed only the most important performances of the city's musical and theatrical season, carefully doing her research ahead of time; and after they went together to the openings, Gigi would help her refine the articles. They knew they could have more work and make more money if they had accepted the offer for him to go to Milan and her to Rome, but they had refused without hesitation. At least their rather narrow-minded and provincial city was more restful. A secure frame for enjoying harmonious hours together.

From Toni Gigi learned that every choice should be weighed not only by what one acquired, but also by what one could lose. She had taught him to conquer anxiety. "Remember that every moment is a blessing, the only sure one." And she added, "But you have to play it right," as though for her time was only a musical score, and the music of the hours more important than any other. Her ear was also attuned to that kind of listening. Rarely would Toni be too distracted to read the pain or joy on a friend's face. This attention was so concentrated that it had frightened him a little in the beginning. "You have to love me, especially when I don't deserve it. An unhappy person is mean, malicious, uses words as shields; life becomes an articulated, contrived lie."

Toni said, "This is so nice! Who knows how that poor woman spends her time alone. . . We must never forget to be grateful."

"To whom?" queried Gigi.

"Grateful, period. To God, if you like, to chance, to your horoscope." She felt playful and hints of laughter were in her voice. "To Tommaso who told you about me, to Laura who invited you on my newspaper's trip, to the fairy who held you at your baptism, stupid, stupid man who doesn't understand anything!"

She was joking. Gigi was afraid of hurting her when she burst out so passionately. He pinned down her threatening arms. The game unexpectedly changed. "Shall we make love here?" Everything evolved naturally under the sky that had grown dark and studded with stars.

3

On the last flight of stairs Toni stopped in her tracks. Paletta was crying again! She wasn't mewing to ask for food or water or companionship, or simply to give notice of her existence. It was the tearful cry of any living being.

Paletta was the cat she had found in the street, and who had grown up forgetting the discomforts and the abandonment of her earlier days. She had been a funny, joyful adolescent with her and Gigi, a capricious and amusing witness to their life as lover-friends, who immediately regressed when cuddled, stubbornly demanding what she had been denied as a kitten. She would suck on whatever came to hand, a sweater or shirt collar, purring with the strong illusion that she had commandeered some deprived maternal warmth. Toni had had both pain and tenderness from her and Paletta knew it. As soon as Paletta heard her, and it was a mystery how, even before she entered the house (at Genoa when the elevator brought her to the fourth floor, at the sea when her clogs came up the three flights of stairs) she would be at the door, caracoling like a circus pony as soon as she saw her, passing rapidly between her legs, dashing like an arrow through the hall, returning and zipping away again in an insane display of joy.

It was impossible to ignore her, and if Toni called to her laughingly or affectionately, Paletta would respond with what resembled words. Even cats that don't like you, Toni learned, make you feel more at home than the person living there if he doesn't like you. And if cats like you they don't hide behind walls of silence or mental reserve. They express it and demand reciprocation, and take offense and punish you if you deprive them of what they consider their right.

Now Paletta was crying. Like a baby, perhaps. Toni had never had one, but she could still remember, when she was going to middle school, how she couldn't bear to hear her newborn sister cry. Toni would run to her every time her mother was slightly late, and so a bond sprang up between them that nothing had been able to break, not the misunderstandings of her first loves considered betrayals by the younger one, nor the inevitable jealousies between two sisters of such different ages. Now her sister was twenty years old, a full-grown woman, and it was as if they were joined by an umbilical cord. More than their mother, each sought out the other for support or help in difficult times. Once Vera told her she recognized her smell. It was the smell that had remained in her nostrils from the times Toni would pick her up, furious and crying, from her cradle and put her sweaty little head on her shoulder, in the hollow of her neck. Toni learned that was the quickest and best way to calm her. Soon her mother would come who knew what had to be done, but in the meantime the passage from desperate solitude to comforting warmth had been initiated by her intervention. Even Paletta must consider her a mother substitute for the real mother she didn't have, and whom she loved with redoubled anxiety because of it. She lost her real mother; she couldn't lose the second one.

Paletta didn't get up when Toni entered the house. Stretched out full length on the floor, she was trying to find a cool spot, turning over, touching the widest surface possible with her tail and flattened face. Those grieving sounds were unceasing, punctuated with shrieks like cries of desperation among sobs. Bending over soothingly, Toni tried to caress her. The cat avoided her without running away by twisting as though she couldn't muster the effort to get up and move.

Paletta wouldn't look at her. In the circle of that lamentation there was no room for anyone or anything. Toni went to the kitchen. Paletta's bowl was full of milk. In two other bowls with fish and meat, not even the cat biscuits had been nosed around out of curiosity. Everything was just as she had left it. Paletta didn't have the time or desire for anything but her erotic needs. Going back to the vestibule, Toni saw Paletta hadn't moved; now her little head resting on her front paws seemed smaller, and her whole body shrunken, noticeably thinner in just a few days' time. Toni tried to pick her up again, but Paletta snarled menacingly and sharp claws appeared from the velvet sheath of her paws. Toni moved away, scolding her, a drop of blood running down her hand. At times like these she regretted ever bringing her into the house, and told her so. But Paletta barely looked at her with eyes that were hostile, impenetrable slits instead of the usual crystal-clear green, open to observe the world impassively.

"There's no way. I'll never understand cats, and even less anyone who loves them like human beings," Toni began as she entered the large room that was the heart of her and Gigi's vacation home. They had furnished it together after they had decided to live together. Gigi had inherited the apartment from his family along with old buffets and uncomfortable sofas. The clutter of too many useless things left little space, but the balcony facing the sea was beautiful and airy. They had eliminated everything — furniture and walls. The furniture had been loaded onto a truck and taken to a colony of nuns in the village, and Toni appreciated what this decision must have cost Gigi, lazy as he was. With the elimination of every piece some image of his past must have stirred in his memory, but he had been good about it. He hadn't complained, and when they returned the following weekend she found a large pot of flaming red geraniums in the empty space where the dividing walls had been torn down, with a tender note of good wishes for their first house together, made by their love.

It was Toni's third summer to vacation there, and now they also lived together in Genoa, in the large and comfortable house that remained hers after the divorce. She had changed the arrangement of the rooms and furniture in that also, so Gigi wouldn't have to suffer from retrospective jealousy, a sickness he had often been prey to in their early days together. Instead of tearing down the walls in their permanent residence, she had them raised. Each of them had a studio and a bedroom. Her failed marriage had taught her that no love lasts without freedom, and there is no freedom without the protection of one's own private corner. Like cats, Toni thought, while Gigi brushed her cheek with a distracted kiss, his eyes glued to the book he was reading when she came in. Toni grabbed it away from him with a teasing laugh, and Gigi, who raised his eyebrows in surprise, went along with her. The second kiss was attentive, while Toni led him to the divan covered with enormous cushions that was their bed.

"Something has to be done about Paletta," she said. "We can't go on watching her suffer without doing something."

"You don't need to tell me. If it were up to me I would have already made that decision, and I assure you that this morning while you were at the beach, I had to restrain myself. A muezzin is more entertaining than your cat when she's in love."

Toni laughed. "You men are all the same. If she bothers you, she's *my* cat; if she's sweet, if she amuses you, if she purrs for you, she's yours. My father was like that with Vera and me. We were his or mama's according to his convenience. It's not a coincidence you said a muezzin. Every man is basically a sheik, a ras, an autocrat, a. . ."

"Stop. Don't get started!" Gigi protested. "And don't change the subject. You decide. Either sterilization or outside."

"Outside," she answered. "But I'm afraid. What if she doesn't come back? She's so used to being with us. What if those other sly, wild, underworld cats around here tan her hide?"

"What a sense of theater you have, darling! Underworld cats! Which are they? I've seen only the most average kind of cats in the neighborhood."

"Yes, because you never pay any attention. There are some that could kill a dog in a flash. They're used to defending themselves, taking care of themselves, finding food. Compared to them Paletta is a young lady from a good family, a virgin compared to those street beggars."

"All right. Have her sterilized. But I'll tell you right now I'm not holding her."

"Let's wait one more day, please. If she keeps on crying I'll open the door and she can do what she has to do. Basically she has the instinct to defend herself; she's no blue blood. There's an army of tabby cats like her. If she meets one of her kind, he'll defend her."

At this precise moment Paletta stopped crying. A paw silently pushed the door open, and rubbing against the door jamb the cat came into the room. With two leaps she was beside them. She sniffed them, her big clear wide open eyes like the tender green of two budding leaves, her muzzle extended like a girl with a passion for love written on her face, and her wonderstruck eyes wanting for the first time to be reflected in the mystery of someone like herself. She climbed up lightly on the woman's legs, and nuzzled against her cheek. Toni felt the rough contact of the tiny tongue, then she handed her to Gigi. Paletta kissed him, too, and went away as soundlessly as she had come.

"She wanted to excuse herself, to say she felt better, perhaps. Who knows, maybe she had a stomachache, and between one pain and another came to say hello," Toni said.

Gigi admitted that might be true, but nevertheless it was hard to know who was more imaginative when in love, a cat or a woman. That same evening Paletta decided her own fate. When they opened the door to go out after supper, she slipped between their legs and shot off like an arrow. Toni went to the railing to call her and then she saw him. At the foot of the stairs in the lobby a tabby was waiting that looked gigantic, his round head as large as a baby's. Paletta hadn't reached him yet, but it was only a moment before they disappeared.

"So small, with an animal like that! God help her!" was Toni's comment and Gigi somehow felt accused and found guilty.

4

The days flowed by calmly by at the beach in a succession of hours of conscious enjoyment. Just the kind of vacation they both needed after the joust of obligations in the city.

At his desk Gigi leafed through the newspaper while he waited to have breakfast with Toni, who had gone down to buy bread. He had already taken the cups and milk to the balcony. The gurgling of the *Moka* pot told him the coffee was ready just as he heard Toni's clogs coming up the stairs. Just at the moment when Paletta seemed to rouse from her lethargy and darted ahead of him to wait by the door.

Toni focused all her attention on Paletta, stroking and talking to her, while Gigi took the package of warm bread to the balcony. They drank the coffee that seemed more aromatic in the cool of the morning with the rustic fragrance of the bread, and Gigi commented with satisfaction on the first of their common pleasures that made the day good. Toni's distress had been momentary, a threatening but passing cloud in their marine sky, and Gigi was able to joke about his own jealousy. "You made over Paletta and didn't bother to look at me. Obviously, I'm just part of the furniture and she's not. One should feel honored by her presence, as one does with tyrants or divas."

Toni smiled at him, but something was going on in her mind. Although she continued eating, her attention was clearly turned elsewhere. Eventually she explained it to him, after a careful inspection of all the possible hiding places in their small house, including wardrobes and cabinets. "I have a problem," she told him, "I can't find one of my blue bedroom slippers."

"One is already too many," was Gigi's swift reply, and Toni grew morose. She had an old slipper in her hand which had once been blue, but now the color of the soft goat skin shone through on the outside; and inside, perspiration and wear had left no trace of color. Even the original shape was lost. The weight of her body had worn the outer side more, as if her foot had always pressed hard in the same direction. In fact, the hollow made by the last three toes, was deep and clear, while the space for the big and second toe had only the suggestion of a depression. As Toni held the slipper close to her chest she gave Gigi a caustic look. "Yes, for you it's too many. But not for me. Some people just can't remember," she said stressing her words, "that there are anomalies, diversity, differences between people. . ." She paused and then concluded, ". . .that can't be changed."

Gigi realized his error, and back-pedaled to neutral ground. "Where do you think the other one could be?"

Immediately pacified, Toni drew close to him and explained she couldn't imagine where it could be. "I'm sorry, I know it's stupid to worry so much about an old slipper. I also know it's old and ugly, and nearly worn out. But when I'm dead tired I can relax only with them, my life-long slippers. . ."

Gigi listened without interrupting. Perhaps the moment had arrived when, by talking about it, Toni could overcome the last vestiges of panic she had been dragging behind her.

"You know I haven't worn them since we've been together, don't you? But I need them with me just the same as. . . an exorcism. When I'd come home from the university, my little sister Vera would bring them to me triumphantly to show me how happy she was to see me. One of her first long words was "swippers," and come to think about it, I call them "swippers," too. . .

"Then, when I began to work and travel I took another pair with me in a leather case, elegant and shiny. But I always knew I could only feel comfortable and breathe a sigh of relief at home with the others. I hid those slippers so mother wouldn't throw them away as she threatened to do so many times. But little by little over the years even she came to accept them. I changed newspapers, loves, friends, I got married, divorced, I've been desperate and happy, and each time I've gone back home to talk about it, and each time I looked for them before beginning a private talk with my family. Now I'd have to say a talk with Vera, since she's a woman, and a woman who understands me. My mother has tried to understand us without being able to. My father is just there, and that's enough for me."

Gigi didn't interrupt her, not even to agree, and now Toni's eyes were on the sea — a luminous blue under the morning sun after a big wind sweeping off the mountains had cleared everything, sky and water.

"If I lose them, I lose a part of myself, and I don't care if you call it stupid or something worse. I think everyone has a right to his. . . irrationality. Dreams, memories. . . everything we've loved that's no longer tangible, but ours in a different way, whether more or less real. I don't know. Anyway, it's not a matter for debate because it can't be proved in everyday terms. Not with language or with reason. It's a little like entering a sacred place."

Toni looked in Gigi's eyes a moment, giving him a brief, nervous smile before turning back to the horizon. "The things of long ago, the things we think about without thinking, that live in us miraculously, because they're alive even though absent. . ." She lit her first cigarette of the day, drew a long breath, and looked at him resolutely. "When I went to live with you I took them with me and hid them. They represented my time before you that existed alongside with my present time with you, and I didn't want to throw it all away. It was something I had been, something I could think about without pain anymore. Those old slippers of mine that I could look at if I wanted to, but never needed to, reassured me that I hadn't just dreamed it all and wasn't dreaming now.

"In Paris, I felt awful. And I wanted them. I can't tell you why. Perhaps the strange city, perhaps just a physical upset, perhaps the feeling of not being myself but someone else I didn't recognize. I wanted to come back and the feeling passed. I brought them here with me from Genoa. Like a good luck charm. Yesterday, for a few seconds I was feeling bad again and looked for them. The bottom of the sack where I had put them was all in a jumble. I found only one, and I'm afraid Paletta stole the other one. I must find it. That's the whole story. You have to forgive me."

Gigi embraced her and went straight to the door. Puzzled, Toni followed. On the landing, next to the case of mineral water that was delivered every week, was a pile of newspapers and magazines to be taken away. Gigi bent over. The top layer of papers was in a precarious position. Under the first two the once blue slipper appeared to Toni's immediately smiling eyes.

Gigi didn't touch it. "I've seen Paletta here many times. My alien hands might desecrate it." He was joking, but he looked at Toni in all seriousness. "Take it, it's yours."

It was the last time Toni retreated into herself that summer. Sometimes he could read a plea for help in her eyes, but never the anxiety of being unable to ask — the closed, mute anxiety that frightened Gigi. And without discussion Gigi took in this information in his progressive understanding of Toni and their reciprocal friendship. There were two old slippers in their house able to open a sealed door for her. Two worn objects that would never wear out completely, like childhood memories and dreams.

5

That night no one slept well on the Riviera. In the evening thunder began rolling closer, a roaring wind rose to bend the palm trees on Via Aurelia, and the sea swirled below lightning flashes. Toni ran to close the windows, and stayed just as she was — in a nightgown sticky with perspiration — on the balcony to watch the breakers lapping where prudent fishermen had pulled up their boats at the first storm warning. The next morning her voice was hoarse and she felt weak. Gigi sent her back to bed, but that evening, when her fever began to rise, he called the doctor who diagnosed a bad case of tracheitis.

The dry and annoying cough accompanying it kept her from resting. Gigi told Tosca about it when they met in the butcher shop. She was ahead of him in a long line of customers. That was the only sour note of their vacation: the loss of time that Toni, and all the vacationers, complained about.

Tosca gave her order and Gigi took mental note of it. The reality appearing before his eyes was clearer than seeing it through Toni's accounts.

The woman asked for two cans of Kit Kat and when the butcher asked, "Nothing for you?" she replied firmly, "No, I don't need much." On the heels of which she added, happy, it seemed to Gigi, to have a friendly witness to her profession of faith, "I live for them." The butcher put on a little ironic smile, while silent disapproval ran through the waiting women like a perceptible breeze. They all had children and husbands to feed. They were oppressed by the cares of the family ménage. Nothing seemed more futile to them than that love for cats. But Gigi felt he wasn't mistaken to weave his plot around that unusual love, like a spider weaves filament around an insect it wants to make his. Except that now he worried about his ability to capture in the woven words the meaning of that life alongside what others considered the only right and normal one.

And so when he saw her in the tobacco shop he waited for her and they walked back home together. Tosca wanted him to see the kitten sleeping under the oleander bush. By now it had filled out and was covered by a coat of silvery fur, and "a little medallion" decorated his chest, an almost perfectly round white mark that Miciamore's firstborn female also had, she told him. Tosca had called her "Fifi, the czar's pet." Gigi smiled with amusement as Tosca told him she had once read a serialized romance with a satanic monk (her words) as its main character mixed in the court adventures, where a scintillating aristocratic friend of Rasputin wore a "charmed" diamond at her neck with the czar's emblem in the setting. They were beside the oleander in the small garden of an anonymous condominium on the Riviera. Tosca's soft body was covered by a worn housedress, but as she talked she looked up and an indescribable smile, a diffused light radiating from within, spread over her features making her look younger. She had a dignity that inspired respect. Gigi reflected that perhaps it was precisely this natural autonomy that kept an inner kaleidoscope of images intact through which she filtered the world where chance had brought her to live. That was the challenge. The parabola is always the same. We hold in contempt what we don't understand, and irony is the easiest defense for cowardice. He watched her while she tenderly cradled the kitten in her hands, talking to him so he would open his eyes. This was an image of maternity, too. The little one's eyes were a tender light blue ("the color of milk") and its nose a pale pink spot in the fur. "He takes milk now from a medicine dropper. Giulia feeds him with it so he'll get used to her. Poppa is already making her rounds, and you can't count on her. Tonight Giulia's going to take him home with her and I donated a bottle, a little ball and a pillow. A newborn shouldn't change smells and routine. He'll be a beautiful big cat like his big sister, with the family coat of arms — the white medallion on his neck."

Later, when Tosca telephoned about Toni, Gigi invited her up to their apartment. It was a different kind of evening for all three of them. Toni was listless and silent. Stretched out on the divan she urged Tosca to talk, understanding what Gigi wanted. But the woman seemed to feel her responsibilities as guest and didn't more than mention herself or Miciamore, as one alludes to a constant in one's life. She was more concerned about Toni and launched into a topic she seemed to know very well. It was another revelation that opened up new prospectives on the village for the couple. That very evening Tosca had brought the sick woman ingredients for a tea, a decoction she assured her would "wash the bronchi," and which actually did help her breathe easier and stop the coughing fits.

Instructed how to make it, Gigi fixed two batches, and after Tosca left, wishing them a good night, Toni was happy to sip the brownish water made from a mixture of mint, thyme, and one crushed juniper and cypress berry. Tosca also brought a jar of honey from Finale, dense and unstrained, but extraordinarily sweet smelling to use instead of sugar.

She knew formulas for curing any and every illness with herbs. "I've taken too much medicine. If my health doesn't improve with herbs I'm no worse off, and at least I haven't wasted a lot of money. Anyway, I feel good while I'm making them. I'm passing the time."

Tosca told them that two years ago she went into the highlands of the Manie with an old pharmacist from Biella who came there for the offseason. He was the one who had shown her the herbs and explained their use. She began to put together her little herbarium that she added to on Christmas or weekends in February or March when the old gentleman came to the village drawn by his longing for the sea. His legs were bad and Tosca accompanied him to the country. "That way," she concluded happily, "little by little I stole his knowledge. I wrote down the name of every herb we gathered, and every time I picked one by myself I compared it with a sample I had collected with him, and with pictures in my books."

She had a number of books, all with colored illustrations, that she proudly showed Toni once she was well and they went searching for herbs, because it was her turn to guide the discovery of Mediterranean plant treasures.

Tosca's house had a collection of the most curious and incongruous objects and furniture. The door of her bedroom was propped open by a large jar as was once used in Liguria for olive oil; it held a large yellow umbrella that Toni recognized as the gift of a tanning lotion advertised on the beach. Above a well-made nineteenth century chest of drawers was a mirror in an ugly gold frame. On the chest, next to some framed pictures of various sizes, were glass bottles from Murano and a collection of little boxes and medicine bottles. From the living room only the end of the bed was visible, covered with a brightly flowered material, a calico with a pretty design giving a cool, delicate impression in the semi-darkness. At the foot of the bed a little Bukhara, a "prayer rug," was a touch of refinement in contrast to the other things, especially to the disorderly array on the chest.

In the tiny anteroom the space was almost entirely occupied by a settee such as Toni remembered seeing in modest homes, and even her grandmother had one in cherry wood with a sculpted leaf border along the back. The settee was old and the seat didn't close well. A cat was playing with a red rag protruding from it. Tosca chased it away and furiously stuffed the cloth back inside. "Ugly beast, you'll drive me crazy!" she said and led them into her "living room-dining room-do all and have nothing," as she said, clearly embarrassed. There were several framed pictures on the walls, and Gigi stopped before a series of four prints lined up between the windows over the little table holding the television set. Tosca brightened at his interest. "Yes, they are nice, a gift from my Mario on our first wedding anniversary. You know, he wanted to celebrate our meeting, the meeting of Tosca and her Cavaradossi, and so, when he found them at the 'O bei' fair, he bought them and had them framed in time for our anniversary."

They were prints of the first production of the opera at the Costanzi theater in Rome, and Tosca commented with a sigh, *Vissi d'arte*, oh, yes! That must be the destiny for Toscas, but just what mine is for art, I don't know yet."

On the wall near the prints two oil paintings in wide wooden frames portrayed two bunches of flowers, hydrangeas in a vase in one, and roses lying on a table covered by a Kashmir shawl in the other. The violent colors and crude execution stood out next to the simple elegance of the prints. "They're ugly, aren't they?" Tosca said at once. "But they were my mother's, and it seemed a shame not to have them out where I can see them. We get used to things and have feelings even for ugly things," and she pointed with pleasure to three ceramic pieces attached to the wall, handmade sculptures of a green sea horse, a red polyp, a blue grouper: "another anniversary gift from Mario."

The table and other furniture were the simplest and most ordinary mass-produced kind that were practically canceled out by the presence of so many objects covering every surface. The useful next to the merely ornamental, a fruit bowl full of lemons near a Sicilian cart, a nineteenth century kerosene lamp near a modern opaline lamp; a "Twentieth century" style coffee service surrounded by a dance of fake Capodimonte putti. From the ceiling hung a ceramic chandelier with fruits and flowers, a good imitation of rococo, revealing the good taste and skimpy funds of its buyer. Above all, Tosca was anxious to show off her books, lined up in orderly fashion on a red lacquer bookshelf. "Mario made it, and I have some other bigger shelves where he kept his books, but I left them in Milan because I have a problem with space here."

Tosca was ready for the outing and had everything neces- sary for gathering the herbs: scissors, a little knife, some string and rubber bands. Toni provided small sacks and identification tags. Tosca asked permission to bring the two brothers who were almost always with her during mealtimes and now came home more often at night. "I want them to get used to staying with me even outside, because on the long rainy cold days I go to the beach whenever there's a little sun, and it will be nice to have their company. And they can stretch their legs, too."

The day was absolutely clear, the whole coast was sharply visible: promontories, bays, islets on both sides, an arc that be- gan at the Genoa lighthouse and ended at the rocks barricading France. The tense air vibrated with the continual buzz of hornets along with the choir of cicadas. The mixture of a hundred fra- grances made breathing as perceptible as a drink enjoyed drop by drop. Among rosemary and juniper bushes, between mastic, arbutus and gigantic heather, the gold of the broom plant gleamed, exhaling a sweet odor that attracted swarms of wasps and bees. In the small clearings between the olive trees, pines, and cypresses Tosca wandered sure and intent "as an indige- nous gnome," Toni said to Gigi, naming plants of every kind (generically anonymous to them), among which were, to Gigi's surprise, rue, wormwood, mallow and mint, thyme, sage, marjo- ram, and almost all the herbs epicures cited for their recipes. They carried home an abundant supply for meat and fish dishes, and Tosca picked wild fennel for a spaghetti sauce with sardines, a Sicilian dish, and branches laden with capers. Toni wanted to make a decorative arrangement in a vase with the caper stems and leaves, and Tosca told her how to put the little buds in salt.

An excursion in which Gigi got, among other enjoyable things, a little bit of local color for his cooking column that up to now had weighed on him like a scholastic problem. When they arrived, Miciamore's two offspring, Puss and Bisi, shot from the car where they had been crouching with fur bristling, not in the least inclined to adapt. They disappeared into the bushes where they became indistinguishable from the spotted green-gray of the shrubs. After the three finished collecting herbs and were sitting on the grass in the shade of olive trees smoking and talking, Tosca declared she would go find them, and didn't need any help.

Her voice reached them from a distance, crying joyfully, as though she were taking advantage of the opportunity to exercise her vocal cords in the happiness of that open space. Low tones alternated with sharp, prolonged modulations of her call. There was no impatience or anxiety in those repetitions that Gigi and Toni followed skeptically, certain they would have to go back home without the two. Instead, suddenly, the voice descended to speech. Tosca was promising the two better fare than the biscuits she had brought along to appease their hunger after the romp among so many new odors.

In a moment she appeared in the lane that went from the scrubland to the state road. The cats were walking on either side of her, occasionally stopping for one of their unfathomable reasons or to make short excursions from which they returned at the first call. In the car (no longer a suspicious novelty) they lay quietly. They were tired and hungry and dozed between one bump and another until they reached home. Tosca got out with them like a queen with her escorts while Gigi held the door. Two local woman talking on the sidewalk turned their heads simultaneously at their arrival, breaking off their conversation. Before their astonished looks, pregnant with all the gossip they would immediately dispense, Tosca walked by majestically with Puss and Bisi, her pony tail waving like a flag. Gigi, who had not missed the unexpected addition to the script of which he was both writer and director, got back into the car next to Toni who had turned her face away to hide her overpowering desire to laugh. "No doubt we've initiated a new phase in Tosca's story. After the resistance begins the liberation!"

Gigi didn't reply. He was asking himself whether, when life has formed us in a certain way, it is possible to escape the conclusions that our own choices draw for us. Though our choices seem clear and obvious, we are never really capable of knowing them in depth. Watching Tosca go by, happy at that precise moment, with a boldness he was sure would be extinguished the moment she returned to the things that serve as background for the drama of her existence, Gigi suddenly superimposed his situation over hers in a way that showed him a self he had never seen with such cruel truth. Everyone recounts his past to himself by changing it according to a preferred plan. It's an unconscious mutation that can last for years, until the day comes when the image of one's self so long contemplated with pleasure and painted with the colors of faith, and also of hope, mysteriously fades and crumbles, and in what remains you see yourself as you have really been, because only now you see yourself as you were and are. When he had come back to Italy after the successes, as exhausting and ephemeral as they were, in American movies, it had been painful to take up his newspaper work again. New editors, some of his friends cut down by illness, others by the corruption of political games, made Gigi feel very much alone.

But a person has to live. There were the two children to raise and he had obligations to his wife, even though he was no longer with her.

At the paper where he had sent the pieces from abroad as required by contract (and only published in part), he was forced to face the hostility of a completely changed situation. He defended himself because he had to, but the desire to throw it all away and resign had been the greatest destructive temptation he had had to fight during those first months. He kept his job because he had to, and at times the situation was humiliating. Gradually he became less a target for maliciousness and even found support. When the offer from the food magazine came, Gigi accepted it as a liberation. The morning he had asked to speak to the director in order to tender his resignation he always remembered as windy and gray. There was the sharp smell of mimosa rotting in water, the leaves still green, but the flowers withered to dry colorless little balls. He had always remembered the firmness of his voice, controlled so as not to fall into a pathetic tone, while he announced his decision to leave, and the director looking at him with cold eyes.

Now he suddenly saw himself as he said good-bye to the portiere for the last time, and as he went on his way to meet three "important" colleagues. He spoke to them, appealing to his dignity not to let him lose his temper when their sarcasm concerning his new activity had grown heavy. He even joked and left them perplexed. Now he knew the memory had been deformed by his wounded pride. The smell of bad water was true, but the day had been beautiful, with a blue sky such as is known in Milan only on a rare winter day. The gray was inside his twisted imagination. The director's eyes were not cold from bureaucratic practice; they were indifferent. Whether he stayed or left was of no importance. His colleagues told him gaily, "You're nobody, you're just one less person to pay." His measured step through the street in Milan (that he had loved more in the early days of his work and grand dreams) was the result of extreme control over his tension-exhausted body. His dignity had saved him from running down the street screaming in rage. He was going away and would never return. Away, better any work whatever than the hostility written on every face, the trap lurking in every conversation, the humiliation of silence and alienation.

Dignity, yes. Tosca had no less than he. But what was it? To shield defeat? And what good was it? You show it to those close at hand, but what good is it if they don't notice? His entire performance that morning in Milan under a clear sky over the roofs on Via Solferino had no audience but himself, the actor. "It served only to keep me from despising myself; the others were left unmoved."

My God, how can you live next to other human beings like yourself without pretending? Now he knew his decision at that time had been right. Life had become sweeter for him, but that wound still hurt. Of those three colleagues, two had fallen in the tempest of scandals; one survived, and perhaps only his dignity had kept him from fleeing. All true, but not enough to justify the pitiful deformation those years had worked on his most searing memory.

While they were getting out of the car Toni asked him, "What's got into you? You're in a black mood!" Gigi was jerked back to the present. He had her, some new friends, some faithful readers he didn't have to lie to or slyly communicate his indignation about every slimy dirty thing that happened in town. He had made a good choice.

Tomorrow his children would arrive with some friends before starting their drive toward northern Europe. He wanted to see them, to touch them, the young man and young woman he hadn't deserted even if he was a neglectful father. He was happy they were coming. Except for the fact, and he finally told Toni calmly, that it would cause an unavoidable break in the thread (though tenuous and illusory) connecting him to the cat woman.

6

For days now, since she was no longer so preoccupied with Miciamore's family, Tosca would surprise herself with the beginning of a song on her lips, as when she had been Mario's wife, and as sometimes when she had spied through the slats of the shutters waiting for Bruno to come from the beach. That shadowy musical presence kept her anxiety company on dark nights, just as in her youth it had registered her desire to live. She was happier—that was it, she told herself—because she was having a free exchange of experiences and opinions, without feeling as though she had to weigh her words according to the imagined ill-will of others, those others she had gradually shut herself off from the past two years. It was the wall of distrust she felt around her that kept her from wanting to do or say anything. Her life had been reduced to ever-narrower circles, but maybe things would change, she hoped, if the kindness of two outsiders was enough to give her relaxed and even joyous moments, and a less resentful state of mind, such as she had felt during the concerts and in the country. For days now she had carefully fixed meals for herself, and her health began to improve. She had slept better since she drank wine only during meals and had started reading again before going to sleep.

Two days after the trip to the Manie Toni told her she was planning a big supper for seven young people, Gigi's two children and their friends. The friends would be sent to sleep with a family that rented rooms in the old part of the village.

Tosca watched them arrive while she watered the garden after supper in the cool of the oncoming night, the sky still blue. She recognized Gigi's children by their common features: long gray eyes rimmed by very dark lashes. A girl pale and small, except for her eyes, and a thin, awkward giant. His wide shoulders and much greater height than his father's had surprised her, or perhaps it seemed excessive in the boy because his movements were disjointed. His long stride and swinging arms gave the impression of someone not in control of himself.

She was curious to talk it over with Toni, but for three days she hadn't seen them and they hadn't called. Only on the fourth day, while cleaning the stairs at dawn as usual, did she see them all file out with Gigi, carrying nets and poles. The journalist told her they would be in a friend's motorboat all day. Tosca took heart. Now that Toni was alone she would certainly call and Tosca waited. But the phone didn't ring. No one looked for her, and when it came time to go down to the garden for the usual evening tasks, she had a heavy heart and felt a weariness in her legs not justified by what she had done during the day. It was natural to turn to the bottle for help. The thread of song was broken. The house was empty; no voice interrupted the silence, and the recorded music was ineffective. It didn't move her. The deafness was in her, she thought, as the cool white wine slid down her throat, but it didn't give her encouragement as at other times. She didn't even feel like talking to the cats. Anyway, "the cats know," she told herself, and it made her melancholy because those weren't her words, but the poet Cesare Pavese's that Mario had given her to read at such a different time which (the alcohol beginning to move her blood) she now doubted she ever lived.

Perhaps she had dreamed it, as she had just dreamed of having friends who weren't cats. Bisi was making a little methodical, rhythmical noise like the low clack of a loom, or a steel point on a turning lathe. Tosca got up from her chair at the kitchen table and went to her bedroom. The rug at the foot of her bed was covered with a light cloud of tiny woolen tufts. With a scream, Tosca flung herself at the animal that shot like an arrow in the opposite direction.

"You just have to put your damned claws on the only precious thing I have," she panted, the light tufts floating up to her nose and perspiring face. She began to cough and sneeze. Bisi disappeared, and Tosca sat down on the rug where the animal's claws had managed to remove a top layer of the woven fabric like an outer layer of skin.

"I forgot about your claws. It's my fault," Tosca moaned, half-drunk, and weak from coughing. "Now I have to find Miciamore's cat tree. Who knows where it is. But it's too late. If he likes the rug I'll have to hide it or he'll ruin it."

Suddenly she heard a noise similar to the one she heard before, and she got up with an effort. Bisi had found another way to sharpen his claws. Stretched out on the floor, his back paws pushing against the kitchen cabinet, he was furiously scratching the floor-cleaning rag.

At the sight of Tosca he stopped, ready to run. But Tosca was too tired to protest; with her hands on her hips she just looked at him. Bisi raised a paw gently from the object of his attentions and looked sidelong at the woman. It was so clearly calculated and such an obvious offer of truce that Tosca laughed, and because she was unsteady on her feet, it was a sweeping, coarse laugh, which Bisi was not accustomed to. The animal began to scratch his ear with the same fury as he had used on the rug and rag, but for an entirely different reason. Now he was expressing his surprise with a gratuitous and ostentatious gesture.

"And they say humans are more intelligent! When did a man ever show his disapproval of me so deliberately and still let me know it had nothing to do with him!" A senseless giggling overtook her. She went to the cat, stroked him, kissed him, and carried him to her bed, which she fell upon like a stone. But Bisi slipped away immediately, and when she heard him in the kitchen sharpening his claws again, on what or with what damage she didn't know, she couldn't find the strength to get up or even yell at him. Sleep didn't come to her aid. Film strips of thoughts and memories, superimposed images, made a painful and diffused confusion in her head that became a sharp pain over her right eye. A migraine had come to visit, the only novelty of another day without human voices. How many days had gone by like this? She had spent almost all winter and spring, and even important holidays, such as Easter and Christmas, with her cats. She couldn't count on her in-laws anymore since they had moved to the house he inherited in Calabria. They telephoned greetings and invited her to visit them. Just imagine such a long trip! With Poppa and the kittens still small. She couldn't face either leaving her apartment or the uncertainties of traveling South, old Lombard that she was, mistrustful perhaps for no other reason than that she had never been able to express an opinion to her brother-in-law without his grumbling. When her husband was alive they could laugh about it together. Later, unable come out from the tough shell of her unconquerable timidity, she finally limited her words with him to the necessary few. Little by little the reciprocal visits had grown less frequent, until now, she was sure, she had become just the crazy sister-in-law who talks to cats. She wondered if she could bear another Christmas like the last one with the wind and rain beating against the windowpanes and the whole building moaning and creaking as though inhabited by devils or ghosts in pain. Enclosed in the few square feet of the living room, where she had to sleep with the cats even at night for warmth (as the doors and windows were drafty in a house built for summer, and on the coldest days the drafts made whirlwinds in her bedroom), she had watched television all day and did the same on New Year's Eve. She drank a bottle of Asti Spumanti at midnight and put a little in the cats' bowl (though they hadn't appreciated the treat), and thus began the new year by watching how the rich and happy of the world enjoyed themselves.

Another year ending this way. No, it wasn't possible. While the last images of shooting stars and glasses of champagne dissolved into a sequence of faces, Mario, Bruno, her brother-in-law, Toni, the Nazi, the emerald eyes of Miciamore in the distance, beyond everything like a star in the sky above a cloud, she found herself in the kitchen, without any plan on her part, opening the bottle she had taken out of the refrigerator. When she climbed back in bed again only a few drops were left to slide down her throat. The bottle held in her fist like a baby holds his bottle was empty and that surprised her, she hadn't even realized it. The migraine spread over her forehead, but benevolently, as if by extending itself it were barely touching the pores of her skin with its slender needles; a thousand tiny, gentle needles substituting for one single sharp, burning needle. The bottle slid without a sound onto the blanket and then to the floor, the crowd of faces disappeared and even Miciamore's shining eyes were extinguished.

7

The children must be getting on well with their father and his new companion, because as the days went by Tosca was aware of a great flurry of coming and going: departures at dawn, evening suppers on the balcony, and the happy confusion of music and youthful voices that Tosca heard at night.

Finally Toni phoned late one afternoon to ask her advice about a worrisome problem with her little cat that Tosca would know how to handle better than she. Tosca offered to come right over. Gigi and the young people were at the beach, so they talked for a long time about children, cats, love.

Toni agreed with Tosca that for everyone, cats included, love was the core of things, the unfathomable trauma. Paletta had tried it and was unsuccessful. The young people, it seemed, were no better at it than the cat.

After her first escapade that lasted several days, Paletta had come home with wet fur, a bloody scratch on her face, and a dangling paw. Toni told how she hadn't touched her food, just licked her wounds for hours in the coolest corner of the house under the window, indifferent to all blandishments, and how she had lost weight at a frightening pace. Sometimes she raised a lament similar to an unhappy baby's cry that kept everyone awake it was so disquieting and imperative—the call for help of a sick body and a soul in pain. How could they ignore it? When Gigi opened the door again Paletta had dashed out with a frenzy that seemed to indicate uncontrollable desire; however, a little later, she came back crying. And from the balcony Toni had watched her encounter with the round head that had been the first to court her. Paletta had hissed, hair on end, claws unsheathed, and when he jumped on her, stronger than she and twice her weight, she escaped and climbed the oleander bush crazy with fear. They had a hard time retrieving her because she was whimpering as though she hadn't the strength to come down, and when Gigi tried to grab her she planted her teeth in the back of his hand.

Afterwards in the house, once again as wild as when they picked her off the street, Paletta behaved as though she didn't know them. Not interested in eating or playing, she spent hours sleeping or crying; if she went to the door and they opened it, she would go out on the stairs and down a landing or two but never beyond. In the mornings when Toni went out to do the shopping she sometimes surprised the proud and stubborn tom into immediate flight. Perhaps Paletta cried with desire, but she still refused him.

Tosca had noticed the forays of Paletta's lover into the garden, and the love summons he brought right to the condominium door, because the steps smelled of his erotic messages. Tosca felt obliged to double the doses of liquid deodorant when she cleaned in order to avoid the customary outrage of the righteous hygienists.

Tosca went over to Paletta, who lay silently in her corner. Bending over, she spoke to her softly. The animal didn't move or try to extricate herself from her caresses. With unexpected tenderness Tosca took her by the nape of her neck in her large white, cellulite-deformed arms, settled her on her breast with continual blandishments, and sat down next to Toni with the now pacified cat. The younger woman was mortified by her cat's unusual show of confidence.

"Don't be angry. It's not that she doesn't still love you, but these days she has such a complicated problem that there's no room for anything else. It's different with me, I smell like cats and she can feel comfortable. Believe me, animals know when they're in an awkward situation, and they don't want anyone to know it, not even one of their own. When she feels better she'll ask for pardon. You'll need to take her to the veterinarian. From the drama I saw in the garden with that big bad male always lying in wait for her, Paletta is still a virgin." At Toni's exclamations she continued calmly, "It happens. The poor thing wants to. That's why she cries, because she's ready to make love, too; but something must be wrong. It's better to take her right away, because otherwise who knows how long it will go on. And as thin as she is she won't last long—either without children, or with them, if by chance that one down there manages it. She's so little and weak it would be the end."

At that moment, almost as if to prove her wrong, when a harsh and repeated call rose from the garden that Tosca recognized as the lover's, Paletta jumped out of her arms so forcefully she didn't have time to protect herself, and a claw tore her dress as the animal touched ground.

"What do you think? Should I let her go?" Toni asked in alarm.

Tosca wanted to talk more, without distractions, about cats and people, and above all about the problem that, according to her, was the same for all.

"If it's like I say, that she has the desire for love, but can't do it because she isn't well or maybe because she's blocked or too little, who knows. . . each one is different, just like humans—anything but the same! Those who say we're all alike make me laugh. Not even two cats are ever alike. Even from the same litter. If she's in love she'll be happy just to be called. You saw how she ran, didn't you? She wants to be desired and looked at, but doesn't want to be touched."

Toni broke in, smiling, "There's a Russian poet, Cvetaeva, who has written that when you love someone, you always want them to go away so you can dream about them. Leopardi says just about the same thing, when he asks himself if it's better to be with the beloved or better just to dream about her."

Tosca settled down in the armchair and lit another cigarette to enhance the pleasure of the conversation. "You see? I don't think there's all that much difference between the way cats and humans love. Jealousy goes with love for them, just as it does for us. And not just erotic love. Take Poppa's first litter, for example. You saw how jealous they were of their little brother. I think we share the same instincts and feelings. We reason and they don't, so they say. But there's always a logical reason for what they do. And cats dream. I always know when they are dreaming, and who knows, maybe they dream about love. And they yearn for what they love, because otherwise why would they come back to me when their bellies are full? Because cats don't love just for sex. They want a bed, a home. I know because I see them when the summer nincompoops abandon them after two months. The first few days after they leave their pets keep faithfully returning; always hoping the door will open again. And they care about people. You can see it when they play with children or with their master (but I don't like that word. Dogs have a master, cats don't, and that's the reason they love a little like we do, because of all pets they're the most free). When they play they do it with a kind of gentleness. I don't know how to put it. They are caring and affectionate. . ."

Toni interrupted her. "I don't love them as much you do or spend much time with them. I couldn't. I probably wouldn't even want to, but it seems to me that they couldn't be more independent, as far as their house and those who live there are concerned!"

But Tosca was on home turf. "Independence doesn't mean indifference. Cats seem indifferent to you because they have different concerns than yours. But the indifference is reciprocal. What could your books mean to a cat? And in the same way you

can't know what's going on in their head, so much more interesting to them, when they refuse your attentions. At that moment he's attracted to or worried about something else. And remember, they can take offense, too, and they take offense because they're stubborn. There's nothing you can do about some
things. You can't train them. Take their claws, for example. If
they decide to sharpen them on your carpet, they'll keep it up for
an eternity. But should we expect a cat to know the value of a
Bukhara? If you punish them it's not long before they ask forgiveness. It happened to me recently with Bisi. As she scratched
away and watched me she seemed to be telling me, 'What's a
rug good for if I can't use it to sharpen my claws?'"

Toni laughed. "Those cats of yours are privileged."

Tosca sat up straight in her chair. "Oh, in that way, yes. I'm
richer than those tightfisted fools who would even rent the tab-
ernacle in the summer if they could. They're just rich in money,
but in every other way no one's poorer. All they understand is
money. That's why they treat outsiders so badly."

Her voice cracked, her body suddenly went limp. Shoulders
slumped, head down, Tosca was just a poor woman who took
care of cats because they were all she had in the world.

Toni searched for another topic of conversation to divert her
from that dangerous precipice. Also, she noticed a strong odor
on her breath, confirming a suspicion she'd had from the first
time she'd met her. She had offered her a cool drink, but not
wine, and now, embarrassed by her suspicions and to break the
pause that had grown too long, she suggested they have something to drink. The other accepted, and as they moved into the
living room, Toni said, "You know I believe in metempsychosis?
And I ask myself if someone like you would want to come back
in the clothes, or rather the fur, of a beautiful cat!"

"Wouldn't I! At least I'd be free and could wander around
the village night and day doing mischief. But I wouldn't want to

be female. I would want to be like Miciamore. I would punish all their cats, one after another."

Toni handed her a drink. "There's a Hindu tradition, based on written laws, the very ancient laws of Manu, a sort of list for transformations after death. If I remember right, there's one that more or less says: he who sins with his body will become a tree in another life. I would like to be a mimosa or a magnolia, or even a baobab. They live for centuries! He who sins with words will become an animal and someone who sins in his soul will return a human being, but like a pariah, on the lowest social level."

Tosca reflected. "Then you intellectuals who sin with words could become cats. Not me. I can only be born as a tree. . . how sad! That doesn't suit me at all. Unless I'm destined to come back as something worse, more pariah than I am now. What does it mean to sin in the soul?"

"That holds no danger for you. Those who sin in the soul have no mercy or tolerance. To your health!" and she raised her glass to Tosca. "To the health of our souls. Now and in a hundred years to my mimosa and to your. . . what tree would you be if you're destined for the vegetable world?"

With a laugh Tosca replied, "A bougainvillea. I like the color and besides I'd have cats playing around my roots."

When Gigi returned after his day of fishing, Toni told him about her conversation with Tosca, and about her suspicions.

"You know, I was thinking today that nothing is more disheartening than solitude," and she gave him a hug. "And that maybe I would drink to fill the void if my life turned out like Tosca's. It must be very difficult to hang on, not to come unhinged, when nothing's important anymore and you don't have anyone to talk to."

"But she can tell it to her cats," objected Gigi, "She always has someone there to talk to, as you know. Even if it's just a pretense of a real situation." And since Toni was questioning him with her eyes, he added, "Because everyone talks to himself when he talks. Our real conversation is inside ourselves. And we lend different faces, ears, language to it as the situation requires."

He realized that hurt her and corrected himself. "But not when we're in love and get back what we give. That's different. Because we see ourselves in the person who listens to us."

And Toni: "But Tosca really believed she saw herself in Miciamore's eyes. I think she understands very well she's reciting a part. Oh, in perfectly good faith! With courage and even with anger, but she knows she's deluding herself. That's why she explains her reality through her cats. She attributes thoughts and intentions to them and sometimes that's enough. But at other times this playacting must be unbearable for her."

Gigi responded: "So, according to you, Tosca's playacting would be a true pretense, or a false truth? I don't believe it. I think she wisely keeps herself from looking ahead or behind as much as she can. She trusts in the moment, in the evidence of things before her eyes, in what the animals ask of her with the strength and grace of their naturalness. She becomes nature, too, and that way protects herself from the awareness of her real situation. She turns to wine only when reason, with its treacherous logic, suggests she has invented everything. And maybe it happens when she runs up against the indifference of others—or even worse, their spite. If she were. . . I don't know. . . more educated, or maybe not, only stronger, or had a strong faith, she could reach a state of perfect autonomy in her solitude. But to get there you need to be a saint or a genius or an artist. She is only a woman who hasn't had good luck."

Toni didn't reply. She was thinking sadly of the waste of such a capacity to love, in a play where the cats would only have been painted by an ironic and tender set-designer like Luzzati.

Lagorio

Wasn't a scenic backdrop enough for the monologue of a great actress?

8

They invited Tosca to supper the next evening. Gigi wanted her to taste a summer substitute for alcohol he had invented for his own problems of high blood pressure. A mixture where the sour taste of black current quenched the thirst with a pleasant illusion of wine. The food was also fresh and light. "I enjoy working in the kitchen when I'm here to test the credibility of the silly things I write about." He didn't add that it seemed more honest than transforming gastronomy into a literary genre, a thought that irritated more than amused him, as he would have preferred, since his colleagues of more refined writing practiced cooking by buying kitchen equipment and citing learned sources. The cultural revolution of food had taken off from Lévi-Strauss, they seriously maintained, and they attempted a committed descent through time. They dined in serious gatherings *d'après* Luigi Filippo or Beatrice d'Este, as one used to paint *d'après* Modigliani or Cézanne. Gigi's irony was bitter because he hadn't forgotten the many little smiles of condescension that had accompanied his passage from writing about films to writing a food column. From the polis to sex, the throat was the final shore to reach with the dizziness of words.

Gigi had discussed it with Toni at length and proposed to help Tosca conquer her weakness. Aware of their intentions, Tosca praised Gigi's innocent mixture and the food prepared by Toni, gratefully giving in to the feeling of being cared for. The evening was spent talking and listening to opera records. As Tosca was saying good night the children came in, Gigi's and the friends traveling with them, along with the young couple from the apartment downstairs. Tosca knew the girl's parents and asked why she hadn't seen them at the seaside for a few years.

"Your mother," Tosca said to her, "was at the condominium meeting, but she left right away."

While the girl responded— "her father's medical office closed due to an overdose of stress," her mother "a vagabond," both "scatter-brained and unmotivated, wandering around the world"—she looked no one in the face. Her name was Lavinia and her beautiful straight blond hair hung loose on her thin shoulders. Her large and slightly watery eyes, with light green pupils swimming in a wide expanse of white cornea, avoided their faces, resting only on objects or the sea. Even her low, warm voice, with its professional, cadenced tones, seemed to reach the ear through a filter. Tosca didn't like her, and inwardly disposed of her with one word: false.

But she noticed Gigi's son, the awkward beanpole she had seen juggling suitcases like a performing clown, didn't let her out of his sight for a moment, to the apparent indifference of her fiancé—or as kids say today—her man, at least ten years older than Gigi's son and at least five years older than Lavinia. Enrico and Lavinia had worked together from the time she graduated from the university. He, as an assistant to the head of sociology, had helped her. Now, under the guidance of their common "patron," who even Tosca knew from seeing him on TV many times, they were conducting an investigation about something Tosca understood to be the games of certain peoples of the South, but described in words she'd never heard before. "With those jaws, he looks like a guard dog, but he's an insensitive drudge, a real drudge who only understands books and doesn't notice what's going on right under his nose," she concluded as she listened, smoking. After they came in she sat down again, instinctively moving her chair to the corner farthest away from the group gathered on the balcony. Her question to Lavinia about her parents had been made to cover her embarrassment. She was the woman who washed the stairs, after all, and Lavinia never had seemed to see her the few times they happened to meet at the door. Tosca had her own small right to be a part of that gathering, but she felt uneasy and tried to find a way to leave without seeming rude.

Gigi came to her rescue, turning to Enrico with a smile, "You could write a much more entertaining book about the games animals play. This woman is an expert. She could write a book about her cats, which would certainly have a wider audience than yours."

Lavinia made a little sarcastic sneer and bleated, "We know, we know. Miciamore is a legend by now." It could have been a kind overture, but in that voice and theatrical manner of speaking, it seemed impertinent. Tosca reddened and Toni raised her voice to ask if anyone wanted a nightcap.

It escaped no one's notice that Lavinia was talking under her breath to Enrico, and that Enrico was annoyed. In fact he got up and went back into the living room, picked up the first magazine he found, and began flipping through it. Immediately Gigi's son Matteo took his place, amid the not-too-well-restrained giggles of his friends, and Gigi was able to joke about the seductive power of blondes without fear of offending the boy whose gangly physique had a pathetically timid aspect. But Toni was annoyed. She was always tense when Gigi's children were in the house, and she had told Tosca that she had found Matteo "almost as thin as her cat."

Luckily, Matteo's friends were at ease. Noisy and happy, they seemed to appreciate everything — the company, the sea, the wine. They quickly took up Gigi's quip about blondes to launch their zingers at Matteo who seemed to be their usual target. One of them put on an exaggerated performance to imitate his Casanova friend whom no woman, blonde or brunette, could refuse. Matteo parried the thrust, but was hurt. The others continued relentlessly to remind him of improbable erotic conquests and the perverse adventures of a male chauvinist. Tosca was embarrassed for the boy and for Toni and got up to leave, but Lavinia went ahead of her. Her face had remained impassive during the humiliating demonstration, a manifestation of boredom behind curtains of hair. Enrico was at her side.

On the stairs Tosca heard her voice stomp on the word "puppies," while her companion's irritated voice was lost in the sound of the sliding bolt. A nice evening had ended badly. Living with her cats had sharpened Tosca's observational skills. "Tabby cats are all alike," Toni had said, surprised Tosca could call them by name and distinguish them by character and habits. Not to be able to recognize them was only laziness, Tosca had replied. The same reason why a group of Japanese or Chinese look alike to us. Her eyes could measure a cat's physical dimensions, and she was sensitive to their individual personalities. And since she spent her time studying them, catering to them, protecting them, it didn't take much for her to "read" them. Now she was thinking how human faces are often more ambiguous and closed than a cat's. For example, she didn't like the girl with the classical name she could never remember—Elena, no, Cassandra, no. Lavinia, that was it. She was cold and must be heartless. She would make Matteo suffer, who certainly didn't resemble his mother, from the little that Toni had told her about Gigi's wife. She seemed to hear her Mario accuse her of partiality. Women who take the place left empty by another are short on compassion for the one they replaced. But she believed what Toni said about the ex-wife because Toni was good, kind to her as no one since the Milan days. And Gigi was easy to talk to, also, aware of the subtle needs of others; therefore, his son must take after him a good deal. And how men were attracted to that lunar creature! That evening she had watched two of them conditioned by her reactions. Reactions! As though her white face (it seemed more white among all the tanned faces, and even pale

Enrico had an olive tint to his brown skin) was expressing anything really decipherable. "Her face is her language," Tosca thought as she went down the stairs; she wasn't ready to go to sleep and preferred to prolong her memories of the evening on the beach in the cool of the evening. Maybe she would meet up with her three musketeers and bring them back with her. They had gone out at the same time as she, filing out the door in a hurry, anxious for some cool air. It was very hot and the breeze blowing from room to room wasn't enough to give relief.

Who knows what men see in some women. She wasn't even pretty, except for her long, silky hair—a powerful attraction for many men. She remembered how every summer Bruno begged her not to give into the temptation to have her hair cut, and she, during that time of love, had let it grow. When they embraced after hours of waiting he wanted her to let it down. She had taken good care of it, buying a dryer and every kind of shampoo advertised by television actresses.

Perhaps Lavinia had a nice body, but Tosca only remembered her too thin arms and neck. Who knows what those two ate, typing all day and going to the beach only in the evening for a quick dip. Yes, her face was attractive. But Tosca couldn't remember her legs or breasts because it was natural to concentrate on that pale mask half hidden by hair. Words issued from that mask as though recited on stage. A curious way of talking, strange for such a young woman. . . Perhaps her power of attraction, her seduction, was just to allow a glimpse of a mystery which, if there was one, she wasn't inclined to reveal it. Toni was entirely different. Emotions passed like visible waves over her delicate features. Fear, disappointment, joy were there, observable to anyone who looked at her with a little love. Lavinia, on the other hand, was wrapped in her mystery, like Turandot. Opera libretti always suggested an analogy that she used to illuminate the impressions others aroused in her, and so she met

Amneris and Don Carlos, Marcello and Pinkerton walking down the street. Turandot was cruel, and Lavinia resembled her. She tried to remember her mouth, applying the old canon of judgment in which thin mouths show meanness, but she couldn't. She couldn't recall the white mask. The white blurred and dissolved. While she was thinking on the beach, sitting on a rock still warm from the heat of the day, Lavinia was for her only a young woman without apparent emotions, ironic and detached, as far from the warmth of life as the moon from earth.

Hearing voices behind her, she turned. Along the wall bordering the beach two figures moved side by side. She recognized Matteo's awkward gait and the other one, of course, was she, the daughter of the moon. "Look at the little bitch," she muttered to herself, so she *was* playing at love! Tosca had been right about that. But where was Enrico? She had heard their voices after they went into their apartment. Maybe they fought and Lavinia returned to the others.

It was late, and a weariness from the whole day now weighed on her bones. She was getting up with difficulty when she saw Matteo take Lavinia by the waist, who broke away abruptly and ran toward the sea. They were far away and Tosca could distinguish their shapes but not their words. However, Matteo shouted loudly, "Don't go in. Wait for me!" The girl was already at the water's edge; with a single motion she was free of her tunic. For a moment she stood still and naked against the black sea in the defused moonlight, then she went in. Matteo followed her, but he had lost time getting out of his clothes and Lavinia was already far out. Tosca stood still, as though spellbound. How beautiful that amphibian creature was, terrestrial and marine, alone and silent in the sea, and Matteo's cry was the cry all men and animals make when pursued by love.

She walked slowly home, turning every so often to look back. Now Matteo was swimming beside Lavinia, their heads side by side in the moon's silvery stripe on the water, and at every embrace a little glistening rain fell around them, their movements in rhythm with the fabulous air and silence. That is what touched her heart: the beauty of the world and the enchantment of youth, of young bodies experimenting in a freedom as yet unconditioned. This happiness was unrepeatable. Perhaps Lavinia's feminine curiosity was playing with his infantile need for love, but she had given him, before Tosca's eyes, a moment the boy would always remember.

9

Those hot summer days rolled by in the same way for everyone in the condominium of cats and bougainvillea. In the stairway to the right the young sociologists didn't type anymore, but joined the journalist's children and their friends. The Audibertis went through the garden in their daily routine of shopping, beach, afternoon nap, evening walk, sleep. Each day at the same time, as punctual as the family of a retiree from Piedmont can be. In her stairway Tosca met the mother of the three little children and her husband who had joined her for the holidays. He brought a friend of hers with him, a tall, well-shaped woman, who introduced herself with an unthinkably energetic handshake considering the depressing sultriness brought on by the scirocco. Fortunately Tosca's landlady was away on a trip to Norway, or somewhere near it, with her husband and son. And so she didn't have to work so hard at keeping the stairs clean, especially during the hottest hours, when it was already hard to breathe.

Life slowed down for everybody. Food, sweat, dips in the sea, sleep, and all in slow motion. Actions were reduced to the minimum, as were plans and thoughts, each one trying to survive, putting aside every task, including mental. Physical effort was carefully measured in the torpor that bound living beings with land and sea.

A gray and downy mass spread over the horizon like a blanket. Sometimes it descended to obliterate the furthest point, and then haze shrouded everything like winter fog on the northern plain. Even the sound of voices grew infrequent. Tosca only heard the cry of the smallest of the three children, restless in the great night heat, and angry outbursts from the mother who never smiled at her children, but nonetheless seemed happier after the arrival of her husband and the friend who now shared the domestic chores.

From the other stairway voices were heard only at night. During the day the young people lived on the beach or in boats, and even Toni and Gigi had, for the convenience, chosen to substitute lunch with a sandwich for everyone, prepared by Aldo, the elderly employee of the beach concession. Tosca was alone for hours during the day. Poppa disappeared, followed by Fifi. Female cats are precocious and are ready to make love before the males. Puss and Bisi went out only if they had nothing to eat, but they slept outside at night. It was a time of freedom for them, too. Tosca noticed that if they happened to encounter Fifi by chance, Puss (the brighter of the two and Tosca's favorite because he had something of Miciamore's looks) would begin to play erotic games with her. Suddenly he would bite her neck, and she would immediately rebel, bristling and angry. Then he would move off and watch her, quiet and determined. Tosca knew cats had no incest taboo, but this time (and she didn't know how to explain it), it bothered her to watch their skirmishes. And since Fifi didn't seem to like her brother, Tosca would chase him off when she was present to observe Puss's proposals.

Three times a year a cat brings a litter into the house. This was too much, even for her, and now she had two of them, mother and daughter, who were cooking up who knows what kind of amatory capers in the bushes on the hill or in alleys and gardens at night. She gave both of them a pill when she could get hold of them, but wasn't convinced it worked. Animals can easily vomit up what they don't like.

In the silence of the house, with her frig always full because the appetite fades in the heat like colors in the sky, the rooms cleaned and aired the first thing in the morning, Tosca would go down and pass a damp cloth over both stairways, water the garden and, along with the plants, have her first shower. At times she went back in without seeing anyone. She would throw herself on the bed for some extra sleep and wash after she got up. Afterwards, when the water had restored the illusion of will and strength, she didn't know what to do with herself, where to move her burdensome body she couldn't immerse in the sea as everyone else could. Just the thought of such a transgression made her heart pound and her breathing harsh. She felt no worse than usual. In fact, if she wouldn't let herself have bad thoughts, she could keep her illness in check. She had to work at it, however, and to work at it was difficult now that she couldn't hope for an invitation from Gigi and Toni, who must be tired after that too long invasion of outsiders on their routine. They had lent her some books, and Tosca made an attempt to read them in bed, but she couldn't find one that really struck her fancy, like waiting anxiously for someone you wanted to be with. Angelica's adventures were too many and too complicated for her. She couldn't remember the foreign names and always had to go back and look for them. The classics, such as Hawthorne and Stevenson, were grim and sometimes her eyes drooped out of boredom from so much rationalization. Perhaps it was justified, but to her it seemed cruel, especially *The Scarlet Letter*. She leafed through the pile of magazines Toni had given her, and read some articles, but rarely found anything that really interested her. It was already too late for beauty treatments, and anyway they cost too much. And when would she ever be able to travel? She liked to read about the movie stars' affairs, but she only felt more miserable afterwards, and was left with such a thirst in her body for liquids, companionship, love, that the only comfort available to her was a venial sin.

And so, in that great rotation of days in the summer heat, Tosca poisoned herself little by little with the sweetest poison she knew.

On the day that a storm came up to whip the awnings and blow away some large umbrellas carelessly left open, she lay unconscious in bed, covered in icy perspiration. After a few moments she came to in the blast of cool air that came from the shutters thrown open by the force of the wind.

She looked around in a daze and tried to get up to shut the banging doors.

Her legs wouldn't support her, every muscle trembled, and she was afraid. The bicarb was in the kitchen and it took all her strength to get it. She dissolved a spoonful of soda in water, and seemed to feel better immediately. That's what her mother did for her grandfather when he had a bad spell. Tosca could still remember his sour smell like green apples when, pale as a sheet, he fell onto a kitchen chair, unable to speak.

It wasn't an unpleasant odor, just as none of the childhood memories she had of her grandfather were unpleasant. She would take his damp, ice-cold hand to comfort him, while her mother put a vinegar-soaked cloth on his forehead and scolded him at the same time for bending his elbow too often, and she spoke of "acidosis."

 The doctor said her grandfather suffered from diabetes and a story began that would grow sadder every day. Her grandfather hated the insulin which he called "my slavery." At home he followed the regime they imposed on him, but away he transgressed with his friends at the local tavern. If he felt bad, her mother gave him some sugar. When he recovered his breath and color, she helped him change his perspiration-soaked clothes. Tosca remembered the complaints, scoldings, fights repeated like an unhappy old couple. Little by little her grandfather stayed away more often; like a cat he escaped out the door at the first opportunity and forgot to come back, reduced to living like a tramp wherever and whatever chance provided. He died younger than necessary, considering the family history. But he was right. Better to live a shorter time in freedom than languish in boredom. However, Tosca was just trying to fool herself with that kind of reasoning while her heart recovered its normal rhythm. In reality she was frightened, and perhaps she hoped that if someone knew about it she might be forced to take care of herself.

The storm drove off the great heat, and also the bathers who had no house to go to and who found the bed and breakfast suddenly expensive or the hospitality boring.

Toni's guests left and Tosca again heard the click-clack of the typewriters, theirs and those of the two young scholars below them. She was curious to learn about the developments of the moonlit evening that now seemed as beautiful as an invented memory, or a moment more dreamed than real. The beach had suddenly turned gray; the sea was no longer the blue of calm water and didn't reflect the brilliant sunsets. It was colorless and cold, and Tosca sadly realized that summer was beginning to die.

Before long the exodus would begin. The outsiders would gradually leave, and she would exchange a few last words with the bathing attendant who, immediately after the cabana doors were nailed shut and the boats and equipment put away, would go home to Oneglia. Finally, the private beach concession would also close where Matteo had experienced the enchantment that emanates from a woman's body, and even Lavinia had been happy with that body she had brought to swim in the moonlight.

Soon only she, her cats, and the sea gulls would be left on the beach.

10

She had been frightened too soon, because the bright sun returned, other bathers came, and she felt better because a cool breeze rose in the morning and evening, and the nights were mild and pleasant.

But Tosca couldn't get her attack during the storm out of her mind. An attack strong enough to make her lose her memory. She had struggled to recover at once, and had believed the season over. When her grandfather drank he forgot the date, the names of things, what he had in his pocket, and her mother would yell at him because she couldn't trust him with the smallest task. Tosca knew a few medical tests would be enough to determine the validity of her fears. Diabetes is hereditary, and she had reacted instinctively during the attack when she remembered what had been done at home for her grandfather before he took insulin; the soda had been good for her and this was a sign, too. The more she tried to chase the thought away the more it gnawed at her, forcing her to be active, to replenish the food supplies for herself and the cats, to stop and talk in the garden with whomever came by, to take care of the plants and windows more diligently than ever. But working in the summer made one thirsty, and being thirsty meant running up against the thought that made her feel guilty even before she gave in to temptation. She had a way of lying to herself that hurt no one but herself. It was an alibi that had nothing to do with her education—what she had received and what experience in life had taught her. And if she gave in to alcohol it was a vice she forgave herself for, though shamefully, a secret vice like masturbation. The wine was tranquilizing and justified by the miserly fate that had reduced her to a category that others, better off and more privileged, despised. Now that she knew she had or was afraid of having a sickness in her blood, the vice of drinking became a deadly sin. The most serious, because a one-way street, a sin that not even God pardons because the dead can't ask forgiveness.

Tosca had a horror of unnatural death, and in her present solitude the news related on TV of ingenious or unusual ways to die, the mysteries of certain violent acts that remained unsolved, had the ability to terrorize her to the point where she wanted to go out into the street among strangers, just so as not to be alone.

Hers was a pitiful life. No one reckoned that misery better than she who lived it, but it was hers, it belonged to her. She didn't believe anything could change it. If she went to church sometimes it was to be with people in an illusion of community. She didn't call it communion, because she didn't feel it was. She was alone, and alone she remained among strangers indifferent to her and to her little life. And up there no one must love her if she was left alone like that, to grapple with solitude and sickness in silence and emptiness.

But in that silence and emptiness she moved and dredged up memories and dreams, the only positive things she had, and if they were lost nothing or no one could give them back. Sometimes she tried to tell herself that not being, not thinking, not suffering, was better than living as she lived. But something always kept her from the temptation of believing completely in the total uselessness of her life. She had lived for Miciamore, and could live for Poppa or any creature alive in need of protection. If the wilderness of voices became agonizing, she could contain, dominate, annihilate the anguish by the becalming descent into drunkenness and forgetfulness of the present that alcohol provides. But it was not a choice; it was a means, cowardly perhaps, but so worthy of pity and forgiveness!

If there was a God, He could at least look her way, indulgently shaking his large head with flowing locks and beard. She was certain God would never condemn her to hell for having invented that oblivion within the four walls of her house inhabited only by ghosts and cats. In these days images of men appeared in her mind she had seen sleeping on benches wrapped in newspapers on cold days, women in rags holding a metal cup before the rectory door of a merciful priest at the end of Corso Garibaldi, and the whole miserable crowd that acted in Bertolazzi's *Nost Milan*. She remembered applauding, but she had also told Mario she preferred a different kind of theater, light and happy, because all that gray fog and misery wrung her heart, even though she knew it was all make believe.

Their conversations about fate came back to mind. Mario had been strong and able to calm her resentment about the injustices that discouraged most people into resignation or reduced them to hate. Mario said everyone had the wherewithal to play the cards he was dealt, in order to live humanely. But she didn't think it worked that way. Mario had his life cut short in a most unforeseeable and senseless way, a life so capable of spreading light and warmth around him. A life that chance had once saved for him while stealing it from his soldiers. Now Tosca asked herself: is it possible that destiny is so determined to make me feel guilty for a weakness that everyone more or less indulges in? By what evil trick of fate or pitiless God must her only cowardice, and also the only life preserver in her empty life, become a deadly choice?

She was floundering around in the sticky mire of these uncertainties that nevertheless reduced the number of concessions to her thirst (ever alert like a poisonous snake), when the soccer world cup came to save her. One afternoon her mind wandered back to a trip she and her mother had made right after the war. Unable to find a hotel room, they settled down to spend the night in the train station waiting room. Across from them was a disheveled drunk; in the folds of his colorless and shapeless pants his genitals were visible and she, a young girl, was fascinated by the sight. Her mother had made her change her seat several times because the drunk fondled himself in his sleep. She still had a confused horror of that night, even a feeling of shame — when she was startled by a shout coming from many mouths at once like a triumphant blast. She went to the window. No one was in the street, but through open windows she saw groups of people with their engrossed faces looking in the same direction. Someone gestured and she remembered: the soccer world cup. Tosca didn't care to watch sports events, not since she had been alone. Sometimes her husband had taken her to the stadium and she had enjoyed herself, getting excited about the game because of his enthusiasm. After that she never followed sports, either in the newspapers or on TV. She switched channels whenever soccer or tennis or some other game came on the screen, even if she recognized some of the faces and knew about their amorous goings-on from the illustrated magazines.

Almost without thinking she turned on her television, a big black and white set, but with many channels — her only luxury, except for the telephone, that she never wanted to give up. In a few minutes she was immersed in such a state of tension that she forgot her worries. Italy was playing Brazil, and even she knew they weren't good enough to win. While watering the plants in the garden she had overheard the conversation of some vacationers sitting on the lounge chairs beyond the bougainvillea bush. She hadn't followed their discussion because she wasn't interested, but something had stuck in her mind. In fact, without any particular interest she had reflected sadly that by now everyone was so accustomed to bad news, scandals, and crimes that people had little faith even in sports competitions. But what she saw now was wonderful, and even noble. She immediately felt Italy could win, and began to wish for it. Many times she had tried to reach out for something desired until the desire itself became a will that joined to someone else's who wanted the same thing, influencing it, bringing it to what she wanted. She had done this while waiting in darkness at the window for Bruno. Every time he appeared around the corner of the private beach she would see his coming as the incarnation of her desire.

At the second goal Tosca jumped to her feet. She cheered like all the neighbors whose various and yet uniform shouts of exaltation reached her ears. Those young men were fighting for her, also, she felt sure of it. Fifi, who was probably pregnant because she had come back home, dashed off in terror. She stayed close to Tosca, as though to be assured of her protection, and had been lying under her chair, the only cool one in the house with its Viennese straw seat.

For the next match with Poland Tosca would go to the rotunda of the private beach, since Aldo the bathing attendant told her that because of renewed hope for Italy's chances a television had been temporarily installed. Aldo and the villagers would be there. She would be with people and out of the house. During the day thoughts of such an out-of-the-ordinary event never left her, and she was able to go there in the evening calmly without any worries about her breathing. She hadn't had any wine except with meals, and then she had been very moderate.

It was agony. The Poles were big and aggressive. The boys, as she called them (and by following the interviews and discussions, she had learned to recognize them during the live transmission), fell like nine pins at every turn. She began to perspire nervously, but even the children around her were shouting their indignation at the adversary and their blind love for the Italian team. Their parents did not quiet them. In fact, the exhortations peppered with anger soon became a chorus. Tosca smoked one cigarette after another. When God, and not his Polish representative on earth (as someone observed), willed it, the game finally ended, and it was another victory. Joy exploded on the rotunda and Tosca took part in it. Aldo offered her a drink and a gentleman from Genoa she didn't know treated everyone.

Now even Tosca had something to look forward to, and she made it a point to watch "the marvels" of the Franco-German game the television announcers talked about, in order to be better informed about the adversary for the final extraordinary game they were preparing for. Also in training, with a solitary exercise of will but equal to that of the players, she abstained from drinking. It was a challenge she renewed in the mornings without allowing distractions, and she cheered herself on like the most avid fans watching every program devoted to the championship. And when she watered the plants in the garden she didn't miss a word of the discussions beyond the garden that were now about nothing else.

The old pharmacist who had taught her what he knew of herbs suggested one day that there were other more important competitions for us to participate in, but he was overruled by angry and derisive voices. Tosca never forgot the comments of the old gentleman who had seen many governments fall and had watched so many championship games. Offenses received are not forgotten, but such afflictions fly away when the merciful wind of glory blows. He kept newspaper articles from the past, and never lost an opportunity to quote their arrogance and inaccuracy with wicked regularity. The ballet of legislators transformed into pipers was conjured up by his bitter voice at every enthusiastic statement his friends made on lazy afternoons. Tosca didn't understand all the implications underlying the old gentleman's words. She got her news from television after she had reluctantly ruled out the expense of a newspaper, a luxury she had come to enjoy during her marriage. However, the language of the political game quickly tired her, because the meaning of life at the pinnacle of power was beyond her understanding; she knew, however, that it was something that did not mirror nor protect her life. It was something she could watch like a poor performance that didn't involve her as this other one did, on days a little drunk with heat and absurd worries. Days with all the notes outside the line, as Mario would have said, who had scolded her for her emotional tears or laughter at the performances they attended together.

She remembered it, a little ashamed of herself, on the evening when the boys scored three times against the Germans and she had followed them with stubborn expectation, and a hope as angry as she hadn't felt since the days with her family in the Brianza countryside. Then, as now, she hadn't understood the fundamental scheme of things. She was a little girl who was always hungry, and afraid when she saw a swastika. But clear fragments of one final episode had stuck in her mind: revolvers hauled up from wells or fished out of haystacks, her heart pounding in the dark countryside between gun shots, and afterwards the celebrations and light when the Germans went away.

She was shouting about past memories in front of the TV, too, and was not astonished when a boy she had never seen before, who was jumping around on the rotunda like a crazed cricket in his bathing shorts, gave her a big hug. Later she had gone into the street along with the others. She couldn't imagine where all the tricolored flags came from — in windows, in children's hands, in automobiles passing by with horns honking. The whole village was out; the houses had spewed everyone out, the locals and those who came from who knows where. She found herself in the middle of a group from Savona who had drums, trumpets, and metal plates to bang together and who hoisted a large sign in German, edged in black, that even she understood. They danced and played in the palm-lined street. Finally she sat down on a bench, dazed and breathless from all the ruckus around her, but someone took her by the arm and led her to a bonfire on the beach where a figure made of cane and rags was burning. A swastika sign hung round its neck.

She wasn't thinking, she was living. She realized at a certain point that she was laughing, but tears bathed her cheeks, and she remained where she was, there in the shadows, when the young people carried their happiness off to other places. And gradually at the waters' edge the shadows became more infrequent, with just those who had been walking in the night to escape the festivities or to shake off exceptional emotions. But behind her the roar of automobiles and honking horns on Via Aurelia continued for some time.

Tosca looked at the ashes of the bonfire and asked herself how it had been possible. She had run into Bruno's friends. One walked along beside her for a stretch on Via Aurelia and offered her a cigarette. Among those dancing in a ring on the beach she recognized some of the village boys. Perhaps one of them had given the poisoned food to Miciamore. . . Could one be happy in a crowd, be part of it with others, for something like this?

One could. It had happened. And now that the celebration was over, the fires extinguished and the flags put back in drawers, she would again be the cat lady, "the furiner" they smiled at and shook hands with only when the shout of unexpected victory exploded to drown out the whispers and silences.

Yet that happiness everyone felt was real. But was the innocence of one night enough to erase the fierce ostracism that had gradually forced her to restrict her life almost completely?

It had been wonderful to be with so many faces all reflecting a common emotion, never before imagined, and to feel herself taken by the hand. She hadn't been alone anymore, she had been the same as the others, and her face shone like theirs. Everyone needs happiness, she thought, everyone wants to be happy and to feel worthy in the eyes of others. For one evening it had been like that for her, too.

I'm the same old naive woman, she said to herself, but maybe not. Maybe I'm wrong to live in solitude out of fear for the contempt of others. It was a serious matter, it was her life in a situation she didn't like, and it wasn't right to throw it away because of a suspicion. She felt stronger and better immediately being with others to watch those boys committed to a game of skill and honor. And now what? With a sharp pang she missed Bruno. She moaned softly at the image that wiped out the evening: his head next to his wife's. She saw him looking resignedly at her pale face sleeping next to him in the blind sleep of the drugged. Not even on this evening had she seen him. He couldn't leave his wife alone with the children, and maybe now, in the silence following the merry making, he was thinking of her, alone, as he was alone.

Tosca could no longer make out the remains of the bonfire on the deserted beach, and the night dampness made her shiver. Cold nausea gripped her again at the thought of the hours that would come in the series of days awaiting her.

She should get up and go home but lacked the strength. What awful new thing might tell her savagely, as had happened with the poison administered to Miciamore, that, no, no one loved her, and her life with cats merited punishment?

Tosca got up, her entire body trembling, with warm waves alternating with chills. My God, she prayed, what awful thing did I ever do to be abandoned like this, to have to decide every day and every minute whether to defend the only things I have, my life's blood, my tired but warm heart, my head full of images and memories, or whether to despair and end it in the surest and sweetest way. The intoxicating liberator, then unconsciousness, and the long sleep without return. . .

The celebration, the brief inebriating proof that she could be happy with others, was really over. She had to go back into her house, to encounter the same ghosts, with no voice to greet another sun with her. Lighting her last cigarette, she tossed the empty package into the bonfire. She looked at the quiet sea, barely lapping, like many voices in soft and continuous prayer. Let's prolong this blessed night, she said to herself, don't think about tomorrow. Something good can happen. This night has shown me I can recognize myself in others without the selfishness of love or hate. The bad things that have happened to me up to now haven't been my fault. If I have lost love's thread with people, perhaps my poor cats have helped me not to forget it completely. Now, Tosca, get hold of yourself, don't be discouraged, stay at the window to drink in the night breeze until it grows light.

11

Tosca was in the garden toward evening, after a long sleep following the night of celebration. As she watered the plants, with Fifi amorously encircling her legs with her tail, the car of the two journalists stopped at the gate. Toni got out, and while Gigi parked the car in the garage, the two women exchanged news, both still excited about the events of the previous night. Toni had come from Verona where she had seen *Aida* and *Otello.*

"I'll tell you about *Aida* later—a wonderful performance— but the *Otello*! You can't imagine what happened! Gigi didn't want to miss the championship game, but now he's sorry he didn't go with me, because I saw both. The first half in a bar, the second half in the Arena on the radio. And I can tell you it was a marvelous spectacle, with the audience exploding at the first goal. There must have been a thousand little radios in the arena. Then the opening was delayed and at the second goal people rushed on the stage with Cappuccilli in his Iago's costume watching the audience and the chorus all hugging each other. At the final whistle the orchestra played Mameli's patriotic hymn while the cast waved the blue flags of San Marco. I don't think I'll ever see anything like that again."

Gigi joined them and learned of Tosca's marvelous evening. "Come have dinner with us when you're finished. I'll take you both to a restaurant so we can talk."

Tosca knew the libretto of *Aida* and the most famous arias. "I always sing *Radames discolpati* to my cats when they're up to no good in the house." And she listened to the news of the opening in Verona with obvious pleasure. Toni knew how to tell a story. Her vivacious expressions were able to conjure up in her listeners the images moving through her mind. The Egypt reconstructed by De Bosio on the model of the first performance (Gigi had the latest essay about that research), and the singers who brought Verdi's arias to life, were vividly described over a plate of fried fish. Toni was weaver of the tale, and Tosca the ingenuous, painstaking embroiderer of it, with her questions and comments revealing how much she relished creating an imaginary performance of her own in the greatest possible detail, superimposing it over the distant memory of an *Aida* given by Carro di Tespi.

Gigi enjoyed listening to the women and finally said, "It's a play within a play listening to you two. I was there, but I must say that for someone who doesn't love opera I am enjoying this more than at the Arena. But tell us what happened here."

Tosca was happy, and began to relate her story carefully, since it was difficult to conceal her thoughts that had caught fire afterwards on the beach at the end of the celebration. She told about the sparks rising from the bonfire, the sparks of joy squealed by the children, the sparks of tension in her and the others in union with the soccer players, and then of the collective exhilaration in the drama she had been a part of. The emotional charge of that night came alive in her sometimes hesitant words, checked by the overlapping of her private thoughts, but still capable of transmitting what had happened in the village similar to what Gigi and Toni had seen happen after *Otello* on the streets of Verona until dawn.

Gigi wanted to rummage deeper into the chinks he had sensed in the controlled compactness of the woman's story. "This time our little village has shown you an amiable face. Don't you see there's always hope for one's neighbor?"

Tosca was unable to respond at once, surprised by the transparency of the thoughts she had believed hidden. She tried to reply, but from her contracted throat came only general sounds of doubt, less expressive than the shake of her head and tight smile. Toni came to her aid. "What does it matter? We have to take what comes, and this was a happy time for everyone. Isn't that enough?"

"That's just what I meant. There are almost magical happenings — like this unexpected Italian victory — that can fill the emptiness, soften the harshness, and unite everyone in a common enthusiasm, at least for one evening."

Tosca's reaction came quickly. "That's exactly what is most discouraging afterwards. It would be so much easier to live together if we all wanted to!"

A black shadow fell over her eyes as she continued. "Nothing is more satisfying than feeling you are like everyone else. . . for once I didn't see sly little smiles. They let me be." Her voice rose with emotion. "Don't believe those who say you don't like people if you like animals. It's not true. I like to be with people, I like to be with you, I need to talk, but if I don't have anyone, what can I do? At least Miciamore rubbed against me when I cried, and his children come looking for me."

"There'll be other opportunities to meet with the villagers, you'll see," said Toni, who couldn't bear to see her suffer. "And besides, if you really don't like it here you can always leave."

"If only I could!" Tosca replied, now absorbed in her biggest problem, as she emptied her glass and lit another cigarette. "If only I had the means to do it, and a reason, a real excuse, I'd take my cats (somehow I would manage) and go to someone who might love me a little. But I don't have anyone anymore, and I can't get my place back in Milan. I lent my apartment to a girl who needed it, and now she thinks I'm a big pain when I talk about wanting it back. She wants to get married and with the shortage of apartments these days, the easiest thing for her to do is to bring her husband into my house, pack up my things, put them in storage, and good riddance! Anyway, Tosca is used to getting wet fish thrown in her face. And who protects her? The courts? A poor childless nut who talks to cats!"

"Stop it!" interrupted Gigi. "You two have the same fault. Your imaginations run away and you know the end before you've taken the first step. No wonder you love melodrama. There's still time, for heaven's sake. There's something you can do for yourself. Don't give up so soon at the first thought of going back to Milan. Anyway, didn't you come here for your allergies? Maybe it would be bad for you to go back there."

Tosca looked at him a moment before responding, and Gigi noticed how liquid and tender, almost childlike, her eyes could become when she felt compassion — for herself, as she did now, or for others. "My allergies don't matter any more. They're the same here or in Milan. I'm allergic to life," she corrected herself, "to solitude. And that's a sickness that doesn't get well, not here or in Milan."

Dinner was finished. There was nothing to counter Tosca's truth, nothing that would sound authentic. Gigi asked for the bill, the two women started walking toward Via Aurelia. Toni took her friend gently by the arm without speaking. Words are so empty, so useless, in the face of real agony! And now she was also infected, now she wanted to free herself from it in the only way she knew how, by embracing Gigi, but she thought any tenderness would be offensive to Tosca, and she moved so Gigi could be at the woman's other side. With her between them, speaking of the heat, the evening breeze that gave some relief, innocuous mouthing so as not to irritate the pain wounding Tosca, they reached home. When they entered the lobby three arrows shot into the darkness and disappeared. Tosca's spirits immediately lifted. "Come here, you big lugs, it's me!" she called them in a stronger and more assured voice. And even a wave of laughter trembled in her apostrophe to Fifi, Puss and Bissi.

"How could I not love them? They're my family. You saw them, didn't you? They were waiting for me, but who knows what amorous plans they have for this evening! They're certainly hungry, but before going out on their adventures, they want to know I'm all right."

She smiled at Toni and Gigi and thanked them, her face returning to its normal expression of childlike trust, and said, "Excuse me for complaining. I really shouldn't, I really shouldn't do it. How many people have three creatures waiting so patiently for them as I do?"

As she went up her stairs. Fifi stuck close to her legs. "Get away, you flatterer, or you'll trip me!" The two brothers had already preceded her. Until Toni closed the apartment door she could hear their mewing synchronized like a duet.

12

Tosca distributed the mail in the afternoon. The postman had fallen into the habit of handing it over to her when he met her at the condo doorway while she was taking care of the stairs and garden, or was out with her cats. For the two journalists there were three postcards from France and a letter for Lavinia with the same kind of stamp. As she put them in the mailboxes, she felt sure the letter was from Matteo. Who knows what painful longing the boy carried with him in the midst of those merry companions so much more sophisticated than he, as he navigated through the shoals and currents of early youth! She felt kindly toward him, so ungainly and so little master of his quickly growing body. She could see him staring at Lavinia, more like praying than looking. And what casual pleasure it must have given Lavinia to make him fall in love! Now if Tosca happened to see her, even from a distance, she was not indifferent as before. She followed her with her eyes, trying to imagine the plot of her day. If she heard her voice it made her uneasy, because she feared the irony in it, and she carefully tried to decipher the message. There was something disturbing about her, barely out of adolescence, because it did not coincide with Tosca's idea of a woman.

Toni, so soft and feminine in her actions, belonged to another race. Her appeal came from something else, from the beautiful, open face that expressed her emotions like a mirror, from her willingness to participate in the joys or concerns of whomever she was with. Tosca recognized this fascination, secretly comparing it to herself, seeing in Toni an embellished and refined image of her young self when she had loved and been loved by Mario. But Lavinia. Lavinia was something else; and it

wasn't her youth that made the difference. It was something Tosca couldn't quite grasp, but felt sharply, almost with repulsion,
at the same time experiencing the enchantment in spite of herself. When Lavinia went for a swim after the beach was deserted — it stayed lighter now with daylight-saving time — her
slim figure with hair cascading to her waist immediately acquired a kind of unreality for Tosca who watched from a distance. Lavinia was fascinating in herself, but it was also the appeal of youth and beauty. It was the mystery in every human
body radiating Eros through natural endowment and their
pleasurable awareness of it.

Her pale, colorless face nearly covered by ash-colored hair
had something that kept Tosca from giving in to her initial instinctive aversion. She realized she could be attracted to it, but
like a fledgling in the sights of a beautiful, languid reptile. Fear
makes it die a hundred times a minute before its actual death,
which it cannot avoid because it stays where it is, fixed in fascinated repulsion.

Poor Matteo! The envelope was thick; there was more than
one sheet inside. If he was like his father he must know how to
write; she seemed to remember he was studying world literature. What a beautiful love letter he must have sent Lavinia. Tosca visualized her reading it, a smile playing on her lips, her long
freckle-covered hand moving the curtain of hair, and a pang of
incomprehensible jealousy surprised the older woman. Jealous
of whom? Jealous of what? Of Matteo? Of that young woman
more remote from her than the moon, who seemed to be a part
of its pale shadow? And yet there it was. That love, given with
such enthusiastic innocence and regarded with such detachment,
hurt her. It wasn't jealousy — it was compassion and envy.

As chance would have it she had the opportunity to watch
Lavinia read the letter. Tosca stayed in the garden in the afternoon. It was sultry, but the sun was obscured by a mass of uni-

formly gray clouds, when Lavinia appeared while she was watering. After their meeting at Toni's Lavinia greeted her less coldly. Now her dissonant voice came to her with the body that surprised her each time. "Sprinkle me, too, please! The house is unbearable!" And holding her hair aside like a scarf, she stretched her slender neck to the water jetting from the hose.

Tosca complied with a smile and Lavinia let the water run over her with a sigh of pleasure. She stood beside her for a moment, drying herself in the air before she went back to the portico where she had placed her straw bag. She took out her cigarettes and offered one to Tosca, finally sitting down with her back to a column. Out from the bag came an envelope and just as Tosca had imagined it, Lavinia read, or reread, the letter from Matteo as she stroked her hair. Tosca held her breath for a moment in surprise at those two superimposed images, the real one coinciding with the imagined one, and for no reason a happy feeling kept her where she was, still and silent. She wouldn't dare distract the reader with any gesture or sound. Matteo had the right to that moment, and it was nice, she felt, because the sharp odor of oleander was in the air, and a breeze from the sea moved Lavinia's hair. She wasn't smiling, but when she said good-bye her pink face looked less severe. Even her parting words were kind, as though she were happy, "Thanks for the shower. This is a nice place to be this time of day. I'll have to remember that."

Tosca had to tell Toni about it. She was curious to know something more about those two, and even about Enrico. But what could she know? Their paths never crossed. He didn't like to spend time on the beach, and his work kept him busy all day. Gigi spoke of him with respect. Enrico was brilliant, he said, and ambitious, but a lack of sympathy in his appraisal hadn't escaped Tosca's notice. Just as Toni with Lavinia, Gigi couldn't recognize his own youth in Enrico even slightly. Where Enrico analyzed with Marxist scientific tools, Gigi drew from intuition and instinct, with more enthusiastic curiosity than logic. If the object of their studies was more or less the same, their ways of perceiving it were so different that the results belonged to two parallel worlds, each completely estranged from the other. Tosca felt Gigi didn't care much for Lavinia, either. He couldn't, she told herself, if he loved Toni; the incompatibility was obvious. But actually Gigi often thought of Lavinia and not only because he had noticed his son's infatuation. He had never been able to resist the attraction of that kind of woman, the insinuating erotic baggage of that body more effeminate than feminine, that low, warm, accentuated voice as if two natures, masculine and feminine, coexisted in her without contention.

Toni was the first woman in his life who had asked for what he could give her and reciprocated without deception. She had responded to his need for love in a moment of fatigue and distress for both of them, and it had been an unambiguous gift that little by little had become a barricade for the two against the world. For that reason Gigi's reaction to Lavinia hadn't escaped Toni. She felt tensions in the girl's presence from the first, and they alarmed her. Not only did Matteo's disheveled head flutter around the slender stranger, but also Gigi's orderly strength seemed electrically charged in her presence. That was the real reason, more than the extra work of so many people in the house, that made Toni breathe a sigh of relief when the two of them were alone again.

Some of this she hinted to Tosca, speaking of the preoccupations Matteo's father had for his son's fragility in a world made for the strong. "His mother," she said, "doesn't understand him. She can't—not because she's bad, but because she's different. She manipulates people like she wants. No one truth exists for her, but hundreds, according to the moment and her interests."

"Some women are more cat than woman," Tosca replied. "But even some cats drive males crazy and others don't. If Puss takes Fifi by the neck, she hisses and pushes him away. Then, while he's asleep (you should see her) she embraces him with her two front paws and kisses him all over, but if he wakes up, she begins her dance of refusal. Really mean. But then there's Poppa, a tiger among cats. It took Miciamore to tame her."

Toni was smiling as she listened, amazed at how their conversations always had a double meaning for Tosca. Human images moved on the stage created by their words and simultaneously velvet paws, sharp claws, sinewy bodies danced their parallel dance in Tosca's mind. Toni had brought Paletta into the garden with her. For some days now she had been more tranquil, and the large tabby that had courted her at the beginning of the vacation left her alone. Now the thin little cat was smoothing her fur with her tongue. She didn't stop licking herself for a minute while her mistress cuddled her in the shade of the portico.

"She's changing fur," announced Tosca, and at her friend's surprise, she explained, "Don't you see she's a lighter color? That's because the old fur isn't as thick and the new fur is still short. Look what she'll do if you want to make her feel good." She took a nylon brush from her linen bag and began to gently brush Paletta's back, who closed her eyes and immediately turned on her back, stretching her neck. Tosca substituted her hand for the brush, and Paletta began a low rumble. "She purrs like she did when she was little and sucked on my dress when I held her," Toni said. The sensuality of the little body tensed with pleasure was so apparent the two women broke into laughter.

"She's the picture of lechery," Toni said. "We should learn that much from animals. To allow ourselves to have what we want and to enjoy it without shame."

"If only we could," Tosca concluded, but she wasn't sad. She was happy with Toni and liked to imagine Lavinia as Fifi or Paletta, but Matteo was no Miciamore, she thought disparagingly. And neither was Enrico.

13

Almost without realizing it the two women had slipped into the habit of meeting in the garden at sunset, when the heat abated and the light was still pink on the sea and behind the coastal hills. Toni would come down from her apartment with Paletta to get some fresh air while Tosca finished up her garden chores. Fifi would crouch next to Toni's little cat and sometimes they played quietly like two little girls who preferred to be alone, away from the boys. If Komeini came around (Tosca had so baptized the big cat that had failed to seduce Paletta, because the thick fur on his head resembled a turban, and also because his eyes were as ferocious as those of the sinister Ayatollah) the two cats would lower their ears to a single horizontal line, their lower lips disappearing below exposed teeth, their backs arched. With a menacing whistle that went through their fur like an electrical charge, they would crouch, watching him. Komeini would look at them stock-still, decisive, insufferable and unconquerable. He wouldn't move until one or both of the women couldn't stand it any longer and chased him off. That anti-masculine alliance amused the women and they joked about the Feminist Movement of the village felines. Lavinia sometimes laughed with them, too. But there was always something about her participation in their conversations that wasn't convincing. Perhaps she was making fun of them, and who know if she didn't make Enrico laugh by telling him about those garden get-togethers!

Two more letters arrived from Matteo, and one day Lavinia asked Toni off-hand if she knew when Gigi's children would be coming back from their trip. Toni said she didn't know, having received only a postcard, and Lavinia said she'd be glad to see them if they arrived in time. She and Enrico would be leaving soon, Sunday, because they had to turn in their work to the university. "Was that a message?" Toni asked herself and Tosca.

"I think so. It's a way to get you to act as messenger if Matteo calls."

Matteo phoned the next day and Toni, on being questioned, couldn't refuse to tell him. Matteo arrived alone on Friday. He said he had hitchhiked because his sister and friends wanted to stay longer and he was tired and didn't feel very well. The air in France had worsened his allergy out of season.

"He's like me," Tosca commented when Toni told her three days later. "He has one of life's allergies, a very common one. It's the love allergy."

Toni smiled, uneasy because she couldn't grasp just what game Lavinia was playing. Toni invited Lavinia and Enrico to welcome Matteo the evening he arrived, and all evening the girl had done nothing but provoke Gigi with the most outwardly restrained discussions, but which nevertheless created an unnatural tension in everyone. The discussion had been sparked by an article about ghosts that had appeared in the newspaper. Gigi told some Peruvian stories about dead people more alive than the living. Enrico countered with his sociologist's need to define and catalog, basing his argument on the snares of the unconscious and irrational. Lavinia said something Toni couldn't exactly recall as she repeated the story to Tosca, but it was something that had keenly impressed her, about the legitimacy of what one doesn't understand because unseen, but which is invisible only to those who are blind. The argument got heated. Gigi siding with Lavinia, Enrico alone and polemically more tenacious than belligerent, Matteo in dismayed silence.

Tosca was not surprised. She had seen Matteo and Lavinia having another swim late at night after all the festival lights had been extinguished or towed away by boats. Toni didn't know anything about the festival. Saturday evening she had been with Gigi and the three young people at a ballet in Nervi, and she hadn't realized there was anything going on in their part of the marine world.

Tosca told her she had gone to the beach while it was still light and the little children, helped by the older ones and Aldo, prepared the illuminaria.

"I went there because the mother of the three little children asked me to give her a hand watching them. When it gets dark it's not easy to see them, and she had other things on her mind. . . But that's another story." She stopped, hoping Toni would ask her "what story," but she went on without much encouragement from Toni's silence. "Children of all ages were there. The tourist agency provided the luminaria — a kind of flared oil paper — and the candles, and a flower for each one. The smallest children placed them in shallow water, and the bigger ones swam out with them or carried them out in boxes on paddleboats. For a while the sea was full of lights. Then the current carried them off, and gradually they all flowed out to sea. Last night the weather was perfect, and it was beautiful."

Toni noticed that Tosca seemed a bit distracted and asked her if anything was wrong.

"I don't know why, but with all those lights on the sea, when it grew dark I 'felt a shadow pass over my heart.' That's what my mother used to say when she was down in the dumps. I had to watch that woman's children; I don't have my own to look after, and will never have children or grandchildren. . . At a certain point one woman said it was a pagan festival like they have at Rio, in Brazil, to send messages to the dead, and I have so many dead now!"

She lit a cigarette and tried to shift the emphasis of her words. "One woman said she likes this festival because the lights on the water are like poetry, each one a wish sent out to sea. And why not hope they'll come true? That's what she said, and she's right."

Toni replied: "We have to remember that dreams are a part of the game of life. If not, everything becomes so gray."

She wasn't in a happy mood, either, as Tosca pointed out. She was worried about Matteo, she said, but in her own mind Tosca substituted Gigi's name, and for that reason told her what she had seen afterwards, when the festival was over, late at night.

Lavinia and Matteo met again beside the wall of the private beach. They talked for a long time and then went swimming.

"I was there to get rid of my sad feelings."

Toni asked what time that was. "Three in the morning," Tosca replied, and Toni remarked they must have made their plans during the trip. They left Nervi at two.

Silence fell in the garden, and Tosca interrupted it following a new thought. "The beach is a curious observatory at night, you know? You can't imagine what goes on while most people are asleep." She waited for a comment that was not forthcoming, so she went on. "For one thing there are the drug addicts. Always someone sleeping in a sleeping bag. At first there were a lot of them, but because they left their dirty syringes on the sand they had to move. There's a kind of radio communication among them. Some leave, others come, and the new ones receive instructions from the old ones. So now you don't see syringes any more. They toss them in the containers on Via Aurelia and go freely about their business on the beach. They aren't bad; they play guitars and harmonicas, and there's even a flute. But only before midnight. After the other people go home they do the drugs together. It scares me, but they just seem oblivious, like fakirs who don't feel the nails. Sometimes I've even wanted to try it, but I'm afraid to; if I got the habit I wouldn't know how to pay for it."

Toni expressed her irritation with the subject. Drugs were one of the horrors she dismissed as cowardice, and she'd just as soon not know about it.

Her companion went on, coming to a topic that would interest her. "Lately I've also seen the two woman in my stairwell. The mother of the three children and her friend, that big woman built like a gendarme. . ."

Toni didn't know what Tosca was driving at and made a weak interrogative sound.

"I didn't like her the first time I saw her. She's hard, with something military about her, just so, in her eyes and in her manner. The other one, who never speaks to her children in a normal tone of voice — she either screams or lectures — isn't the type for a friend like that. You hardly remember her because she's so little and skinny. If you didn't know her you wouldn't even notice her. It was a big surprise. You should see how gentle that big woman is with her! Always helping her. If it's rocky, she hands her her sandals, if she has a purse the other carries it for her, a real gentleman. And the little one, you should hear her! Prattles away like a girl."

Now Toni understood, but she didn't seem impressed, so Tosca became more emphatic. "On the beach they behave — I don't have the nerve to say it — like two lovers."

"They probably are," the other said calmly, "and that explains why the woman is smiling. She has her friend; her husband is gone. If it's as you say, she's finally enjoying her vacation."

Tosca didn't add a word. She arranged her garden tools, feeling disappointed that this evening's conversation with Toni wasn't as spontaneous as other times. Lesbianism had the same importance to Toni as drugs; that is, none at all. I'll bet, she thought with irritation, Toni sees and hears everything with her job, but I never would have imagined anything like that. She could have answered me in a nicer way and come down from the heights of her great experience. . .

But she immediately reprimanded herself. Maybe the reason for Toni's indifference was something else, something that was bothering her. And so she wished her a good evening. Toni replied she didn't feel like fixing supper another time for everyone. Lavinia and Enrico were coming again. And she smiled ironically. They had postponed their departure again.

The way she said it was enough for Tosca to excuse her, and even to feel guilty. She wanted her forgiveness. "What a lot of nonsense I've been talking! You have things to do. Do you want any help? I could run an errand for you," and she gave her arm a little squeeze, a gesture of affection she never allowed herself, even though sometimes tempted to show her friendship more openly. "You'll have to excuse me if I seem like a gossip. Nothing ever happens to me, and so I watch what happens to others. And besides, the beach will be deserted soon."

Saying good-bye with any warmth was an effort for Toni, just as everything else that evening. Toni was thinking that for too many days she hadn't spoken to Gigi about her friendship with Tosca — or about anything regarding just the two of them, and she strongly resented the hours of general conversation she had to prepare herself to undergo.

14

Instead of playing a passive role, Toni attacked with a vehemence that stunned everyone. The objects of her polemical passion were Lavinia and Enrico. Certainly she hadn't known she would unload her jealousy for the one and her resistance to becoming friends with the other until she did it — she ordinarily so timid in society, and at home if there were outsiders. What set her off was the declaration by the two that they hadn't watched any of the soccer match on television, hadn't gone outside when people poured into the streets, and hadn't paid any attention to the extemporaneous concert (in which Tosca had participated) that took place under their windows.

"Underdeveloped, third world, tele-plagiarizers, unconscious masses, mean power-brokers." Toni had caught only the nouns in Enrico's elaborate discourse. She hadn't followed the logical connection whose arrogant thread was always as thick as a plank (oh, as though it had to be!) that can neither be grasped nor bent. With such thoughts her nostrils dilated and her face grew red. She didn't even wait for the end of his argument before interrupting, her voice steel-edged in her final interrogative. "Have you ever mingled with the masses you're talking about?"

After a moment's surprise, Lavinia opened her mouth to respond, but by that time Toni had taken off.

"Touched them, smelled them, lived with them? What kind of sociology is yours if you never experience life? You do everything in the abstract. Yours should be the science of the many and instead it's a laborious study of the few. You think you know everything but you don't know anything, because to know is to understand, and I doubt if you even know what it means to understand: to contain, to embrace. Your knowledge of books is not the knowledge of things. Life is outside and stays there, and you stuff yourself with words that have no meaning. Understanding is alive. Your words are dead. People are blood and meanness, why not? But also desire, insecurity, the will to live. They are everything and the opposite of everything. Your theory is more anemic than a dry stick, disinfected like the books and typewriters you use instead of knives for always dissecting the same cadaver, thinking you're cutting into the live body of life."

She stopped to draw a breath, and when she took the tall drink Gigi handed her like a playful rebuke, her hands were trembling.

Lavinia remained silent. Sitting by herself, she passed her hands through her hair with frenzied regularity. A neurotic sinking into the pool of her neurosis, thought Gigi, leaden as the silence into which she had fallen under Matteo's lost look. Enrico tried to defend the concreteness of his work, but it was difficult for him to recover from the surprise of that open hostility. It was Gigi who made the first move against the suddenly oppressive atmosphere on the balcony.

"You caught us off guard, Toni, dear. I didn't know you were so critical of sociologists, and so indulgent of sports fans. But basically you're right. Lately I've been asking myself what understanding is, too. You say it is to look inside. But with what? Reason? Intuition? Instinct?"

Toni shot back immediately, "I'm not at all indulgent. Certain things bother me, too, but because they bother me doesn't mean I must condemn them. I try to understand them instead."

Enrico was the one to answer her, calmly. "Understanding is critical by its nature. For this reason it's unaccepting. It digs, suspects, doubts, and even refuses."

And Toni, "All right, but certain understanding, or rather, certain operations codified by understanding are just that, codified. In abstractions they become prejudices. You say 'mass' and everything's settled. An avalanche of commonplaces, statistics, data accumulated and classified, come under that one word alone. That's what is so discouraging and takes one's breath away. But where, how, do we get fresh insight for understanding people if it's so much work just to understand just one individual? It takes—what to call it?—intense concentration that mulls over what it knows and even veers off course, but is never separated from what it's investigating."

A pause, then looking straight at Enrico, "I know it's difficult, because your kind of understanding comes from what is studied. But it can't be done abstractly. That's what I mean. Because you who talk about everyone and would like to speak for everyone must be a sounding board for so many things. Not only gestures, actions, cries, contemptible behavior, songs, like those we've heard and seen, but generous or piddly feelings of every kind, false or shady aspirations, full or empty lives that are undeniably banal. You also have to understand the deep reasons, compromises, the origins of self-interest, the corrections and deviations, sometime the renunciations, that make life worth living."

She grew silent, realizing she had talked too much, but she hadn't done it for herself so much as for Tosca. Her pure joy in telling how beautiful it had been to hear her own voice in the chorus shouldn't be dismissed with assumptions that diminish her, such as her lack of culture or spiritual underdevelopment.

Gigi noticed the shadow that had passed over Toni's face and voice and understood the reason for it.

"You should have seen how our neighbor reacted!—Miciamore's widow, just so you'll know who I mean. It was a vital reaction, which I believe did more for her than all the medicines and herbs she thinks help her allergies. Do you want to tell me she's also part of the masses? She could be, if you put a good individual standard of measurement in your concept of the masses. Discouragement is her bread. Does that seem to you a sentiment of the masses?"

Enrico retorted, "In this case we have an anomaly. When you study behavior you assume what has the highest percentage of examples. . ."

Toni interrupted, "Yes, certainly, but when you arrive at a law that you define as 'the masses,' you haven't yet touched on the point I'm talking about. The individual sense of belonging and individual suffering within that law that you want to spread over everyone like a gigantic net."

Enrico smiled, "Well, if we looked at it that way we'd never get anywhere."

Toni wanted to extend an olive branch. "I know, and excuse my outburst that must have seemed a little too. . . fiery. However, I really believe one thing. I know the importance of absolutes and general truths organized by knowledge, but I don't forget, and never want to forget, that there is no absolute for people, for us, we're all poor people who have to endure a common reality. It is quite an illusion to believe that absolute truth is experienced in daily life! And what a stumbling block for anyone who works from that premise."

Lavinia got up, looked straight into Toni's eyes as though challenging her, and announced to the room without speaking directly to anyone that she was tired and was going to bed. "I'll walk you home," Matteo offered and they went out the door. Toni's courage had given Matteo courage. At the door of Lavinia's apartment he took her arm and headed down the stairs. "Please!," was all he said and Lavinia followed him.

Without speaking they took the street to the private beach. Matteo slipped over the wall and Lavinia after him. The boy's heart beat as if something were collapsing inside him, an earthquake roaring through his head that kept him from seeing, hearing, reasoning. However, in his agitation there was the very clear need to save himself. It's not reason that looks for a breach in the ruins when everything collapses around us, but instinct that makes us like animals that flee a moment before death falls on them. Impulsively he turned toward the girl and embraced her in his long arms. One hand sought the nape of her neck, his mouth clung to hers with such desperation that Lavinia once again consented, and gradually the kiss became an exchange, a sweetness given and received. Then Matteo held his head in his hands and quietly, shamelessly, allowed the tears to run freely down his face. Lavinia sat next to him silently. Impulsively, Matteo wanted to give back what he had just stolen, but the moment was gone and Lavinia pushed him away, saying, "Everyone in your family is a little mad. Or am I wrong? Even your father's friend. Or maybe it's just that she hates me. I don't know — anyway," and her voice sounded bitter, "I don't care anything about her opinions or her women friends'."

Matteo was suddenly apprehensive again. He had reached the safety of the narrow ledge, but the darkness of the ravine still loomed wide below him. "Let's not talk about them. They're not important. Maybe Toni realized that I. . ." he drew a deep breath and threw himself in headlong, hearing the air whistle in his buzzing ears, "that I love you. Why didn't you answer me when I wrote? Why didn't you come yesterday? I waited so long!"

Lavinia looked at him for a moment and smiled, coldly, like the light coming from the blue lamp the nuns leave as a guard light in their garden, giving their faces a sickly pallor.

"Why should I? I'm not alone, and, anyway, it's better like this."

Matteo's objections couldn't find the right words to line up in a logical order; he babbled love and desperation.

"I don't understand you." Lavinia had the authority of both her greater age and her indifference. "Aren't we friends? You talked to me, I listened, we went swimming together, you wrote me. Isn't that enough?"

"But you're going away!" the boy shouted, now lost in the vortex of what was collapsing internally, dragging the brief past and an eternal future into his present.

"Exactly. I'm going away, and you are too, each of us in different directions. Maybe you'll write me sometime, and we could even meet."

"Marry me!" He said it without thinking, as though pushing the button of "save yourself who can," when fire bursts out or the ship lists, and he was surprised by the cloud that broke into a tiny rain of crystals around him. Lavinia roared with laughter, her head slightly back, a lock of hair brushed her face. She was so beautiful and so happy the surprise blended with shame, then humiliation. He laid his trembling hand on that throat until Lavinia screamed and jumped up, just as Matteo, full of fear, had eased his hold.

"Wait, please, forgive me, don't go away like this." But now he knew everything was lost. He had tried and failed. Lavinia still listened to him, while with every wrong word Matteo became more discouraged, and he writhed in helplessness and pain.

Suddenly the boy got hold of himself. "I'll walk you back. Good-bye, Lavinia. If you can, remember me like I was before. . . before this evening. I'll write you, but don't worry. I won't bother you."

In the morning Tosca saw a large envelope in Lavinia's mailbox and recognized Matteo's handwriting. Toni had told her he had written poetry for several years. And Tosca imagined he had told Lavinia the pain of his farewell in poetry.

15

Matteo left before his father was up. He left a letter on the table that Gigi read to Toni. "Papa, please excuse me if I don't wait for you to wake up. I should be ashamed of myself for being so rude to Toni, and I am. I don't want to talk, about myself or anything else. But I'm grateful, and especially grateful to her for all her kindnesses that have allowed me to have such an unexpectedly nice and important vacation. Because, and I this I say to you who always look at me with such alarm, it has really been important. As I leave this morning I feel I've aged ten years. I'm leaving my boy's skin with you and go away skinless, but I hope capable of growing. I didn't tell Enrico good-bye. Do it for me. I was afraid to tell him what a lucky man I think he is, and deserves to be. Bye, love to both of you."

Toni observed that behind all he said and left to the imagination was Lavinia, the original cause and effect and end.

"Do you think she realizes it?" she asked.

"There are women," Gigi replied, "who are never affected by the love they arouse."

"Women, women! I'm talking about that one, who is still so young! And I ask myself if anything will ever touch her."

"She'll have children and, don't worry, even she will suffer. Besides, what do we know about it? Maybe even her sorrow would seem cold to you."

"She's too independent for her years, when I compare myself at her age. She knows what she wants and goes after it." After a pause, "How can Enrico love her so much?"

Gigi: "He's intelligent and good, and that lets him love her with true passion, even though he knows it's not reciprocated. It happens much more often than you think. He knows he's getting something essential for his life from her, and even if Lavinia allows herself some caprice, or lets herself be loved out of inertia—women like her are too lazy to oppose strong desire—Enrico understands and doesn't overvalue it."

"Words," Toni broke out. "It's pure and simple meanness, ugly selfishness."

"You're too hard on her," Gigi objected. "The real attachment of Lavinia's life is Enrico, he knows that and it's enough."

"And what about Matteo? Does the same thing go for him, her laziness, et cetera, et cetera?"

"She let herself be loved, like a cat if it suits her at the moment. Then she was through. That's all there is to it."

"But he's just a child! Ten times younger than his years, just as she's older than her age. And stop being so roundabout. I don't see how you can bear for anyone to be so deceitful to others. Pain is pain whatever the reason, and don't tell me she didn't realize how much Matteo was suffering."

"Certainly, she did. That's part of the game. She gave him both love and pain, only she herself was barely touched by love. She sipped it as pleasure, or maybe as vanity, and doesn't know the pain. And why should she care if a boy cries over her? Tears are salty only for the one who cries."

Toni got up brusquely. She didn't want to argue with Gigi. Her irritation kept her from being as sympathetic as he would like her to be. She became intolerant in such cases, and friendship went out the window, tossed out by her desire to wound. Gigi noticed the bitter fold of her mouth, her bent shoulders, and how her tan was turning yellow. After so many days in the boat with the young people, his own tan was still glowing. With a pinch of remorse he remembered how she had often given up the beach to look after the guests, and in the last ten days had worked more at the typewriter than she had rested on a mat by the sea as she would have liked.

August was slipping away. Summer would soon be gone. He took her by the arm. "No work today. Total vacation, only the beach, and tonight we'll improvise."

"If there's a concert somewhere around shall we ask Tosca?" She was herself again, his woman who needed so little to get her back on the right track of openness toward the world.

They spent the day on the beach in pure physical pleasure, and by sunset Tosca was dressed and ready for them in the apartment doorway. Gigi had reserved three seats for the concert at Cervo.

Via Aurelia was nearly traffic free and they arrived while it was still light enough to show Tosca that special corner of Liguria they loved. It was all new to her. The beauty of the rocky peaks against the blue sky, the gray of the olive trees, the long descent down arch-spanned little medieval streets to the little square enclosed like a shell among houses, and the church barely tinted rose and green in the uncertain transparency of twilight. She could only express her delight by repeating, "If only Mario were here!"

Tosca wanted to go into the church while Gigi told her its history. She sat for a few minutes on the stairway that curved like a baroque backdrop above her, in order to enjoy the revelation of that new and beautiful scenery in a single embrace.

"I'm getting ready for the music," she said to Gigi, her face flushed with emotion. "The whole place is music. . . with this church, like the fulfillment of a vow. And especially if it was built with the coral fishermen's money."

Toni was sitting on the low wall smoking while she waited for them. Flowers blooming on the small balconies perfumed the air. She was glad to see Tosca so happily immersed in the atmosphere of the place, but she was afraid Tosca might be disappointed with what followed. The musical program was so unlike anything she knew.

The concert began. A dignified, serious quartet from Rome. First it was Beethoven to flood the space with notes that separated and joined like a necklace, then Mahler, and finally Schumann.

During the intermission, Tosca said calmly, "I didn't feel anything or understand that first piece. Maybe it was beautiful, but with the breeze in my hair and on my neck, and this moon and the sea down there, I was too distracted to know who I am or where I was. It's too much all at the same time. I couldn't remember one note in a thousand. But the second one! Do you think I could buy a tape of that "Quartettstatz"? I don't know anything about the composer, but if there is a paradise the angels must play music like that."

Now the excitement over her new experiences was overpowered by her abandonment to the music, and after Mahler Tosca listened to Schumann carefully and surrendered to that musical wave she couldn't sing, but whose strong impression remained with her like a memory. "I'd like to buy all three of the pieces I heard, even that poor Beethoven I didn't appreciate!" she said to Gigi while they were walking to the car parked under the olive trees. "Though I think it must be impossible to learn music like that. If I try to hum it I can't. I don't remember anything—but that's not true. I remember it, but like the poetry I learned as a child. I know it is inside, but the words don't come to me anymore."

Gigi took the two women to a restaurant by the sea. After those words that had cost her such an effort, which she had interrupted with an embarrassed, "How stupid I am to be talking about something I don't know anything about," Tosca ate with pleasure, but left the conversation almost entirely to her hosts. She seemed suddenly intimidated, and Gigi wondered if she wouldn't miss the different life they had showed her after they left.

Tosca must have been mulling over the same thoughts, because while they were drinking coffee she asked, "When are you leaving?" and suddenly, without waiting for the answer, as though concluding her troubling thought, "It's true I'll miss all these things, the music, the dinners, but it's also true that I'll have some nice memories."

Toni couldn't reply and looked at Gigi, but Tosca again forestalled them. "Isn't it better to have something to remember that you have lost than never to have had it? I think so."

Gigi squeezed her white, plump hand resting on the tablecloth. On her ring finger a gold wedding band and an aquamarine stone glittered in a fine setting. "Good for you. You've scored again. Did you know that a poet has written almost the same thing? An English poet said, listen, "It's better to have loved and lost than never to have loved at all."

Tosca sat a little straighter, her eyes looking beyond the terrace where they sat facing the sea shrouded in darkness, sporadically revealed by boat lanterns. Her voice had a sudden intensity. "Will you say it in English again? I studied English a little in my time, after school, but I've forgotten everything, even French; but when I get the chance I like to hear it."

It was Toni who repeated in English Tennyson's lines that the cat lady had recalled to Gigi from his long ago studies and loves, both romantic, that he had kept wrapped in that melancholy couplet like an antique jewel in a swatch of faded velvet, secret and sweet.

While Gigi drove on Via Aurelia over the steep curves of the capes separating them from their stretch of coast, Tosca observed, "It's hard to drive with all those headlights in your eyes," and she curled up quietly in her corner, "so as not to distract the driver."

"How many days (though with interruptions) have my thoughts revolved around her," Gigi thought, occasionally looking at the woman's profile in the rear-view mirror. As usual Tosca had refused the seat Toni wanted her to have. "I was interested in plotting a story about eccentric behavior, to be the cool observer of a dejected human condition. How stupid I've been! Now I'm as melancholy as she. I still feel her warm hand under mine. Toni has helped me catch some of the flavor of her life. I've used her reflected memory and my eyes and ears to write about her, but something I didn't expect has happened. My investigative coolness has failed me, or is no longer with me. Conversations with cats! Someone else might consider them foolish, extravagant, or, even perverse, but me? Tosca is only someone very much like myself, I believe. The friendship I offered her like bait has become an exchange. I'm ashamed of trying to entrap her."

He looked at Toni and immediately wanted to tell her what he was thinking. Toni smiled at him, and Gigi reminded himself she also felt a friendship for Tosca — one of the many ways to love, and perhaps the longest lasting and most faithful.

He tried to joke about his own frailties; he couldn't tell these thoughts to his long time friends at work. "Who knows how far below Miciamore I am on her scale of values." But irony didn't help. At least one truth was certain in the uncertainty of that friendship born of a cold analytical project. It's not the object of love that counts, but the ability to love. And Tosca, imprisoned in the indifference of others, had found an emergency exit in her cats. Was it enough? Why not?

To break the silence he threw out a suggestion. "Maybe Tennyson fits Matteo's situation, too. . ."

Tosca was the first to speak, leaning toward the back of his seat. "You mean it's better for him to have met Lavinia than never to have known what it means to fall in love?"

Toni had a ready reply. "Meeting a girl like Lavinia can be an exhilarating experience — I don't deny it, but it can also mark you forever. Won't he be unsure of himself with every woman he meets? Sphinx women, cat women, who seduce and run, who are always sought after and followed? God, how I hate them!"

Tosca sat up to look at Toni, who reassured her. "I talk like that because Gigi knows how I feel, and you're a friend."

Tosca leaned back happily. "I think you're right. There are woman who use their bodies like hunters use a birdcall. I don't like them either, but I realize if they can do it well, it's better to be followed than to follow, better to be waited for than to wait." She paused to sigh briefly, but she wasn't finished. "For a boy like Matteo, who's still so naive, an experience with a beauty like that—Toni knows what I saw—will certainly stay with him for a long time. Maybe forever. The violin is short, but the sonata is long, my grandmother used to say. I think it's better for him to have loved and lost than never to have loved at all." And after a pause and a little laugh that brought a youthful tone to her voice, "My grandmother, who knew a thing or two, also said one happy surprise made up for a hundred disappointments! Matteo has had the happy surprise, time will take care of the disappointments."

"Certainly he'll philosophize about love—it's the fashion—and write poetry for his beloved. Isn't that a nice present? Your first crush is hard to get over. The rule is that you pay what it's worth. We'll phone him to see how he's getting along, if there are any new developments. Maybe this vacation has given birth to a poet!"

Tosca seemed to have stopped listening after the mention of the telephone, because she said no more. When they arrived she asked Toni, "When are you leaving?" and learned that it would be within the next couple of days. Tosca forced her lips into a strange smile, a toothy whiteness in pale lips mechanically accepting the news, revealing nothing of her true feelings. She would have time later, at home, to prepare herself for the parting and to plan for the death of summer.

16

The opportunity to talk about herself these two months (something that hadn't happened in a long time) had been both good and bad for Tosca. After such a long time, it had been good to relive moments that had counted in her life—choices, jobs, changes, and also the happy moments that were mysteriously detached from the river of time and still glowed with the intensity of the emotion, whether happy or cruel, exalting or desperate. It had been good for her to realize she had lived everything with a will, sad or happy, but honestly, completely herself with her character, her nature, her opportunities, her destiny, ("on the journey of life," as Mario always said), just as she was and as others saw her.

The bad part came from continuing to go over those moments afterwards. Sometimes she would elaborate on these stories of her life, telling them to Puss and Bisi and Fifi, but no longer just to keep company; she did it to keep swimming backward in the river of time that she had rediscovered the taste for with Toni and Gigi. She had recaptured time. It was still hers, and perhaps she had arranged it into a less chaotic perspective from the many lines that intersected the experiences lived, choosing or submitting to them as she had them. She noticed everything became clearer, in better proportion to the whole, when thought about in this way. Every moment connected to the preceding and to the following one, and even the bad things— mediocrity, wickedness, sin, sorrow—had a necessity and a justification that gave it now, from a distance, looked at with pity for the past, a precious and unalterable value. As if by losing the instant, the continuous thread of time grew stronger. The thread of her long time that had slipped away but that flowed again in her present life without losing any of its intensity, even though different, as though mollified.

She knew it hadn't been like that, the instant she lived it. For example, when she had held Mario's waxen face in her unbelieving hands, or when she had heard Bruno's broken voice tell her he would never be back. She knew fire or ice had burned her heart and nerves for long moments and ferocious seasons, but now even they belonged to her, and remembering them meant not discarding or denying them in the present emptiness.

This passage from yesterday to today was the bad result of the summer meetings. When she had finished walking through the great boulevards of the past, with a weary sweetness, but without torment, the present appeared before her in the objects and beings in her house. The bowl of cat biscuits, the unmade bed, the TV's white eye, a gray tail around a chair leg. That was today.

It was the natural, irresistible effect of comparing today with the yesterdays. Now she had no heart to tell Fifi about the dress her mother had made for her first dance, or, like a fairy tale, to go over the roads of Brianza that the war transformed into death traps, but also into appointments with hope. She was forced to look around herself, to look into herself. She looked and thought. Then the tranquil awareness of what had been gave way to a tension that gradually became unbearable. The emptiness was awful, and all her games of fantasy, her mental gyrations, her trapeze of dreams thrown out in front of her were only distractions in the emptiness. There was no present Tosca. There was only a mishmash of nothing in the nothingness of everything. This was the terrible part to get through, because if this was the way it was, she couldn't help but wish it would end.

But it didn't end, it never ended, because she still had to ask herself if it was right to want it to end, and if she was allowed to accelerate this end with the only mercy that held out its arms.

She didn't give in at once, sometimes not for an entire day, and not only because she hoped to meet the people who gave her comfort and didn't want to show her weakness, but also because she knew she could do it, had always managed to do it, and this was essentially her real condemnation. Now she had to postpone the problem as long as a semblance of summer remained around her. Toni and Gigi would be leaving, but the Piedmont family was still here, and also the mother of the three children with her friend, and the herbal pharmacist would be coming back the first week of September.

Oh, there wasn't much to be happy about. People were in the garden and could be heard on the stairs. Immediately the memory of her landlady's arrogant heels made her shudder. At least she wouldn't be back! But once the two journalists were gone there would be no one left in the condominium who treated her like a human being. But there was still La Tedesca at the bar, and Aldo the bathing attendant, to smoke a cigarette with.

She could wait until the cabanas were dismantled and everything was nailed shut and stacked. Then, if she could manage to stay sober, she would make a decision about the winter. Suddenly, while her thoughts were running along these lines, the conversation after the concert at Cervo popped into her head. What will I decide to do? Whether to leave or die? Her future prospects were so absurd that she said to Fifi, "Did you understand the plans? Tosca's playing for big stakes this time. I could break the bank if I went to San Remo with a scheme like that!"

The forecast of the near future was so bleak she made a conscious decision to drink to it. One glass more or less wouldn't change the situation. And while drinking, sitting on the kitchen chair with Fifi who had jumped on her lap (and didn't even make her too warm because the air had turned cooler), she observed what she was doing and absolved herself. After all, there wasn't a law that you had to protect your health beyond a certain point; she had already had plenty of tests. Wasn't it enough if she continued to take care of her asthma? And anyway she had so much to do in the house with the cats that she'd be in good spirits and the wine would keep her company only occasionally, without constituting a mortal sin, like cigarettes.

Tosca had never been able to tell a lie. Mario had scolded her about it many times. Certain harsh truths were more harmful than a white lie. "Better peace than truth, it says so in the Bible," he told her, and she had admitted that merciful omissions or deceitful veils were sometimes a virtue instead of a sin. But admitting a defect did not mean knowing how to correct it and so, between indignation and silence, vehement declarations and remorse, Tosca was to this day incapable of lying. Even to herself. In fact, after polishing off that glass of wine she immediately poured another one to make a toast with Fifi who was looking at her with ears rigid, surprised by her loquaciousness. "To Tosca and her sins of cowardice and mendacity." That was the word she used. It was an unusual word that was familiar because they had used it in a play, and each time she had objected because it seemed false and pompous to her. A lie is a lie. Mendacity is only for important people. A poor person tells a lie. Only a general can be mendacious. The wine mildly excited her, added to what she drank at supper, and her hair began to feel damp. Perspiration always started with her head, and it was pointless to blame it on menopause. There was no way out; if she drank she was taking a risk. She knew it and nothing could make her forget it.

She got up with difficulty, her legs no longer as steady as when she had come home. She took off the dress of happy evenings, put away her shawl, and washed. Mahler's music was only a memory of a forgotten yearning, a sweetness without echoes. She hoped to go to sleep immediately, because now she didn't want to talk to anyone, not even to herself. Fifi rubbed against her. Tosca bent over to pet her. "Go away, poor little thing! Why not leave, if you can?" She opened the door, but the cat drew back, arching her back, frightened by the empty darkness of the stairway. "Do what you want. Stay if you want to, but not with me. You're sleeping in the kitchen."

She closed the door again and went back into her bedroom.

Tears suddenly constricted her throat. "My God, my God, if you exist, why don't you help me? I'm so tired, so tired of everything!" As she lay down she asked herself what that everything was. That everything was nothing. A few cats, sickness, no love. Yes, the everything was nothing. Tears returned, the pillow was uncomfortable; alcohol was always hard to digest lying down. It wouldn't be easy to fall asleep, that much was clear. With a sigh she turned the light back on and tried to read a few pages. She had begun a Japanese love story Toni gave her, but it wasn't convincing. She couldn't visualize exalted female beauty in the young Satoko, as she had never seen a Japanese woman she thought beautiful. Her tired eyes ran over the words, but her mind wasn't following the story. Dropping *Spring Snow*, she turned out the light and closed her eyes. Anguish, after making its way surreptitiously into her thoughts and actions, now completely dominated her. Cold perspiration covered her body; she might as well give up. But with an extreme effort of will she tried to put off the surrender. "If you exist," she prayed, "why not teach me to protect myself without killing myself? You know I'm happy with very little, and that every time I wake up I thank you in my own way, without naming you, for what I have that perhaps you gave me. I haven't cursed you when you've struck me down. I kept on living and didn't hurt others. Isn't that enough? Do I have to go to church to get you to pay attention to me? And if you don't hear me when I go to church, is it my fault or yours that you don't call me?"

Sleep caught her while she was rocking in painful uncertainty between faith and anguish, a floating wreck tossed by the waves, her identity erased at last in merciful oblivion.

Part Three

1

I've been distracted by Lavinia and Matteo's amorous episode, and haven't followed the cat lady with the same concentrated attention as I did in the beginning. It's still hard for me to call her that; she is Tosca to me, too, as to Toni, and maybe it was she who diverted my thoughts to the two young people. Because she is very attentive to the lives of others. And by following her who had observed them from a distance, who had seen them without being seen, who had reinvented my old Tennyson, I was lost in fantasizing about the cold, sinuous blond and my son. He is unsure of himself only around people, but bold as a knight in Ariosto's *Orlando Furioso* in declaring his love.

His poems are very beautiful. Toni says "not bad" to avoid a judgment that would expose her. Beyond the rough technique and the naiveté of a tired erotic lexicon (but one he discovered for himself), the boy tells the surprise of self-discovery in the adoration of another with a purity that seems poetic to me. I liked the shadowy atmosphere, the said-not-said, the shades of color, which were once called mysterious. Every love affair is mysterious for the one who lives it. And he lives it twice by putting it into poetry.

I fear for Matteo if that's the way he is, if the only divinity he worships is pure beauty, flesh and word, vision and representation. What will he do when he must work, exchange words for money? He wants to be a journalist — the bad example I've set for him — but I bent my back much earlier, forced by necessity. He has come this far without material difficulty. He has read and studied, looked and observed, now he transforms the still innocent fruit of his vital contemplation into poetry. That's a lot. It's a way of living, not dying, and even a way of soothing the burn of an unhappy love. In fact, Toni is afraid his sadness will become an obsession. She didn't tell me so, but she was locked in her obstinate silence, where she curls up like a leaf and refuses to open up. I'm sure she was thinking of the suicidal temptations that have seduced her enough to recognize them when she reads them in another's eyes. Her hasty departure for Turin can mean only that she wants to see Matteo for herself, to reassure herself. It will reassure me, too, if she comes back more settled. It wouldn't have helped a thing for me to go with her. Matteo has never talked much to me. Something keeps him from it. It may be my bad rapport with his mother and a kind of moralistic jealousy he has toward me without realizing it. I, too, had looked at Lavinia, and a person in love doesn't miss that kind of look. I would talk to him paternally and he would hear only the ambiguous, or worse, the hostile words of a male rival.

But Toni keeps telling me I should help him. How? At this moment the future for him is only the black hole of not having Lavinia. What would I say to him? That he will see her next summer? Or some other such stupidity? The silence of the lunar blond has been deafening. At least she could have dropped him a line, telephoned him some consolation, but she's not a woman given to impulse. Matteo has already disappeared from her horizon, if he had ever risen so high. Perhaps it was only heat lightning, one of those thin streaks we see plowing the sky in the heart of summer, nothing more. However, for him she is the queen of his nights, the light of his days, Isis and Osiris all together. He despairs in the emptiness and fills the silence with his words-prayers to his distant goddess.

But he is young, and he told me he's going to take two exams instead of one in order to finish sooner. If I know my son, at least the part he inherited from me, he is trying to overcome desperation with work. Hotheaded in passion, but hardheaded in renunciation. He wants to hurry up and be somebody, and won't let anything stop him. Obviously many things will happen to him and to her in the meantime, and I hope other Lavinias will illuminate his nights, but for now he will cure his wound of love this way, going in other directions. Or so it seems to me. But Toni, pragmatically, goes to "see." It's right for her to do so, just as it's right for me to keep my counsel. I could tell him that every blaze of passion dissolves into sparks, that every ball hurled into the sky falls back to earth, but whatever discourse my old and therefore more subtle soul could make would be dismissed as a boring sermon. I know, not he, that it is better to live everything, good and bad, not to avoid anything, not even the poison, because in time — whenever that may be — it's our only honey. It's useless to imagine what will come; if you let yourself live, suffering without demeaning yourself with resolute decisions that are always vulgar, you'll find yourself outside the cyclone without realizing it. In time some help will come that is always wiser and more imaginative than we are. He writes poetry and poetry is his first ally. Unless. . . unless he gets stuck in the snare of words inspired by something so far away. It would be absurd for him to do anything foolish by keeping faith with the words he finds by digging deep inside himself. To lose one's life for words has already been done but, my God, no longer, and Matteo knows enough about linguistics and psychoanalysis to know how to extricate himself from the pitfalls of the metaphysics concealed in rhetoric. Matteo is faithful to life, I hope, and not only to the idea he has of it, which he tries to transfer onto paper.

Matteo, Lavinia, Toni, Enrico — how many images have become part of the portrait I wanted to make only of Tosca!

I admit that my not seeing her any more, as happened only a few days ago, makes my imagination less sure. I write, but enveloped in the fog of distance. Is that good or bad? Hasn't it been said that the only possession is in absence? Perhaps it takes a more profound mind than mine to "see" Tosca moving in the distance, in the continuity of her life that I can't touch or save. I, who can't even save my own. In any case, I telephoned her. At first she responded in her hoarse voice that also sounded tired, and became animated only when she heard my name. But then we were cut off, and when I called back she was all primed to show herself in the way she thought best for us, formally correct and in good humor, even playful. She gave me news of the cats using expressions unusual for her, as though she were communicating a weather bulletin. It didn't help me. I won't call her again. Rather, Toni will do it for me. Tosca will tell her if something is bothering her.

But one of these days I'll go to the village early in the morning. I want to see what it looks like empty, as it soon will be for Tosca. It will be my last swim this summer in the sea that the cat lady will watch grow pale in the winter sunsets, the smoke of her cigarette rising with the flight of gulls.

If I were honest to my bones, I would confess I'm thinking of changing the point of view of my story. That is, I want to try to live from inside Tosca's story, almost performing a graft on which I'll no longer allow myself to be ironical about my soul or mind or spirit, whichever you prefer. I've done it partially, but always in the guise of an interpreter. Now I want to face the sea alone, stripped bare of myself, with the will to chew the thoughts I know as hers, as if I were responsible for them, too. Symbiosis, transplant, osmosis. A hybrid, certainly, but if it breathes I will have achieved what a friend of mine said was the only justification for writing. What you write makes sense "if it rises," he said, and I believe that leaven is the key to all my problems. Also because at a certain point this treacherous observing of mine has made me feel guilty. "I'm a peeping Tom," I said to myself, a filthy, lazy, nosy peeping Tom. And when I

took Tosca's hand it occurred to me to kiss it and beg her forgiveness. I didn't do it, naturally, so as not to embarrass her, but
this role of voyeur makes me feel sticky and smelly. The meta-
phor of an ancient Frenchman suits me better, which I applied to
my case with my usual presumption; he compares the reader
sucking the marrow, the essential meaning, out of the book to a
dog chewing a bone. I, the dog-writer, circled around Tosca's life
to find a readable, recountable, unifying sense. I didn't think my
curiosity was squalid, or my ambushing her on her daily rounds
to get a better look was depraved. It was only a game, but the
absolute always sets its traps, and I now realize I was cheating.

But am I so wickedly responsible? Aren't the eel-like characters responsible, those who escape from the nets of the writing? And don't the ideas themselves change, also, without the
mind that produces them realizing it?

If only the hybrid that is being born from Tosca and me was
autonomous! Leaven is necessary for that hybrid, as for every
human game. The trapped butterfly that I, Tosca, everyone carries inside must finally find the opening and fly away, free. I am
waiting for this miracle, and I believe it's a common desire, conscious and unconscious. I would like for that hybrid, like my
liberated butterfly, to lightly touch the earth in that place without boundaries or laws that is halfway between life and literature.

But this, dear Gigi, is no longer a desire; it's a prayer.
Prayers fly high, like butterflies. That's fine. I pray. And so be it.
If Ruggero were only here! Only he, among so many literary
friends and so many Marxists and so many halfway between
involvement with politics and involvement with literature,
would be able to understand me and absolve me. Only he could
get to the heart of something and reveal its unifying sense, if
there was one. Who of us has believed in the grand hopes and
lofty projects of the left without surrendering to some other,

more remote, utopia of words? Or vice versa? That day at Gaeta (I had been back for a year) during one of the hundred round tables in which we hoped to reconcile reality and project, life and poetry, when Giuliano attacked him. Realism in the narrative was one of the issues, with that great red backdrop of socialist realism. Ruggero grew more passionate and since Giuliano, stubborn and persistent, didn't give in, he pounded the table and, the only time I can remember in the years of our friendship, shouted. "Your communism comes from Marx, mine from Breton." He cut it short like that. His intuition saw further than his logic, his freedom as a man was the prism that shed light on every other freedom.

At times I feel that writing is an act of obedience, like a monk and prayer. Can I put it that way? I could say that to Ruggero, and I'm sure that he, with his vibrant face, sweet smile and shining eyes, would reply, without judging me, "At times we seem to possess the key even without Fourier, and we can send the magician-philosophers out to pasture." Yes, the magicians. Are we all forgetting perhaps to call a spade a spade? Ambiguity displaces authenticity in everything, Benjamin said. Benjamin, one of the hundred magicians.

2

It seems there were sudden, savage cyclones after our departure. Perhaps the summer heat—a tropical, un-Mediterranean heat—had exasperated the blood and nerves unaccustomed to it, and everyone's thermostat went crazy. Tosca telephoned on her own initiative and thank goodness Toni was there, just back from Turin and still not her calm self. Matteo, she told me, is more spare than ever, in flesh and in conversation; he told her not to worry, he studies ten hours a day, has haunting eyes in his drawn face, is determined to keep others from interfering, thinks of Lavinia, suffers because of Lavinia, wants Lavinia. The clever rationalization his nature suggested to him was to believe that writing poetry and taking exams were the only way not to lose her forever.

Tosca needed to tell Toni about some things that had shocked her. Enrico came back alone (she really wanted Toni to know this because Matteo would be comforted by the news) and began pounding the typewriter again in his empty flat. He goes out to eat at a restaurant, is nice to Tosca when he sees her, and more than ever has the air of a faithful, melancholy guard dog. That was Tosca's interpretation. However, from the little that I have been able to understand about him (scrupulous to the point of Calvinism in his mental discipline and in his research for the greatest and the best), Enrico has decided to make Lavinia choose. I've never seen a guard dog abandon his watch to protect himself. Toni agrees. She says she is certain Lavinia will come back to him after letting him pine a little, just enough not to compromise her monopoly. Without a doubt she used Matteo as a card she could immediately discard in her game with Enrico. An impulse that tried the patience of Enrico, who is tolerant but not at the cost of his dignity (I noticed this word popped up often when he spoke, whether it applied to the dignity of his studies or of moral dignity), and Lavinia is too intelligent to flaunt it. Matteo is not important to her, as far as I know. She must have been curious about the new charge of tension that the routine with Enrico had made her forget, and the sweetness of feeling herself enveloped by innocent adoration, pure of any judgment. But after parading her vain capriciousness before Enrico she doesn't want to lose him. She'll let him wait a little—noblesse oblige—and then go back to him. Toni and I have bet on the duration of the punishment those two are inflicting on each other, both with clear consciences.

According to Toni, Lavinia doesn't love and therefore doesn't suffer. Enrico, on the other hand, monolithic in feeling, is never completely secure. He refrains from phoning her in the absolutely vain hope of teaching her a lesson. But he is troubled by the fear of going too far. She knows it, and every morning prolongs the awaited day. Toni says a week. Lavinia's appearance will coincide with Enrico's Sunday day off. If I know this kind of treacherous Venus I'll win, because I say not before next Thursday.

And there was a real cyclone in Ivrea that ripped holes in roofs. Vacationers from that unfortunate town rushed back headlong to patch up the gaps. Tosca was excited to be able to relate so much news at one time. But the other cyclone, the one unleashing Tosca's outrage and her desire to tell Toni about it at any cost, was the scene on the beach the other night between the mother of the three children and her husband who arrived unexpectedly. Her friend was with her and, says Tosca, they were as inseparable as ever. She saw them from a distance while she smoked her last cigarette before going back to the unbearable sultriness of her apartment. With the hot African wind still blowing, a veil of sand covered everything, suffocating the breath and perhaps the feelings. Tosca froze before the fury of the man who was shouting unrepeatable obscenities in the night and who also raised his hand against his wife while trying to keep her friend away with his other arm. But he was defeated by the Lesbian's strength. His wife hammered him with her small fists of a succubus; the other one held him bound with her gendarme arms—holding him by his neck from behind, Tosca said.

Then they calmed down. Their excited voices became quieter. The next morning the husband was not to be seen, and Tosca surmised he had left that same night. The two women were glum, the little one cried and hugged her children to her as never before, the other lectured as insistently as a pneumatic drill, and the gossip flew. In the beauty shop they whispered about divorce—the husband would try to get the children. Tosca spoke of guilt and reason. In her canonical vision of things homosexuality had no place. The wife is guilty because corrupt, and therefore a dangerous mother. The husband has every right to leave her. The desecrated marriage is over. Toni and I talked about it, trying to take the woman's side, clearly weak in every way, a little thing with an endless succession of pale days behind her. A dull adolescence, an indifferent marriage, a sex life endured, the hard work of maternity. Then the meeting of a dominator who supported her, exalted her, gave her unexpected feelings. She must have lost her customary standard of judgment and substituted another that seemed the only right one. She hit him and didn't feel guilty. Her freedom from him and from everything that had forced her to accept the sacred canons was well worth the revolt. Now she will wake up once the heat abates and will have to consider what she gains and what she loses. The respect of others and peace of mind first of all, which someone like her can't easily renounce. It would take a far greater strength than seems to be in that tiny little body and those lifeless eyes.

But we'll learn from Tosca what happens. I ask myself if this tropical summer hasn't burned not only the woods on the peninsula but also the patience of the timid. In the exasperating heat psychic anomalies had also reached the limit of their endurance. Lavinia flaunted what is usually left understood, Enrico surrendered to the blow of offended dignity, the two women friends abandoned themselves to the discovery of sex beyond all fear of public condemnation, the husband was unable to endure the insult made more to the institution of marriage than to himself.

And Tosca? I guess the goings-on are nourishment for her. Charitable bread. Busying herself with others distracts her from herself. I would like to hear her while she tells it to her cats. Toni is very funny when she imitates Tosca's feline assemblies. Tosca must be especially disturbed by her discovery of the Sapphic mysteries. She still has desires for love, but her desire does not go beyond boundaries that her healthy nature and simple culture indicate. However, on the beach, watching the two women in love, she must have felt her turbid blood run more quickly beneath skin caressed by sea smells. I don't believe I'm wrong in thinking that, though ashamed of her thoughts, when she picked up Fifi to carry her home, she held her closely, as she would a lover, as she would want to be held. A fierce mimesis she doesn't bring to the light of reason, but which I do for her. Charitably, it seems to me. But who knows if I myself don't wrap my dark desire for perversion in merciful shadows. Am I not also blinded by the heat of this long, too long, summer? What yearning, frustrated by the hot winds of tiredness and by the dark cyclone that each day moves more threateningly nearer, makes me hover stickily around the flesh of a woman with a thankless existence, but one not demeaned by cowardice or wickedness?

I have sufficient self-irony to judge myself. And a red light in the obscure tangle of thoughts about this summer warned me I must not give in to the temptation to invent instead of bearing witness. Tosca speaks real words; I babble. That is what divides the non-real, imagined, from the real observed with scrupulous fidelity. Which is, after all, my presumption as realistic narrator. As if I didn't know every truth has two, three, a thousand faces. The cruelest massacres are committed in the name of truth. What are the world's real colors? For me Tosca is colored with all the tints of my passion to represent her: across my spectrum is red, gray, blue, according to the moment and the mood—hers and mine. But the real colors are only those of the one who has put them there, on us and things. I am naive, as so many others, as perhaps almost everyone, and I would like to be reassured, but by whom? Without that painter who alone knows because the colors are his, how can I presume to know? And what's worse, what can I depict? But even this is destiny. And mine is to be forever in doubt, and anxious about it. A confused destiny. But it is mine and I have no other. It's my only small certainty. To which I cling as well as I can, as each one does to his own. And if Tosca knew she would forgive me. After all, my thoughts create a halo around her that protects her from solitude. If I knew more about science, exact or not, or even about parapsychology, I could comfort myself by measuring the energy that from my thoughts springs to her defense in the wide universe and in the small marine strip where she is attached like a plant in the garden she waters, or as I am attached to my destiny that has at this moment put on its peaceful white mask. But from behind the mask gleam Miciamore's eyes, also undecipherable. . .

Which truth, then? Mine, hers, the magic truth of that non-human look, or the truth of the sweet madness that develops its image in the darkroom of its own desire?

Even Miciamore can be the protagonist of a fable. When the fable is told according to its own logic, and is sufficient unto itself.

3

I read Toni the first part of my work as clandestine novelist. She wasn't surprised, perhaps she expected it, and she followed my reading in her totally involved way that makes her a unique collaborator.

She doesn't just listen; she lowers herself into it. She's the reader every novelist would like to have, and perhaps the one he thinks of when he writes. But in submerging herself she doesn't forget herself. She's like someone who follows a concert and vibrates in tune with the music but is aware if one instrument lags or hides or dissents from the whole. She stops, picks out the expression that has disturbed her—it's not only an aesthetic disturbance—and strings it on the pin of her critical sensibility, then submerges herself again, and only in the end, with eyes that don't look at me but that follow her inner images, does she give me her opinion of what she has heard.

But by watching her face as I read, I know what is happening. There is a continuity of reflections under her vivacious change of expressions that shows me without any uncertainty, just as you don't doubt the depth of a lake whose surface is continually rippled by the breeze. And finally, her melancholy, which is one and the same with her capacity for reflection, is also a very adept measuring instrument for signaling useless evasions, unconscious flights, superfluous digressions. She leans instinctively toward the unity in the things she lives as well as in those she thinks. She says she is "fed up" with Croce, but if she didn't know him she would have adapted his literary canon naturally.

This time, however, Toni has been silent too long after I stopped reading, and, anxious for her opinion, I attempted to joke. "Come on, say something! At least it's good as a recipe for cats. Moncalleri's Kit Kat Cook Book?"

She looked at me as though she didn't see me, frowning, and I, querulous and chattering away like an insecure student, went on, "Haven't you read the latest thoughts on writing as a way of cooking? And about the possible two souls of black cabbage? Writers with degrees are stealing my profession, and I'm getting even. But one can't be both frivolous and boring. When I'm frivolous I'm not boring. And now?"

Then Toni told me I had nothing to reproach myself for if our little marine world had taken me by the hand. "Without Tosca it wouldn't make sense. It's what we know and understand." She used the plural and this gave me a pang, whether of tender complicity or of unconfessable jealously, I don't know. But, she concluded, she didn't want to know the end of the story. She didn't want to hear any more. I should follow my own instincts as a novelist. She didn't want any part of it.

And so I am alone today with both Tosca's ending and my own.

It's cold, the first real cold of this year, and Genoa is proud about this also, ignoring the nuances in its weather reports. The wind blowing on the sea off the northern Righi mountains and from Castelletto is winter's peremptory announcement. Continuous, vigorous, insistent, it raises clouds of dust in the streets near the beach and long waves along the coast. Not a hint of blue in the dark sky, premonitions of frost at every crossroads where furious currents of air meet. I went downtown to look in the store windows, but already at Balbi I couldn't walk without feeling chilled to my bones under my too lightwight coat flapping in the wind. I feel well, the vacation renewed my muscle tone and breathing with swimming and rest. I haven't smoked in six months, and I don't have anything to tell my doctor. But this dark Genoa under an already winter sky gives me an uneasiness that keeps me from concentrating on the only work important to me.

I was thinking about Tosca before I went out, while I hurriedly wrote an article, trusting in my ability and in the patience of those who by now swallow everything— catastrophes and recipes, royal scandals—like abstract morality plays. The beach in the village must be deserted today. . .

The bars are closed. The German woman has gone for the last time, but I doubt if she is still thinking of Israel after what happened in Beirut. Aldo is in Imperia painting houses instead of cabanas. The pharmacist has gone back to Piedmont. Tosca is alone with Bisi, Puss, and Fifi. When we left Poppa was still leading her gypsy life. From her difficult delivery only one little kitten remains, adopted by the girl at the beauty shop, and it is very beautiful and domesticated. Fifi, who was not pregnant, as Tosca had thought, was getting the pill. Half of one every week, two a month, "On Sundays, along with Mass," she said with a laugh during one of our conversations, and she told me how she had learned to administer it, pulverizing it in chopped meat, to be sure Fifi didn't make kittens.

I returned to Boccadasse on the bus, but I didn't feel like going in the house. Just the thought of its creaking complaints in this angry blast of wind bothered me. And so I got off at the Boccadasse beach, with the boats in dry dock between the houses. I wandered around among the narrow fishing boats that all have archaic names. Only one "Patrizia" among a series of Annes, Mariucces and Baciccias. I filled my lungs deeply with that sour and a slightly overripe odor boats have on land. The strong smell of natural death. It needs more time to rot to the point of mephitic exhalations; now, so recently removed from its vital element, the boats smell of dead but not rotten fish, the odor of tar but also of sun-dried wood. It's a combination I could recognize from a thousand odors with my eyes closed. Someone dying of a heart attack or waiting to die in old age without having known the slow corruption of a cell-destroying illness must smell like that. Like boats in dry dock. It's an antechamber of death and the smell, sad but not repellent, anticipates it. I wandered around the boats feeling just like them, in dry dock waiting for the last caulker to prepare me for eternity. At the first spring breeze the boats will be floating on the sea all red and yellow, I know; but in the meantime I enjoy roaming around among these brine-smoothed keels and rusty rowlocks like in an old folks home, blending my mortal smell with theirs, enjoying both my health and my old age, my strength to still navigate and the awareness that every day the horizon gets farther and wider for wings I don't have and condemns me to earth without remission.

My waiting seems just to me, even though I'm not sewing my shroud like old Jews in the past. I'm sewing my thoughts around me. I must humble myself for the presumption of guessing the thoughts of others. I write about Tosca, Lavinia, Toni, but with what right if I don't have a clear idea of who I am? I don't know, and yet I let my boat float on the wave of imagination, and free my thoughts as if I were not one, but two, three, a hundred people. Now when it gets cold, as it is today, and my heart is heavy behind ribs bathed in the north wind, I'm afraid of having to die not once but two, three, a hundred times. The half rotten and half sour odor of the boats reassures me. I won't die more than once.

I went home and saw Toni curled up on the pillows in the living room with Paletta in her arms, a cat herself, soft and warm. I embraced her with a gratitude that surprised her, but I couldn't tell her that away from her I had forgotten her like boats forget the sea. To find her waiting for me was to take up the navigation again, the immersion in life, the warmth after the cold, the expectation of new things in the nets I will throw out again with her. We should have started getting ready to go out to supper, but I wanted to make love right then. And afterwards we felt close all evening, munching on whatever was at hand, drinking, watching television, in tender, cradling warmth.

4

Once again Tosca was both the witness and choir in the little marine vacation world. She had been in the doorway doing her cleaning chores when she heard a door open in her stairwell. The husband of the "little one" appeared with two suitcases in hand. Tosca called her "the little one" with a wink that not even she knew whether of scorn or pain.

Soon he returned empty-handed, went back up the stairs and immediately came down with the three children, the oldest girl responsible and aware of her duty as caretaker of the other two sleepy and whiny children. Then the man returned, his unshaved face dark with tiredness. The three children must have been settled in the car. A quarter of an hour went by and Tosca was asking herself if the little one would stay in the village, abandoned and punished, when she saw them coming down together. He was holding her around the waist. On her changed face— younger and brighter—was a wide smile that caught Tosca by surprise. So that was how it was. Accustomed to obedience, she had again bowed her head, and he had forgiven her and come to get his family that had been endangered by the summer cyclone. It was too simple, but Tosca liked to imagine, just like one of the many romantic films she watched on television on winter afternoons, that everything would be different in their house in the city: she less beset by her unconfessable rebellions, he more attentive. However, the relief was evident in the protective way he led his wife, in the gentle way he loaded her suitcases into the car. When the little one came to Tosca she stopped, and for the first time in all those months she spoke some simple, casual words as if she suddenly recognized the person she was speaking to, after passing by her so many times without seeing her. She took Tosca's hand in her small, dry hands, and looked around with bewildered eyes—even her eyes, now, were no longer dull; a blue veil told of her sadness at the moment of leaving a place and a time that had touched her life. Without realizing it or wanting to, she treated Tosca like an involuntary witness to what had happened. Saying good-bye with words that she believed Tosca wouldn't understand the underlying meaning of, she said farewell to the summer, to forbidden love, to guilt. She was returning to order and told it to that woman so different from herself, but whom she had lived near without getting to know, and whom she had neither the wish nor the curiosity to make a less opaque mirror of her personal affairs.

"I'm sorry," she repeated several times. "I'm sorry to be going away. We haven't had a moment together. You'll be staying on? Alone?" A pause, and then, "I hope to come back another year. The children will be older. I'm sorry if we've been a bother to you."

Tosca waffled, embarrassed by being witness to so much beyond the walk-on part the woman attributed to her, and at the same time feeling a sincere and absurd emotion rise in her throat. She smiled at the little one who was trying her husband's patience— inquisitor's eyes, compressed brow—and she wished a good winter, "To both of you and the children."

When they left she drew a long breath, wryly amused at how easily tears come to the elderly, and lit her first cigarette of the day.

She was finishing up her work in the garden when the postman called to her: "This time the special delivery is for you!"

Running up the steps, she signed for it with suddenly shaking hands, and opened it. She had trouble making it out. The name was unfamiliar: a lawyer, but his office address was in Turin. She read it without understanding, then read it again. At the postman's call she had known immediately, but hadn't wanted to believe it. Tosca couldn't follow the turns of the juridical syntax, but the truth she had feared and churned over during her worst nights was there. The landlady was evicting her. Her apartment was to be left free for her son.

She sat on the flight of stairs leading to Toni and Lavinia's apartments. If only there was someone to tell it to, some soul with whom she could give vent to the tears overpowering her! She sobbed without restraint. No one would hear her. Not a soul was passing on wind-battered Via Aurelia. That thought froze her body like a blade of ice.

How long she sat there she didn't know, until Fifi and Puss circled around her, tails straight, ears pointed. They were mewing, complaining that they hadn't had breakfast yet.

She got up heavily, dried her red swollen eyes and followed them into the house. After the cats had quickly emptied their dish and looked at her from mere slits, already disposed to a digestive nap, she thought she should phone Toni. She would tell her about the little one and if Toni asked how she was, she'd explain her problem. She drank her coffee without pleasure. Everything had become more bitter with that threat hanging over her head. Even the frightening prospect of the squalid peace ahead was now a lost blessing. The squalor remained, but not the peace.

Who was that miserable man whose troubles never ended, the one people use as an example of the most miserable of the miserable? Oh, yes, Job. She was like Job. But if she remembered right, he was also in a ditch, filthy with his feces. With an effort she got up, went into the bathroom and filled the tub, pouring in some perfumed bath salts. At least she could be clean. No, she wasn't filthy Job yet, and she let loose with a curse that gave her no comfort, but that made her have to explain herself to the cats immediately afterward. "Let's hope no one heard me. If I don't have even him, I'm lost." Her "him" was always in lower case, when she thought about him, because she only thought about him to scold him for not being there, or if he was there, for not taking care of her. The hot bath made her feel better. When she got out of the tub she hadn't decided anything, but one thing was clear. It would take time. Gigi had said that one evening, too. She would go to the city and get the advice of someone at the Renters' Association. She had happened to see something about it last winter and had been happy to know that it existed.

By the evening of that unfortunate day she still hadn't telephoned Genoa. She was ashamed, afraid of pity, and was big enough, she told herself, to take care of her business herself.

As always, a great weariness came over her body, blood, joints after a siege of tears; therefore, she didn't need too many spiritual exercises to resist the invitation to false consolation. The film on TV was so boring it brought on the sweet desire to sleep, so she turned it off and cut short her nightly routine. The cats had come back and were sleeping. While she languidly ran a brush through her hair a few times and brushed her teeth, the letter she received that morning suddenly appeared in her already foggy mind. With an extreme effort of will she put it aside. She wanted to fall asleep following the natural hazy loop. I can't, she told herself, start taking sleeping pills or something worse. That's enough for today, and she pretended not to notice the trembling that suddenly began to vibrate in her throat. She buried her head in the pillow until the agitation slowly subsided, and she found the security she wanted in sleep.

Tosca divided her sleep into distinct categories, rating them like television channels did their programs. The best was deep sleep, dense as the pulp of a peach just before it was completely mature. From the peach-sleep she emerged renewed, without wrinkles and her eyes shining with a suddenly recaptured youth. Next there was the musical-sleep that unraveled in phases like the tempos of a concerto with continual variations; in the morning she was rested but the skin on her face retained signs of the wrinkled pillow on which she stirred restlessly while following the varied melody of her sleep. The third category was the nightmare-sleep, ruined by distressing dreams from which she would awake with a start, feeling weak. A sleep more exhausting than hard work. The fourth category was the pudding-sleep, trembling to touch the unconscious without ever reaching it, dreaming disconnected images, tenuous visions soon forgotten, a light sleep, but sweet, like the first hours of the cats' sleep. In the morning Tosca was not refreshed or rested, but in good humor. Always something of that trembling pudding sweetness stayed with her, some shred of memory or filmstrip of images for her fantasy to keep her company while she drank her coffee.

That night a Pierrot hovered for a long time near the pillow where her head, exhausted by tears, was tenaciously buried. He was half cloth and half porcelain that an office colleague had given her when she was still young, and which had been lost on one of her many moves. His sad face was made of biscuit with black eyebrows and pink cheeks, and from the wide silk sleeves protruded two tiny porcelain hands with red painted fingernails. His feet were also very small with painted black shoes over the rose-colored biscuit. He seemed like a sick young boy and she had never liked him. Unconsciously she had connected him with the man who brought him one Christmas eve, perhaps offering it as a love message. She had felt an annoying sweatiness on the hands that offered it and he, the colleague who looked at her with hope shrouded in timidity, was awkward and too subservient. She detested him, so humble and always so ready to agree, and had avoided him with the cruel shrewdness of young women when untouched by love. In her dream the Pierrot moved his eyes, and they were those of the man she hadn't wanted. The biscuit hands were damp. She was restless in her sleep but the Pierrot was now laughing and moving his feet and hands as if tied to wires pulled by a puppeteer. His motions were brusque and ridiculous because even the other objects around—she didn't know where the place was or what use the objects were—were also laughing. Perhaps oversized vases or curiously shaped drinking glasses. Surrounding the disjointed and incongruous Pierrot they were all laughing in the dream. Then the wind-filled curtain rose, thin and worn, with the insert of lace, and Tosca recognized her grandmother's house. In the curtain were small mended patches trying to be invisible. Instead it was the grandmother who was invisible, who Tosca knew was there; she shouted at the Pierrot that stopped moving and disappeared.

When dawn broke, all Tosca remembered of her night was that curtain embroidered by her mother and mended by her grandmother and the Pierrot's weird laugh. There were no extraneous images, but those she remembered didn't portend anything or recall anything that especially mattered to her. A colleague she made fun of in her youth, the thriftiness and patience of the women in her house, an ordinary dream to start the day, trying to keep control of everything ready to float to the surface. The embankments were threatened, and it was crucial, absolutely crucial, that the tide didn't flood them. While she prepared breakfast for the cats and sipped her coffee, she wondered what had happened to that young man of the Pierrot. Who knows why that memory came up, buried as it was under the accumulation of years and she was surprised how completely she had erased it for such a long time. But nothing is destroyed of what we are or what we do. Even indifference, even lack of love, everything leaves a trace if suddenly a face can return from far away and reclaim its right to be in our life. Or to ask for an accounting of something. I, too, thought Tosca, was a scatter-brained girl, indifferent to what happened to the souls of those around me. Perhaps I, too, have had my moment of cruelty like Lavinia. Anyway, I didn't kiss him, she excused herself, but immediately told herself the times were different and she forced herself to remember. Yes, when she was working at the counter behind the glass window, giving out and receiving forms from people, she had, on alternate days, been completely indifferent or exchanged glances with the Pierrot whose eyes were always on her, as on a promise of happiness.

Perhaps the dream was not entirely accidental. A shadow of forgotten guilt explained the reappearance of the Pierrot that had good reason to laugh, when you think about it. Oh, he had! We pay for everything, she thought, down to the last red cent.

5

That summer quizzes were the vogue in the illustrated magazines coming into the journalists' home. Once Tosca had found the two of them tallying up scores and joking about their results. The quiz results concluded that Toni was half her real age, Gigi an octogenarian. They explained what it was about and invited Tosca to give it a try, but she hadn't wanted to risk it. She was ashamed of her ignorance and afraid of being forced to make up answers at random to hide it. But now that they were gone, she realized they had taught her to think differently. Even her former letters seemed poorly written now. But on the other hand, she couldn't get interested in any of the novels they left her, and she had to work hard to make sense of individual sentences. She sighed, "I'm rusty, and now it's too late." It had been different with Mario. Even if their education hadn't followed a regular school curriculum, they were interested in everything. They knew people, actors, musician who were motivated by the same lively curiosity, and Mario took up new things so instinctively! Just talking with him made her want to learn more. "I was more intelligent when I was with you," she said to him like a caress, and sighed again. The village, the damned village, so beautiful from the outside, so asphyxiating inside, had dried her up, diminished her, made her regress. With Bruno she had rediscovered life in a more direct and animal way. They held each other, gave pleasure and warmth to each other, but they rarely talked about anything beyond the demands of the daily routine. Bruno was a discouraged man, accustomed to watching his words with his sick wife, and perhaps (she confessed to herself) he had no special attributes either of feelings or intelligence. He had so cruelly canceled her out of his life! Just as she had canceled her memory of the Pierrot. But there had been something entirely different between them.

In the quiz she hadn't wanted to take even love was categorized with specific case histories. She had had trouble recognizing her relationship with Bruno, but hers with Mario fit every category. Yet not any one of them really well.

With the highest and lowest scores tallied, her liaison with Bruno didn't add up to much on the list. Hers with Mario was out of proportion. Perhaps the quizzes had a logic, because he had the winning total. But what did winning mean? The winner is the one who wins tomorrow, not yesterday. She squirmed. A tear in the bus seat was poking her in the back. She hated plastic in every form, perhaps because not even the sea was able to digest it. She moved to a seat in better condition.

Tosca was returning from the city where she had cashed her retirement check and made a visit to the Renters' Association. The bus was half empty. The conductor punched her ticket and sat down beside her. For years now Tosca had taken the bus every month, without counting the extra trips, and by now they greeted each other like old acquaintances. However, this time the man wanted to talk. And he did it with such an air of familiarity that Tosca was a little taken aback. She had come to feel suspicious of anyone she didn't know well.

"What's wrong? Don't you feel well?" She looked away from him to gaze out the window. "Don't deny it. I was watching, and I was afraid you were about to cry. And when you moved, I was afraid you wanted to get off."

Now she had to say something, and while attempting to form any sentence at all, she thought of the face he would make if she told him, yes, he had observed correctly, that she had made lists of the pluses and minuses of her life and they didn't add up. The scales didn't balance. The man didn't persist, but his wide face with the hint of double chin showed he hadn't changed his impression. His body was rather coarse and inelegant, too; his jacket followed the contours of his belly, and he was no longer young. "He must be about fifty," Tosca thought, and so as not to seem unfriendly, asked him, "Aren't you going to take a vacation?"

"To do what? Mix with the holiday crowd? I'll take time off, but later on, when there's no one left on lousy Aurelia." At Tosca's surprised look, he explained, "Look, I've gone up and down this highway for twenty years, sometimes here and sometimes there," he pointed to the driver's seat, "and it gets worse every year. This world is full of crazy people. He took off his cap and passed his hand (surprisingly long and thin) through his grizzled hair, and continued. "Even in the winter it's risky on a bicycle. I go as far as Torre del Mare and plant myself in the coves facing the island and fish."

Tosca asked him about his fishing luck and, immediately cheered, he began a long and elaborate discourse on bait, flies, lines and currents. Tosca quit listening and was astonished when she heard the man's last words:

"If I come to your place with two beautiful live fish, will you cook them for me?"

She laughed with embarrassment. "You don't even know where I live."

"Yes, I do. When I pass your apartment I'm always on the lookout in case you're late."

Tosca's stop was after the tunnel that led to the pink and yellow village, at a place overgrown with weeds between the sea and the railroad tracks, now used as a car park. The man accompanied her to the automatic door and handed her the bag he had taken when she jumped up, surprised to be home already.

What was this new development? An offer of companionship, without a doubt. Maybe the man had a slovenly old wife he tried to forget by going fishing, or maybe he was one of those who never lose an opportunity for variations on the matrimonial theme, but she didn't think so. Everything he said indicated a rather unsociable character, however. . . it was really nervy of him to invite himself to her house in such an direct way—anything but unsociable! She was unsure whether to go straight home or not. That unusual conversation had unsettled her, and to go inside meant shutting herself off from the world of the living. She turned around several times indecisively, and then went off in the direction of the tobacco shop. Sometimes, as right now, she bought things she had no immediate need for just to be able to say a few words out loud to someone besides her cats. Even an episode such as just happened to her (which was really nothing, but in the repetitious nothing of her days was much) would have meaning only if she could tell it to someone. She remembered the evening conversations her mother had had with the other women beside the fire during the evacuation, the detailed comments about what had happened during the day. Each woman brought a piece of wood or twigs, and the day was relived and shared, and perhaps (she understood now) such an exchange helped them bear the misery, the fear, the separation from their men.

The tobacconist was cold and alone in her shop. "Why not put a stove in here?" Tosca asked her.

And the other woman was immediately defensive. "That's all well and good, but to pay ten hours of electricity a day for three packs of cigarettes is no way to run a business!"

Tosca bit her tongue. In the summer money ran like a river toward that door propped open by stacks of toys, toilet articles, flippers and even beach chairs. La Tedesca had told her the number of apartments the tobacconist rented in the summer had doubled over the past a few years. Well, she said to herself, everyone finds his pleasure where he can. This woman is blue with cold but warms herself by counting money. I would give all the pension money in my purse to have someone visit me this evening.

She really had to go home. There were no other distractions left. At the apartment house door she immediately heard the three cats mewing. They were hungry and complained that she had stayed away too long to suit them. All three surrounded her. Fifi, the crazy ballerina, twirled in the vestibule. Bisi with her big head on her thin neck. Puss, more serious, after rubbing against her legs, sat in the kitchen doorway, following her with his eyes.

"Here he is, my man," she said to Puss, "you don't have the words, but there you are, asking me to account for where I've been and why, and how it went." She took off her coat and changed into her slippers. "Now I'll tell you, but first let's see what you've all been up to." There was a bad smell in the kitchen, and Tosca scolded all three of them. One of them had dirtied outside the litter box. That never happened if they were well, and she decided to change the menu planned for their supper. She gave each one a drop of disinfectant the veterinarian had prescribed, cleaned up the mess, and opened the windows. A little later, with the three satisfied and settled down (she hadn't eaten yet, but had drunk a glass of milk), she tried to write a reply to the second special delivery letter from the lawyer, the way the Association had advised.

After such a long time she had lost the habit of writing; and besides, that bureaucratic language frightened her. She had to say and not say, deny the owner's right and defend her own, but in an irritating roundabout way. She wrote a nearly insulting letter that she read to Puss, the only one still awake beside her. It was impossible, pointless, maybe it was better to go back and have them write it. Then it occurred to her that she would have to take the bus, and the prospect of another conversation like the one today didn't sit well.

Telephone Genoa? She hadn't yet and didn't know why. It wasn't pride or fear of being badly received, it was something inexplicable, as if to telephone was to take part in a performance others expected of her. It was pride, then. She wanted to amaze them with her strength. Perhaps that was it more than timidity. And because of this pride that she alone knew and managed, she had turned to drink only a few times. She wanted to hold out as long as possible and refrained from going to the emporium to stock up on wine. Thirst justified it in the summer. However, now she was shamed by her failure to write the letter and took a drop of whisky in order to clarify her ideas.

When she took the bottle from the cupboard it was full. By the time she went to bed the liquor was down to the label.

6

For two days Tosca wrote and threw away unsatisfactory replies. The biggest problem was that she didn't have official residency in the village. She was retired and unwell (the only points in her favor), but she was poor, and the landlady alleged, with all the necessary medical certification, that her son needed to recuperate his health by the sea. The parabola was always the same. An exchange of special delivery letters, a court hearing, postponements, expense, then surrender. And the girl she let use her apartment in Milan wouldn't even deign to answer her letters.

Two days later she found herself at the end of another solitary day, no wine in the house, the whiskey bottle empty, and the TV suddenly gone mad. She had sound but no picture. A big wind the previous night had broken the antenna. What now? "I should call Bruno," she said to herself, and discouragement laid her low.

The cats that had heard her swearing while she fiddled with the television set waked up and began to act nervous with her. They followed her into the bedroom where she opened the wardrobe, then into the living room where she began rummaging in the sideboard. She took a bottle out, the last one in the house, and grimaced in disgust. It was the bitter digestive Fernet that she kept in reserve out of habit from the time she lived with Mario. Indigestion was unlikely, because she had eaten nothing but fruit and bread. She began walking from the living room to the vestibule, from the vestibule to the kitchen. All the lights were on. It was cold with all the inside doors open and drafts coming from the cracks in the walls. Everywhere silence. Turning to the cats, she said, "Tell me what I should do. Christ,

Christ, is this life?" Her voice trembled and her hand as well, as she poured the dark liquor into a glass. It was atrocious to gulp it down that way. But the herbal taste left in her mouth wasn't bad, and it had given her a rapid and pungent shock with its strong burning sensation. Perhaps it wouldn't be so bitter if taken in tiny sips.

The next day she still held out. She didn't go buy anything to drink, but evening came and the man she had called in Finale to fix the broken television set still hadn't come. She resorted to the Fernet again. There wasn't much left, but her throat was dry and the bitterness of the drink was nothing compared to the bitterness she felt inside.

She tried to fight it, but the dark velvety liquid at the bottom of the bottle was the only thing that interested her at that moment. Why fight it? Who for? She poured again and drank it down, feeling better immediately. There was a little bit left and she decided to leave it for the next evening. But the bottle kept calling her. She got ready for bed, but couldn't get the dregs of that bottle out of her mind. What did they call it? Drug dependence. Dependence was deciding not to do something and then doing it, or vice versa. She poured out the remainder and drank it slowly. This was dependence. No different whether alcohol, drugs, or sex. The worst thing that can happen, what she had always despised. Easy to judge, more difficult to resist in order to avoid judgment. As she finished the Fernet in two swift and greedy gulps, she consoled herself with the thought that now she wouldn't be able to give in to temptation. There was nothing left in the house.

That night she didn't sleep with any of her four categories that could sustain her after days such as these. There were waves as big as mountains, avalanches of tumbling water that roared over the beach and each one came closer to where she stood, frightened to death, with her back glued against the wall, a crying baby in her arms. She saw it coming from a distance, a monstrous mass of water that touched the sky. Clutching the baby tightly she screamed and found herself at the foot of the bed with three wide-awake cats.

In her confusion she couldn't find the overhead light and knocked the bedside lamp to the floor trying to get away from the nightmare. When she recovered, she stroked the cats that were still frightened and crying, and they followed her into the kitchen. She looked for cool water in the frig and didn't have the heart to disappoint them. Because they were looking at her expectantly, she filled their bowl with milk. Puss and Bisi sniffed it without touching it. Only Fifi, who was always the most acquiescent, cheered up and showed her pleasure with two or three little compliant licks.

Tosca drank a glass of cold water without any relief whatsoever. Her mouth tasted like bile, and she remembered she had drunk bile before she went to sleep. In the bathroom she brushed her teeth, but the atrocious bitterness wouldn't go away. She poured a little cologne in a full glass of water to rinse her mouth. It was pleasant, and she resisted the urge to drink it. Clear headed and determined she poured some cologne into a glass of water for the second time. Someone once told her crazy people will drink anything if they aren't watched. She wasn't crazy, but she was tired of futile excuses. She wanted to do it, and she did it.

It had a good taste and she didn't have to account to anyone. After reading an adventure novel for a long time, one she knew almost by heart, and which she turned to when incapable of real concentration, she managed to go back to sleep. In the morning she got up with iron bands around her head and didn't make it to the bathroom. "Maybe I'm vomiting up my liver," she thought while wiping at the greenish stains on her nightgown. But she couldn't think of anything else because the shocks of

nausea came more frequently until she felt she was losing consciousness and fell to the floor. When she woke up she figured
the faint hadn't lasted long because it was still early. The nausea
had passed; she felt very weak and her head ached badly, but at
least she could get back into bed.

A vinegar soaked cloth on her forehead helped her to relax.
She wasn't afraid. The bad spell was over; it wasn't her turn to
be called just yet.

7

Last night had been the same as all other nights for some time now, a struggle to keep from thinking in the half-awake moments so as to avoid the nightmares that rocked the world, and even the small part of the world that belonged to her, from which they wanted to evict her.

A persistent nausea sent her out into the garden without breakfast. At midnight she had been wracked with dry heaves in the bathroom. She hadn't vomited anything, but a deep, rhythmic hiccoughing like a funeral bell had kept her awake and in a sweat for more than an hour. Then it had settled, but restorative sleep had not come. She thought she heard noises on the stairs, and Fifi often mewed, restless on a pillow at her feet.

The garden was desolate now without flowers and with half the leaves gone. Those few remaining seemed to absorb the gray of the sky and the branches were dry as though stripped of all vitality. "And yet I always water them," she grumbled, and decided to sprinkle them.

The hose she kept next to the washtub was missing. Tosca looked around, going from one end of the garden to the other. It was nowhere to be found.

So those sounds she had heard during the night were real! Someone had come to steal her pitiful garden hose. God, what nerve! She stood next to the oleander, uncertain what to do. Report the theft? To whom? To the greedy town policeman who was nowhere to be seen now that the source of his fines had disappeared? Go to the town hall to let them look down their noses at her? A hose is nothing, "They'll bring it back, you'll see," she seemed to hear. "Perhaps a neighbor needed it and didn't want to bother you by asking." Yes. That's the way it could have happened. Like that time she couldn't find the rake and hoe. From then on she locked them in the storeroom next to the garage. But not the hose. There was always some water in it and she didn't want it to make mildew on the floor of the small windowless room that already smelled bad from lack of ventilation.

"I'll go upstairs and get a bucket and water the plants that way today." While making up her mind she glanced on the ground where the soil formed a ring around the oleander bush, next to the path of irregular stones for people to walk through the garden.

It had been disturbed. Leaves stuck to the ground as if someone had walked there or stirred them up.

Miciamore! With a furiously beating heart she frantically began digging with her hands. But in her anxiety she couldn't make any headway. Running to the storeroom she got the little hoe she used for garden work and returned to the oleander. "It was here," she spoke excitedly. "It's not possible, maybe more to the left," she dug and talked and her fatigue dissolved into tears when the hoe finally hit what she was looking for. She gently brushed the dirt off a tin cookie box (a memory of a nice Christmas long ago) she had buried Miciamore in. She didn't open it, afraid of what she would see. The little batiste handkerchief embroidered with her monogram was just enough to cover his face, and anyway, the strip of oil paper she had wrapped around the little bier was intact. She looked around, picked a tender shoot of ivy, and covered up the little grave again with the hoe and rake. The effort exhausted her. She got up from that uncomfortable position and tried to smooth the ground around the tree without bending over, using the handle of the hoe as a support. Now it was more or less as it had been before. But she was not the same. She had to protect her still undiscovered secret, or this new worry would make her nights worse than they already were.

Putting away the garden tools, Tosca went back upstairs.

Ravenous cats were waiting for her. The nausea had passed. "One pain drives out another," but the irony gave her no relief. In any case she would have to pass up her morning coffee for her stomach's sake. She combed her hair, put a little rouge on her gray cheeks, and a dash of lipstick that she wiped off immediately with a piece of toilet paper because it accented the deep lines of her face reduced to a mask. She'd go out right away to look for rocks on the beach to put around every tree. That way all the circles would be the same and perhaps it would discourage curiosity. She didn't know whose. People's. The enemy's. Those who didn't want to let her live even like this. For a moment she thought maybe it had been only a cat or a hedgehog, an animal looking for food. Never mind. She would protect Miciamore's grave and was sorry she hadn't done it before. Every once in a while after a visit to the countryside she put a bunch of flowers on it, or some bluebells and flowers from the bougainvillea torn by the wind. Maybe someone saw her and became suspicious.

"Coming with me?" she asked the three well-fed cats. They filed out the door and waited for her at the bottom of the stairs.

Not a soul was on the beach. She walked slowly, searching for rocks similar in size and color, not looking at or hearing the sea — it, too, a extension of that emptiness, an indifferent sound in the surrounding silence.

The shopping bag grew heavy. When a ray of sun broke through the clouds she instantly felt its sweet warmth and went to sit on the beach wall. While watching Puss and Bisi play she smoked a cigarette; Fifi had disappeared somewhere. She was out of sight, maybe enticing some male with her eyes. But she would come as soon as she was called. What Tosca had imagined would happen was happening. Every day the three cats more and more became her shadow, her pages, her bodyguards. She smiled and called the two brothers. In a flash they were beside her and only after she stroked them, talking the sweet non-sense they loved, did they return to their game of investigating the tide-strewn debris.

The sun was pale but already filling most of the sky. That was when she saw the dark, slow-moving group, coming from the long, wide expanse of beach parallel with Via Aurelia.

As they came closer she recognized them. They were the old people, the same and different every year, who came to winter in a boarding house outside the village.

In the morning light she watched their distant shapes against the background of the sea they walked along, alone or clinging to each other. The couples were almost all mixed, but there were also two women arm in arm. A few men walked ahead.

The predominating color was gray. The brown of a few of the women's coats and one man's jacket were the only spots of color in the group whose faces were beginning to be distinguishable.

My goodness, how alike those sad shapes were, and how awkward! Misshapen bodies, massive legs. One thin man taller than the others seemed a god among a tribe of large monkeys. "How mean I am," she scolded herself. "You're walking that same road. In a few years that's the way you'll be moving, with swollen feet and stiff back." A flight of gulls suddenly landed on the beach and the group broke up. Happy shouts reached her. They called to each other, pointing out the large wings of one, the bluish color of another.

Their voices were happy, as though nothing mattered more to them at that moment than enjoying the sun and watching the flight of those happy creatures.

"And yet they must be full of aches and pains like me," Tosca thought while (she really didn't know why) she put out the cigarette she had just lit. She didn't want to be seen smoking. She

was suddenly ashamed of her hair tied in the usual absurd ponytail, but the ribbon was red and even her sweater was bright
purple. Her uniform showed she belonged to another army. But
did she have a right to it? How many years separated her from
those spent women? Here a wool beret, there a scarf, but in dull
colors. And yet, now that she could see them better since they
had continued to walk in her direction, their clothes were of
good, warm material, their purses leather and their shoes well
made. Then what gave that sad impression? They weren't poor,
that much was clear. If there was an economic modesty it was
not without dignity. But they were a dreary lot, all bunched together like a group of students on their way to some kind of un-
welcome activity. All alike, in a group no longer a part of the
greater life. "Old people on the Riviera." That's what made it
sad.

Who knows how many years they add up to all together.
"Next year, some certainly won't be coming back." Watching
them with that thought in mind was as though she were wit-
nessing an odd ceremony that didn't affect her. "That small man,
a little hunchbacked may be taken away by the illness that has
shortened and twisted his bones. And that fat man will drop off
while he's snoring, taking too long a breath."

She imagined their coffins floating in the air among the sur-
vivors on a walk next year. "And not just their coffins, but they
themselves will really be with their old companions, their spirits
liberated from clothes and bodies. To rejoice in their company
and let their presence be known. For all we know maybe one
doesn't die completely. . ." She believed she carried Mario' silent
voice inside herself, now part of herself, like breathing, and
sometimes she managed to think with his thoughts. She was
sure of this. And this, until proof to the contrary, meant that
Mario was still alive in her.

"And when I die who will remember me in order for me to last a little longer?" She heard him speak for her: "Those you have loved or have known for a day or a month, it doesn't matter. You are a woman who gives something to those who know her." But it wasn't enough. There were few among the living now who would want to know if it was worth the trouble to know Tosca!

The old people were talking among themselves, with long pauses. Only two couples didn't speak, concentrating on the hard work of walking. One man helped his companion when a rock was too sharp. The male of the other couple was led more than self-propelled. He walked ahead without looking. She used her eyes for both of them. One woman kept nodding her head at intervals, her way of commenting on her friend's discourse. "Maybe they're talking about children, maybe they're two widows who come here to find company." The tall man, who must be over seventy, was now gesturing to the others in a circle around him. The air carried their scraps of conversation and their accent left no doubt. They were from Turin and they were talking about their local soccer team.

A young girl came by with a cocker spaniel on a leash. She was tiny, but her solid flesh strained against her jeans. The tall old man interrupted the conversation while the girl went by; the others also followed her with their eyes while she ran alongside the dog. Broken laughter in many catarrh-hoarse voices tore at vocal chords thickened by smoke and years. It reached her ears as unpleasant as an obscenity. Perhaps they were laughing at some buffoonery uttered by the tall man and interpreted by each in his own way. "That's the way it is. Sex never dies." Why was that such a repugnant idea? Youth had touched them, and perhaps a shiver had moved their placid flesh. "I also like to look at the young and the beautiful." Everyone has eyes to see. Don't old people have the same right as the young? She defended them in order to absolve herself from the disgust she could feel growing for all of them, the women discarded like old slippers or battered pans, the men female-hunters on closed game reserves out of season.

She got up with difficulty. "Here it is, old age has arrived." It always made her unhappy with herself to discover some lack of compassion for others. Suzanna and the elders. . . Mario had told her many Bible stories, and some she remembered in the same words he had used to explain the meaning that only he seemed to have discovered, beyond the meaning others gave it. Tosca remembered Mario had forgiven the two judges for the violence of their desire, while condemning them for falsely accusing Suzanna of the sin they wanted to commit with her. "When one is young," he said, "everything is permitted. No one is shocked if you look at a beautiful woman with desire. In fact, people smile, and the admired woman struts like a peacock. . . But not old men, poor things, who can only desire and imagine. No one pardons them. Because they are ugly, people make a face and pretty women run away. But I believe," and each time it irritated Tosca a little to see him smile to himself, without sharing with her the real reason for that smile, "I believe there are no limits to a man's fantasies, and an old man is still a man. It's when you don't have it, when you can't do it, that your desire goes wild."

Mario died too soon to know whether his suppositions about old age were true or not, but he certainly understood many things before death put an end to his knowing.

Tosca often thought about how much she missed him, but perhaps, as far as he was concerned, he had got all that he was due, and had learned what there was for him to know.

She emptied the shopping bag in a corner of the garden. She would arrange the stones another time. That was enough air for today and she had sat still too long. The sun hadn't been strong enough to attack the dampness in her joints.

In the house, after giving water and some biscuits to the animals so they wouldn't start miaowing too soon, she looked around. The windows were dirty again. Salt was a problem to remove. The floor could use a good mopping, too, but she was so tired! She flopped down in the armchair facing the TV set and closed her eyes. There was time for work, there was time for cooking, She had a lot of time for everything. She didn't sleep, but as she rested, Mario's voice kept her company, along with images of those old people in the sun on the Riviera. Maybe old age wasn't as sad as it seemed — who knows — but alone it could be awful. No one to give you an arm, no one to give you encouragement when your heart beat too fast, no one to hand you a glass of water. She shivered, unable to rest with such agonizing thoughts, and so got up. The bottle of wine bought the day before was still half full. She poured a glass and drank it down greedily. It fell leaden on her empty stomach but immediately filled her with a warmth that rose to her head. Not sure of what might happen, Tosca fell back into the chair. Nothing happened, quite the opposite. Suddenly an unexpected levity drove away like soap bubbles the melancholy feelings aroused on the beach. Slowly she sipped the last of the wine, enjoying the quiet restorative warmth that blessed her at that moment.

To die now would be a pleasure, she thought, to fly away with the gulls. Didn't Toni say we were reincarnated? Animals, plants, people. . . "Who knows what I'll be next." She couldn't remember the ancient law Toni had explained, but she had responded with something about bougainvillea. She had just been making conversation; she didn't really want to stay in a solitary garden. Yes, she wanted the freedom to fly around in the sea smells, her eyes dazzled by the light. Stunned and feathery light, with wide and solemn wings, she flew beside a gull in the blue and brushed his wing with hers. "It's a beautiful reincarnation," she thought, as the glass slipped from her lolling hand, and no tinkling disturbed her flight because beside the armchair was the army blanket Mario had brought home as a war souvenir.

8

After her television set was repaired, Tosca decided to return to the city on the day the bus conductor told her he was off—the only thing she remembered from his discussion, along with a vague sense of irritation. At the Association they made a rough draft of a reply that she copied in the post office lobby and sent right off special delivery. It was almost noon and most of her tasks were done. She wasn't hungry; she didn't have an appetite any more, even though she had apparently suffered no ill-effects after her last attack. And as she walked under the nineteenth-century porticoes of the little town that served the bureaucratic needs of her life—it seemed neither ugly nor beautiful nor hateful, it was a necessary place like the village stores—Tosca wondered if it was worth the trouble to go home right away.

She was tempted to stay. She could go to a restaurant, and then to a movie, and finally to a hotel. To change the scenery, to go through routine motions, such as showing her identity card to a clerk and taking off her clothes in a different bathroom. Yes, and then what? A slice of her pension would vanish quickly, and afterwards she would have to nibble away at her savings to make it to the end of the month. That idea usually frightened her. Now she felt indifferent. Someone always provides for the funerals of have nots, she told herself, and the thought cheered her. But she didn't want to sleep there. Fifi's sensitive little face looked in on her thoughts, and her two brothers also, who now behaved like perfect gentlemen. They came home at the right time and didn't get impatient with evenings in front of television. Why abandon them without warning? She should have thought about it earlier. They always understood if her absences were to be longer than usual because she left an extra bowl of

food in the kitchen and cleaned their box at the last moment before going out. But they must be expecting her now. She had let
them out when she left and surely they had come home for dinner.

Nevertheless she decided to make some concessions to her
own pleasure. It was half an hour before stores closed and the
bus left. On the tree-lined street intersecting the porticoes at a
right angle there was a perfumery and a wine emporium. It cost
the same for a small bottle of perfume she put in her purse as for
six small bottles of sparkling wine a kind clerk fixed with a rope
handle for easier carrying. It was all done quickly. The perfume
didn't take much time. She asked for the brand she used to wear,
happily and sparingly, when she lived with Mario. Only recently
she learned from a magazine that the great Maria Callas wore it
during the time she was a queen and symbol for her. Tosca admired everything about her — her voice, elegance, authority in
her excesses, her regality, and even her nose and those tremen-
dous sweet and tragic eyes. Those eyes of a seeing blind person
who had prepared her life of music with the same dogged determination as her death when music deserted her.

Still ten minutes until closing time. Passing by an open door
Tosca saw a bench with flowers and green ornamental plants,
and entering into the small flower shop she asked if they sent
flowers to the Riviera. She settled on a price (that was high) and
ordered a dozen long-stemmed red roses. Asking for an envelope, she wrote her address on it, and when the florist asked her,
"And the card?" she answered with a smile it wasn't necessary.
On the envelope she added the date when she wanted them delivered. At the last moment she changed her mind and asked for
the card, scribbled something on it, and sealed the envelope.

While walking toward the bus station, among people who
were hurrying about their business or calmly strolling, Tosca
realized no one was looking at her, no glance met hers. "I'm in-

visible," she thought, and the idea at that moment and in that place gave her a flicker of happiness. "I have a bottle of French perfume in my purse, some sparkling wine in a package. I'm one of the many who has made good purchases in town," and her stride immediately became more vigorous. She was anonymous in an anonymous choir. But not in the village. In those deserted streets everyone she met recognized her. "Buon giorno," "buona sera, " and "come sta," were ritual words that broke the silence. Every time she heard them she felt like disappearing, flattening along the house walls so they wouldn't see her; but instead she had to bolster her courage and go on, while voices grew silent at her passing. Then they would start up again and she would cringe, imagining the despicable things they were saying about her. "I'm invisible there, too, but like a shadow. They see me, but they want me to know I don't exist for them, I'm already dead." Here it was different. Unknown among the unknown, but also alive among the living. When she got on the bus she felt tired but happy, having done the necessary things and some unnecessary ones, like everyone, and now she was returning home to her cats. They needed her and she did as much for them as she could. That was the point. She no longer felt like waking up in the morning just because Fifi or Bisi pulled at her mussed hair on the pillow. They were tender, affectionate, always demanding, sometimes mischievous, but she felt so indifferent now even to their individual peculiarities! She could even predict them, knowing their vices and virtues. With each morning her maternal sense was slower to renew itself. This time they would have to respect her desire for something different and put up with the consequences of her little foolishness.

"If I can't make the pension stretch to the end of the month," she concluded, "I'll buy less meat for Bisi and fewer biscuits for Fifi. If she doesn't like perfume, too bad. I like it." She fumbled around with these justifications because for some time she hadn't wasted any money on herself. When she explained it to her three blood suckers they would understand. She smiled at her own naiveté. As if anyone had the right to be wrong! It's a right people never observe without making a big deal out of it, and she expected a lot from her cats. Tomorrow she would fill the house with Kit Kat. To the devil with stinginess! We'll worry about that at the end of the month. She settled down in her seat, asked the conductor with her eyes permission for the infraction, and lit a cigarette.

Via Aurelia was nearly deserted and the towns they passed through were empty. Under a gray sky the colored signs had the sinister uselessness of an old clown who could no longer provoke laughter. No gulls flying about. Maybe the air was getting heavier. She saw a group of gulls sitting on a rock in a creek as the bus passed.

Strangely, that sky, pregnant with humidity, low and still over the gray road and waiting houses, that suspension that seemed to close the mouths of the few passengers on the bus, was to Tosca like a protective covering. She felt calm and independent, at ease with herself. She had some good wine, some first-class perfume, but was sorry she forgot to buy a new cassette for her player. Drawing her wool scarf tighter around her neck for more warmth, she decided she would cook something. A little spaghetti would be a welcome change also for Puss and Bisi. On the other hand, Fifi couldn't be tempted by pasta. As with everything else—loves and friendships, sleep and rest—it was always she who made the decision. Tosca had learned from her how to defend herself! Of the three, the most congenial and wholehearted approval of her dissipations that morning in town would certainly come from Fifi. "I feel good," she thought with surprise, and remembered reading about a kind of lucid insanity fashionable among important people. An unusual expression. She had recently read it in the announcement of a young man's death. What was it? He had killed himself with drugs, alcohol and sex. He would work for weeks without stopping, then become inert and gloomy for long periods of time. He was ecstatic with happiness and then desperate. . . manic depressive, that was it. An actor friend of his had used that word in an interview telling about the irresistible happy spells of the Maestro who could transform a foggy street of the North into a Rio carnival, and his glum periods that weighed on the happiness of others like a ruinous hail storm on a grape harvest. "I must be manic depressive, too." Yes. Depression and euphoria. Alternating. Irritated with herself, she lit a cigarette. Balls. As if depression and euphoria were things. "Buon giorno, Euphoria!" "Buona notte, Depression!" She felt depressed when her nothing was more nothing than ever, but only two months before she had wanted to sing if the telephone rang, if any plan whatsoever encroached on that nothing. "Don't be silly, manic depressives are rich people who have rich lives. I'm just a poor old soul. So I think I'm manic depressive if just once I don't despair. To hell with such complicated thoughts! I feel good, period."

The day drew to a close in Miciamore's house, and when sleep firm as a ripe peach arrived to award Tosca there were only five bottles of sparkling wine on the sideboard.

9

The sparkling wine was finished in the next three days because a letter arrived from the judge sooner than expected. The Nazi had started proceedings when she went to her lawyer with a precise order. The stages of the procedure were now following their course. The woman hadn't expected a reply, it wasn't necessary. Her conscience was clear because entrusted to the law.

Tosca's apartment was one of many that gave her landlady more aggravation than income. Tosca had heard her say so more than once, hissing it when she rebuked her for the cats' presence on the stairs.

Now Tosca had lost her independence, savored like a miracle unexpectedly revived the day she went to town and returned just before the sky let loose a drenching rain. After the injunction arrived, signed for in the mailman's book with a scribble as agitated as her heart beating in her mouth, she hadn't had a moment's peace. She had to be present in court just before Christmas. She already knew an extension would be allowed her, and the Association had advised her to start looking for another place to live. They said the season was right for it; summer leases were still far off, and someone in the village would want to have a sure renter year round. Yes, they reasoned well, but with city heads! More money could be made in the three summer months than renting for the whole year. And she couldn't live with the fear of being evicted again. Even if she were lucky enough to find another house, it would be the same story all over again because of the mirage of fabulous summer earnings.

And she hadn't had the courage to confess everything to the Renters' Association: that no one in the village would give hospitality to the "mother of cats." A paralyzing fear — of the scornful faces, the half sentences mumbled by card-playing men who had decided to punish her for Bruno by planning Miciamore's death—had kept her from speaking openly with the courteous woman who had written the text of her reply. She wouldn't have understood, she couldn't have, with her papers in perfectly symmetrical order, pencils sharpened to a fine point, erasers in a plastic container, no ash tray on the table and annoyed when Tosca asked for one. "Smoking is prohibited in public places." And she added immediately, acidly, "And you tell me you have asthma!"

In the desperate hours of early evening, with the judge's gray-colored letter in her apron pocket, she admitted to herself she was a coward and shouldn't be. She should go knock on some door where every year they displayed a "For Rent" sign in the early February sun. The idea was horrifying, and she erased it with the second bottle.

However, the next morning she did try. She went to the village, to the old part you don't see from Via Aurelia, where almost everyone had places to rent. She went up and down the main street until she noticed, the second or third time she passed under those slightly ajar windows, some eyes glued on her as sharp and cold as a knife blade.

Tosca returned to her house with labored breath, her good intentions totally defeated. She had knocked on no door. The law did not decree that she must add mockery to her humiliation.

She took care of the cats, touched no food or drink herself, and threw herself on the bed.

She fell into a sleep similar to an anesthesia, detached from all reality, even free of dreams. There was nothing to dream, nothing to decide, nothing to do.

It was nearly dark in the room when she got up. When she turned on the light the sleeping cats woke up and started to play with their little ball.

After fixing their supper, she set a glass and bottle down in front of television. The ashtray was full from the evening before. She emptied it and aired out the room. It was cold and the sea was high. Its constant roaring, a threatening but irrepressible note, comforted her in her deliberate resignation, and she set about to pass the hours in the only way left to her.

10

When the last of the sparkling wine of the oasis she had invented was finished, Tosca resigned herself to going out. The cats were out of food, so she confessed the truth to them. "I don't feel well. You're big now and won't die of hunger, go out and find something." She opened the door and left it ajar, All three rushed outside without too much persuasion. Puss turned back to rub against her legs, but since she didn't make a move or add a word, he went out the door slowly, as though reluctant, and disappeared. Two days went by like that, dragging herself from armchair to bed to bathroom, mixing the wine from the last bottle with water to make it last longer and also because thirst tormented her as during the hottest days.

She hadn't cleaned or aired the house. She smelled the same bad odor on herself that seemed to permeate the furniture and walls; however, in a few days she had become accustomed to the bitter taste in her mouth. Now she really had to go out. No wine, no cigarettes, and the cats had a right to a good meal after their fast.

In the bathroom mirror she was dismayed by her thin, pale face and straw-like thin hair soaked with sweat. As indifferent as the villagers were to her, they must have noticed she was sick. She feared their curiosity, and worse, the initiative of some pious do-gooder's attempt to save her soul by sticking her nose in her house where, except for Bruno, no one from the village had ever entered.

She sighed and decided on what seemed to her an immense, but nonetheless necessary, task to defend her right to live as she wished (but she knew what she really meant was the right to die). She ran water in the tub, threw in the last remaining bath salts, lathered her hair. After she got in she thought she might never get out and concentrated on not losing her remaining strength. She surprised herself by thanking God as she put her feet on the floor and reached for a towel. Just as she was, feeling her way, she made it to the bed. She absolutely had to catch her breath or she'd never get to the bottom of the stairs. Without realizing it she fell into a deep sleep from which she soon awoke surprisingly reinvigorated.

That unexpected surge of energy made her want to hear some music while she dressed. She put in a cassette — Mahler's First Symphony, because the quartet was not available, and it had been the last gift from Toni. At that wide sweet wave of sound self-pity brought tears to her eyes. What a gift music was, what redemption from misery for humanity, what a stupendous gift to listen to it with a loved one! She looked in the mirror; she was ready, a little makeup had softened the grayness of her complexion. She absolutely would call Genoa if she managed to get back home in good shape, because even gratitude is love and she was grateful to that kind woman from Genoa who had listened to her and treated her like an equal, she who was so much more subtle in her culture, manner, ideas. Regretfully Tosca turned off the music. She had to go now because in the winter stores didn't stay open the entire scheduled time, and she was sure she wouldn't make it another time.

"I'll listen to it this evening," she promised herself, and went out with a strange inner lightness, as if her body was weightless and her soul had been transported by that stirring music beyond the confines of the reality in which she lived. She didn't feel alone on Via Aurelia where the streetlights among the palms were already shining, every third one, according to the winter economy. She walked slowly, feeling close to Toni, Gigi, Matteo, Lavinia, the young and lively creatures who had recently showed her she could live freely, following greater impulses than those imposed by her daily life among strangers. And she thought that Mahler had written his music of love for her also. Oh, yes, she had given and received. Just don't ask too much and it all works out.

She smiled at the tobacconist, ever tinier under the accumulation of sweaters that didn't protect her from the cold. She smiled at the man at the emporium who was kind enough to carry her bag of wine as far as the apartment door. She smiled at the butcher when she bought meat and biscuits for the cats and a fillet for herself — she had suddenly felt the need to nourish herself, her legs barely holding her up. She smiled at the shopkeeper where she replenished her supply of bread and fruit.

Getting up the stairs required all the determination she could muster. She didn't want the man to go up with her, and the bag of bottles was too heavy to manage. She was tempted for a moment to leave it on the landing below, but denied herself that momentary relief. She couldn't and she shouldn't. She wanted her supper and her wine and her cats with her. On with it, to the summit!

Again the bed to recover, again a deep and immediate sleep, again a miraculous renewal. She heard a noise at the door. It was Fifi. She let her in and left the door open for the other two.

In the kitchen she moved around slowly, every gesture taking its toll. After a rapid bout of sweating, she drank some water with sugar, recovered again, and finished fixing supper. She had managed to do it.

Tape player on the table, fillet on the plate, bottle open, fresh bread, three satisfied cats. She sighed with relief. Lifting her head slightly, she said, "You're proud of yourself," but she didn't smile. It was too easy to be ironical, and she didn't want to be over dramatic, but it had cost her a lot, that last supper! The expression surprised her. "After all, it's not Easter," she said, trying to master the anxious subterranean emotion disturbing her, making her aware of every thought she had kept at bay.

She looked at the three cats that returned the look. Light as air, Fifi jumped on her lap. "You could be John," she told her, "the one who rested his head on Jesus' heart." That was blasphemy, she reprimanded herself, but she didn't mean it that way. John must have had a feminine nature if his love was so transparent, and Fifi was the only female of the three.

The sacred name brought other words to mind that had resonated in church when she thought she hadn't been listening, her eyes open and blind on the black spot that hid Mario's body among the candles. "In your house, Lord, I shall find peace." And earlier the other priest had remembered brother Mario — how strange it had been to hear him talked about like that, but perhaps it was true, she thought, they were all Mario's brothers — his companions, her, the prisoners, the people he met on the street, in shops, at Milan, on vacations by the sea. The priest had spoken of brother Mario "in faith yet unseen." He meant in life, not yet before God. In life, but believing. That is what "in faith" meant. Tosca had wanted to tell the priest it wasn't that way. Mario didn't go to church, and they had talked about destiny, not about God. But what did words matter? Now it seemed the priest had spoken the truth. Mario had lived in faith, because he always loved everyone.

"And me? I love only cats." It wasn't true, and she knew it. To the very end she had hoped to make friends even with those in the village who frightened her. Now it was too late.

"I'm so weak and tired." Who knows if weak souls still have the strength to hope. . .

The bottle was finished. She opened another, but Mahler was also finished and she turned off the player. She wouldn't clean up now, there was time. Now she only wanted to abandon herself in the armchair as on every other evening of her life for so many years. She turned on television. The images were clear but the thread connecting them was not. She couldn't follow the story, but it didn't matter. A spreading torpor loosened every tension, even the disturbing scraps of thought that had flitted through her mind during supper and immediately afterwards. Now it all evaporated into an absorbing, indistinct, tender silence. Slowly she caressed Fifi who was still cuddled in her lap, but her hand was as slow as her blood, and the little cat was too touchy not to take offense. She slipped away and joined her brothers' play, as always more lively at night than during the day.

Tosca dozed for a few minutes. When she reopened her eyes she wanted to get up to look at the sky. From the living room she could see it wide and high over the sea, a cold and distant (but in some ways reassuring) companion. Perhaps, she thought, with the last flicker of consciousness, I'll be able to pray if I see it. But it was enough just to imagine it for her to see it, one last time, in that muffled limbo she had entered. A shining enamel sky was over-under-around her. It was the sky, but it was also the sea and earth. She went ahead totally immersed, but did not move her legs. Her arms were her wings, but they barely beat, like those of a fledgling gull's first attempt to fly. Strange, this shrinking of her body, but it wasn't strange where she was now, looked at as children are looked at, with tender pity, and she knew she was small. Her mother held her hand and guided her so she wouldn't lose her way in the long corridor she had entered. Stopping for a moment she sank into a cover of low clouds in the corridor. With a little hop she got up. She was still in the corridor, going forward, but it was endless. The faint blue light at the end was so far away! She was tired; if she stopped she would sink again in the soft cloud that opened up beneath her and called to her with Mario's voice. The light at the end went out.

It was the gas meter reader who gave the alarm the next morning. The cats in the house were shrieking with a sound that made his hair stand on end. He went to get a man from the town hall and together they forced the lock. A children's cartoon was on television. Tosca was sitting in her armchair, a slight smile on her half-open mouth, her head resting against the back of the chair. The cats recoiled at the arrival of the two men, with backs arched, fur rigid, teeth bared in a threatening snarl. The men stepped aside and the three ran from Tosca's house like crazed beings.

They were still trying to decide what to do — call the doctor and advise the relatives, if there were any — when the telephone rang. It was Gigi who, worried about the long silence, asked about her.

He arrived three hours later, in time to open the door for the boy delivering the red roses. A card was with them. He thought it not too indiscreet to read it and tore open the envelope. Inside was a date and one scribbled word. It was difficult to decipher, but there was no doubt. The date was that day and the word was a name: Miciamore.

11

I wasn't able to finish reading what I had written because Toni broke into tears, and I had trouble calming her down. To be honest, I would have to say she had a real case of hysterics, because she threw herself at me as soon as I started justifying the narrative logic. I let her hit me to exhaust her overwrought nerves. After she calmed down we talked a long time, and she wanted to call Tosca. No answer. Toni began to be anxious again and ran to look for the summer address book with the phone numbers of our vacation life and fortunately found out from the grocery store owner that our friend had been there the day before. She had lost weight but was all right.

Now we'll do what Toni wants. We'll keep telephoning until Tosca answers and on Sunday we'll go visit her. Agreed. But my book? Can I finish it like this, with the errand of mercy of two outsiders who cannot, fatally cannot, change anything in the only story that belongs to her: her life and her death, with her courage and her cowardice? If we can call courage and cowardice the deceptions each of us holds onto in the only performance we are allowed. And isn't Tosca perhaps the only legitimate writer of the play in which she is the main character?

Perhaps Toni is right when she says I've done Tosca a wrong, that I saw tragedy where it is the comedy of everyman, that everyone is alone, often more when they live with others. But if I have felt Tosca was like this, a prisoner of her imagination, I don't believe it's only a novelist's arrogance. We'll still help her, why not? Perhaps she'll continue living as she has lived up to now, but as a writer I won't surrender. The story of Tosca and Miciamore has a necessity of its own I can't escape.

"She'll make love with your conductor, you ass!" Toni shouted at me, and maybe she's right. And maybe she's right when she accuses me of giving Tosca thoughts that aren't hers. A game of false truths and mixed deceptions, a fiction not hers but my arbitrary audacity. That's what she told me and I listened, but nothing totally convinced me. For one thing, she didn't know what Tosca's landlady told me she was about to do. I didn't tell Tosca because it would only have tightened the noose of the final anguish all the sooner. The landlady hadn't wanted to hear arguments of pity, and was annoyed when I suggested paying an additional amount of rent for Tosca.

Now Tosca's silence makes me uneasy. I don't want to feel I'm anything I'm not, neither abject and guilty nor a demiurge, but I won't be happy until I hear her rather brusque, hoarse voice on the telephone.

It would be too much if I were right, following her from a distance like a gravedigger.

I'll rewrite the last few pages to make Toni happy. Recent studies by some foreign doctors (though contested by us) say that tunnel is the antechamber of a life beyond, not inhuman or lugubrious, but harmonious and warm with memories from which some have returned to tell us about. Tosca could, after her mother, also meet Mario, who doesn't call to her, however, but only smiles. To call to her, to make her come back to the luminous end of this side of the tunnel, into life, would be the voices of Fifi, Bisi and Puss, who mew their fear and hunger. I could do it. It wouldn't even be bad. But afterwards? Everything would start over just as it was before, and I heard Tosca complain, "It never never ends."

I didn't have to rewrite anything. It was almost as I had imagined it. Red roses were on Tosca's coffin. I bought them without Toni's knowledge, and I wrote what I believe Tosca would have wanted, the date and a name on a card that I tossed into the open grave along with the roses. The two of us, her friends, ordered a large bouquet of blue hydrangeas and violet tulips because we weren't able to find bougainvillea. We'll take bougainvillea to her next summer when we return to the house of Miciamore.

The End

About the Author

Gina Lagorio, born in Bra, in the Cuneo province in the region of Piedmont. Having earned a degree in English literature from the University of Torino (1943), she later spent twenty years teaching English literature and history in Savona (Liguria) from 1954 to 1974. She subsequently moved to Milan, where she was a consultant for the Garzanti publishing house. In addition to her literary and intellectual career, Lagorio was a committed public intellectual, having been first a member of Italy's Chamber of Deputies and then a member of its Senate, a career as an elected official that ended in 1992.

She was, one might say, a faithful child of her land of origins; indeed, the Langhe area figures as a major theme in much of her work, as does also the region of Liguria. Cesare Pavese and Beppe Fenolgio were aesthetic and ideological confreres of hers, as were also Antonio Barile and Camillo Sbarbaro. Her "dialogue" with to two of these writers, especially, is evidenced by the following critical writings: *Fenolgio* (1970), *Sui racconti di Sbarbaro* (1973), and *Sbarbaro: un modo spoglio di esistere* (1981).

Her literary writings are marked by a strong commitment to women's rights, their search for independence as individuals, motherhood, sexual freedom, and, hence, self-identity. Her numerous creative works include: *Il polline* (1966), *Approssimato per difetto* (1971), *La spiaggia del lupo* (1977), *Fuori scena* (1979), *Raccontami quella di Flic* (a play, 1983), *Golfo del paradiso* (1987), *Tra le mura stellate* (1991), *Il bastardo, ovvero gli amori, i travagli e le lacrime di Don Emanuel di Savoia* (1996), *L'arcadia americana* (1999), *Elogio della zucca* (2000), and *Capita* (2005). This last novel deals with her illness, and was delivered to the publisher only three weeks before her death, July 17, 2005.

In addition to her many contributions to a variety of Italy's leading literary and cultural magazines, she published numerous books of non-fiction, which also include: *Penelope senza tela* (1984), *Russia oltre l'URSS* (1989), and *Il decalogo di Kieslowski* (1992). Throughout most of her career, she received numerous literary awards: Flaiano Prize (1983), Rapallo Prize (1987), Viareggio Prize (1994), Grinzane-Cavour Prize (1997), among others.

About the Translator

Martha King received her Ph.D. in Italian from the University of Wisconsin, Madison. Her articles and translations have appeared in many periodicals in the U.S. and England. She has a special interest in Sardinia and the writer Grazia Deledda as well as other Italian women writers.

Book publications include translations of *Cosima* by Grazia Deledda, with Introduction (1988); *Family Chronicle* by Vasco Pratolini, with Introduction (1988); *New Italian Women: A Collection of Short Fiction*, edited, with Translations and Introduction (1989); *Elias Portolu* by Grazia Deledda, with Introduction and Notes (1992/1995); *Zibaldone (A Selection)* by Giacomo Leopardi, with Introduction, in collaboration with Daniela Bini (1992); *Chiaroscuro, Short Stories by Grazia Deledda* (1994).

Her most recent translations include: *Teresa* by Neera (1998); Grazia Deledda's *Reeds in the Wind* (1999); Luigi Pirandello's *Her Husband*, in collaboration with Mary Ann Frese Witt (2000); a translation Anna Banti's short stories, in collaboration with Carol Lazzaro-Weis, published in the Modern Language Association Translation Series, 2001; Dacia Maraini's *Darkness* (2002); *After the War: A Collection of Short Fiction by Post-War Italian Women* (2004); and *Game Plane for a Novel* by Gianna Manzini (2008). She has also written a biography of Grazia Deledda, *Grazia Deledda: A Legendary Life* (2005).

Martha King currently resides in Florence; she has lived in Tuscany since 1979.

CROSSINGS

AN INTERSECTION OF CULTURES

A refereed series, CROSSINGS is dedicated to the publication of translations from Italian to English. Open to all genres, translators should first contact the editors before submitting a complete manuscript.

Rodolfo Di Biasio
Wayfarers Four
Trans. Justin Vitiello
Fiction. $11.00. Crossings 1

Isabella Morra
Canzoniere: A Bilingual Edition
Trans. Irene Musillo Mitchell.
Poetry. $9.00. Crossings 2

Nevio Spadone
Lus
Trans. Teresa Picarazzi
Theater. $7.00. Crossings 3

Flavia Pankiewicz
American Eclipses
Trans. P. Carravetta. Intro. J. Tusiani
Poetry. $9.00. Crossings 4

Dacia Maraini
Stowaway on Board
Trans. Gi. Bellesia &V. Offredi Poletto
Gender. $8.00. Crossings 5

Walter Valeri, ed.
Franca Rame. Woman on Stage
Theater. $18.00. Crossings 6

Carmine Biagio Iannace
The Discovery of America:
Trans. William Boelhower.
Autobiography. $15.00. Crossings 7

Romeo Musa da Calice
Luna sul salice
Trans. Adelia V. Williams
Folklore. $9.00. Crossings 8

Marco Paolini & Gabriele Vacis
The Story of Vajont
Trans. Thomas Simpson.
Theater. $13.00. Crossings 9

Silvio Ramat
Sharing A Trip: Selected Poems
Trans. Emanuel di Pasquale.
Poetry. $14.00. Crossings 10

Raffaello Baldini
Carta canta (Page Proof)
Ed. D. Benati. Trans. A. Bernardi.
Theater. $12.00. Crossings 11

Maura Del Serra
Infinite Present: Selected Poems
Trans. Emanuel Di Pasquale
& Michael Palma
Poetry. $14.00. Crossings 12

Dino Campana
Canti Orfici
Trans. & Notes Luigi Bonaffini
Poetry. $25.00. Crossings 13

Roberto Bertoldo
The Calvary of the Cranes
Trans. Emanuel di Pasquale.
Poetry. $15.00. Crossings 14

Paolo Ruffilli
Like It or Not
Trans. Ruth Feldmann
& James Laughlin
Poetry. $16.00. Crossings 15

Giuseppe Bonaviri
Saracen Tales
Trans. Barbara De Marco.
Fiction. $19.00. Crossings 16

Leonilde Frieri Ruberto
Such Is Life
Trans. Laura Riberto
Intro. Ilaria Serra
Autobiography. $10.00. Crossings 17